THE PARAGON

RANDOM HOUSE   NEW YORK

THE

PARAGON

A NOVEL BY

JOHN KNOWLES

FOR PHILIPPE FORQUET de DORNE

THE PARAGON

I

The students were settling into their rooms for the new academic year. Trunks were being trundled, bags dragged, boxes and footlockers and cardboard cartons were being hauled along the stone walks past the red-brick Georgian façade, the green-shuttered windows in Pierson College of Yale University.

Pierson, like all the residential colleges at Yale, had been built to withstand attack. A Bastille psychology had dominated its construction and that of the entire University, girding the campus for obviously imminent assaults by mobs of storming townspeople. Facing the outside world were, at the forefront, the battlements of the Old Campus, frowning intimidatingly down upon the New Haven Green and its three meek churches, inoffensive and cowed. The rear of the campus was blocked by the Gibraltar known as the Payne Whitney Gymnasium, a citadel so formidable that only the most advanced weaponry could have reduced it. In between there were the many residential colleges, designed like the precincts of some long-established and only infrequently attacked permanent military installation. There were symmetrical inner courtyards and blooming shrubbery and tended trees and clipped lawns, stained-glass windows and minstrel galleries and Gothic towers, little and big bells in little and big belfries, fieldstone sunken patios, pillared loggias, winding staircases, sealed rooms for music and for squash, ornamental gateways and echoing tunnels, built-in town houses, stranded gazebos, organs surrounded by immense hanging banks of pipes, sculptural figures, mostly clothed and mostly seated, Victorian porte-cocheres, a defenseless and historic eighteenth-century dormitory completely surrounded by a fortified perimeter, subterranean passageways, white marble Greek temples, numerous bizarre windowless redoubts, greenswards and croquet lawns.

But none of these graces and amenities was ever permitted to interfere with the real purpose of the buildings, which was self-defense. All of the colleges were on all sides enclosed by walls and high iron picked fences, and by dry moats.

Louis Colfax carried a huge duffel bag across his back, his tall, black-clothed frame bending forward under its weight. Two other students followed him, carrying his two cardboard cartons. With his eyes fixed on the stones of the walk Lou suddenly saw a pair of South American sandals, elaborate with thongs and straps. They could only be on the feet of Clement Jonaz, his Afro-Brazilian friend.

Lou looked quickly up into the broad, copper-colored face which had its usual expression of dignity and alertness, and said, "Clement, hi!" with a nervous chuckle.

Clement beamed back and said, "Well, here we are. Another first day. It's an ordeal, isn't it. 'Preparing a face to meet the faces that you meet.' Hard work sometimes."

"It is, it is. How was your summer?"

Clement had spent his summer in an anthropological study of a tribe of Indians in the upper Amazon and began to describe his findings in some detail.

Lou listened, forgetting the weight on his back, and the two heavy cartons the students behind him were holding.

One of them finally yelled, "I'm going to drop this box of yours if you don't get your ass moving."

"Oh, of course, sure," mumbled Lou. "Come on," he said to Clement, and staggered on down the walk.

At the end they went down a couple of shallow steps into a whitewashed brick cul-de-sac opening off the courtyard; it was trimmed with black grillwork, New Orleans-inspired.

"You're in the Slave Quarters," said Clement with mock wonder, "how grand."

All the student rooms here opened directly on the outdoors. Lou pushed open the first door on the left and looked into the living room of the suite to which he had been assigned. It was completely furnished, with a handsome red and brown Moroccan rug, dark brown leather couch, armchairs, curtains, sports prints, pewter beer mugs.

Lou surveyed it. "Guess the other guy got here before me," he said.

"Pretty swanky," observed Clement drily. "What's your roommate's name?"

"I've never met him. His name's Gordon Durant."

"My, my."

"Why 'my, my'?"

"Haven't you ever heard of Durant Chemicals? Money, money, money."

"Well, and so I don't have any money, so what? America's a democracy, right?"

Clement gazed shrewdly at him and murmured, "Are you jesting?"

The student behind, swaying under the weight of his box, butted against them, saying, "Get the hell out of the *way!*" and forcing himself into the room, dumped the box on the rug. "There! So long."

"Wait!" cried Lou. He hadn't met either of these students before, but had recruited them on the street to help him. "Have a drink!"

They slowly drew back into the room.

Introductions took place. The first student was named Brooks Randell, the other, Richard Anders. They were roommates and also lived in the Slave Quarters.

Lou, in his black pants and long black sweater, looked at them through his dark glasses and said, "I wonder where we keep our liquor? And where is Durant Chemicals anyway?"

"Sounds like he's in the shower," said Brooks.

"Does it? Can't hear so much today." He hit the side of his head with the butt of his hand. "I'm a little deaf sometimes. Now!" he rubbed his hands together, beaming, "a drink!" gazing brightly around him. Randell pointed to a promising-looking walnut cabinet under the window. Inside it Lou found a bottle of Polish vodka. "This is *real!*" he said enthusiastically, and poured each of them a vodka on ice, not taking any himself, however. "I don't drink in odd months."

"Odd months?"

"Odd-numbered months. This is September, ninth month."

"Oh. That's funny."

"Yes," agreed Lou.

Lou sat down on the floor to unpack his cartons. The first thing he drew out was a very large Soviet Russian flag, brilliantly red, with the hammer and sickle, and draped it from the mantelpiece, secured by two of Gordon Durant's vases. He opened another carton brimming with paper. "Two thousand letters. I had a pretty big correspondence in the Marine Corps. Nothing else to do once you've survived Boot Camp. If you survive Boot Camp."

The sound of a shower running ceased. The other two heard this but Lou Colfax didn't. He sat on the floor sorting through the other contents of the first carton, which seemed to contain a great many black sweaters. Gordon came out of the bathroom wearing his glasses and a towel around the middle of his tough and rangy body. Without his glasses and without his cultured-sounding voice he would have been taken for a very competent farm hand. "What the hell is this?" he asked hastily in a half-voice. Clement, in his armchair, didn't stir, but the two students on the couch tried to pass from a sitting posture into a standing one without, however, appearing to move a muscle, since to be seen rising when someone entered a room was not part of their repertory. Eventually they arrived at slumped, semi-seated positions on either arm of the couch.

"How are you!" said Lou from the floor with great pleasure. "You must be—you're—ah—"

"Gordon Durant. You would be Colfax."

"That's me!" he exclaimed, pleased.

"Was there enough vodka?" inquired Gordon, at his worldliest.

"Fine," said Brooks hurriedly, and then wondered what that was supposed to mean.

"Lots," said Richard at almost the same time, and also immediately cursed himself for it.

"And this flag," Gordon squinted at it. "Is it to leak on or what?"

Hurriedly getting up from the floor, Lou snatched it with a beautiful maneuver from under the vases in such a way that both were spared. Gordon stared back at his deprecating smile with stupefaction and then looked at the ceiling.

"Just decoration," muttered Lou smilingly, "just a joke." He looked at him brightly. "Do you like it?"

Grimacing back, Gordon snapped, "What do you mean, do I *like* it?"

"As decoration. I mean the color. It sort of goes with the rug, doesn't it?"

"It doesn't go with my rug, not in my sitting room, not here it doesn't go, no."

"Are there bedrooms too?" Lou inquired, "or—"

"There are two bedrooms," answered Gordon, indicating doors on either side of the couch. "I sleep in that one, and I study in that one."

"Oh," said Lou more or less to himself, nodding, also more or less to himself. Hostility in the first two minutes, here it was again, unprovoked and undisguised; this person was already an enemy and he had done nothing to make him one.

Gordon went on through the living room and through the door on the right, which he closed after him. "Well," said Lou very cheerfully, "I certainly do appreciate you helping me carry in these stupid cartons. Got to get myself some bags or a trunk or another duffel bag, I guess."

He sat back down on the floor and began to handle their contents. A sudden and total atmosphere of isolation came over him, pervasive and almost tangible, a spell. The others sensed it and stared. The world of solitude closing around him was at that moment impenetrable, a shield, airless, hereditary, penetrating to his bones, his veins. Sitting in this intense pool of solitude, Lou Colfax went on slowly fingering his possessions.

Then this intolerable shield of isolation faded.

"Let's go and have a beer!" he cried, coming out of it. "I do drink beer in uneven months. And this *is* an uneven one. I'll say," he added, and did not glance at Gordon's closed door.

"I'm in training, not allowed to drink," said Richard Anders, finishing his vodka. They went out, leaving the open and partly unpacked cartons on the Moroccan rug. The Communist flag was spread over the chair next to the fireplace. When Gordon Durant came out of the bedroom in his Hong Kong silk bathrobe, he began talking to himself. "A squatter!" he snarled. "A squatter in the sitting room."

Lou, Randell and Anders went across the street to the Old Heidelberg, a dark, beery, carved-table, sawdusty saloon. "I like this place," exclaimed Lou, sniffing deeply the rancid air. "Great. A real saloon." They sat down in a dark booth, ordered a pitcher of beer, and drained it. Then they ordered another and drained that. Then they asked for the bill and Lou, who had been acting as host to these two new acquaintances whom he invited for a drink and who had done him a considerable service, found he had seven cents in his pocket. So the other two paid. "I'll pay you back, I have something for you," he said, and they answered that that would be fine, and forgot about it. (Some days later, returning from football practice, Brooks Randell found an oxygen tank with breathing tube next to his bed. It had a blue ribbon around the middle and dangling from this was a card reading, "Not as good as the air in the rathskeller but healthier for you athletes. Lou Colfax." Brooks turned the nob at the top, inhaled from the tube and his lungs were instantly flooded with oxygen. A few days later Richard Anders found a Calder-style mobile twirling slowly in his sitting room. Suspended by wires from its four balancing arms were discs showing a mouth, a rose, the view down the barrel of a gun, and a tiny picture of Queen Victoria, all slowly circling each other in changing relationships in space. Anders didn't like art particularly but he loved a good laugh and found this one of the very best, and told Lou Colfax so. "Oh," said Lou cogitatingly, "it's funny, is it? I see. Hm. Good.")

Gordon Durant was not much of a drinker. "I go mad when I drink liquor," he explained to anyone who remarked at his glass of orange juice at cocktail parties. He said this simply, and it was the simple truth. Two years before, at his father's wedding reception in Watch Hill, Rhode Island, he had had several glasses of champagne and then several glasses of Scotch and the next thing he remembered, he was aboard an airplane bound for Shannon, Ireland.

The tension caused by the Squatter in the Sitting Room, however, was too much for Gordon's resistance, and so he was only semi-sane at 12:30 A.M. when he walked into his darkened room and discerned in the murk Lou, wrapped in the flag, asleep on the couch.

"*Achtung!*" he roared.

Lou Colfax snapped upright into a sitting position, and next he was on his feet. Laughing irresponsibly, Gordon moved past him to his bedroom and, still full of mirth, slowly shut the door. Lou sat down on his couch and waited to see whether the pounding in his veins would subside enough for him to fall asleep again, ever.

The next morning Gordon woke up and, sorting among scraps of memory of what he had done the night before, felt something which, if it had been stronger, could have been described as remorse. But then he took a long hot shower and began to think about what his family had done for the Yale endowment and how he had never asked a special privilege of any kind here.

This spooky wraith Colfax just wouldn't work as his roommate, that was all. It was only because Gordon's great buddy, Harper Van Ingen, had flunked out at the very end of the previous year that this vacancy had occurred, leaving him open to invasion by this phantom. It just wouldn't work. Gordon knew that he was not a snob; he was a realist. His roommate should wear gray flannel and tweed and cashmere sweaters and striped ties and English shoes. He should be able when he was in New York to get into the Stork Club and El Morocco without trouble, he should play squash, he should ski, have a certain amount of money, have his friends among a certain kind of people. None of these characteristics was possessed by what's-his-name. Gordon had a right to be comfortable with his roommate, damn it. He reached for the telephone beside the couch and dialed the University Operator. "Give me the President." Pause. "Um-hum." Pause. "Is this the President? . . . Well, I want to speak to him. . . . When will he be back? All right then, the Assistant to the President. . . . Hello? I want to see about having the person assigned to my rooms changed. . . . .

That kind of procedure is going to take all week. . . . .

Look, I don't have time for all those steps, this is urgent, I've got my nerves to think about. . . . See the *psychiatrist!* . . . . . . Well, it was a poor one. . . . Yes. My name is Gordon Durant. . . . Is that right? Yes, well I think so to . . . . Good. I'm so glad. Very good. The family's always glad to know the things it's tried to do are worthwhile. . . . . Well, of course lunch would be fine, because I do have this problem. . . . . Right. Will the President be coming to lunch? . . . .

Um-hum. Right. Okay then, Mr.—Mr. Peake? Today at 12:30." He hung up. He would get a little action around here. If there was anybody he detested it was somebody who used the accident of birth to get his way. He never did it himself. But this was different. This was desperate.

He had done some checking into this squatter's background.

Everything he had learned had been bad, very bad. Colfax had spent a large part of his freshman year working on some cockeyed perpetual motion machine. He also did chemistry experiments in a basement room on the Old Campus. There had been an explosion. He also concocted gases there, and one story was that these had caused temporary blindness in several students. A bumbling amateur in chemistry living with, let's face it, the heir to Durant Chemicals! Gordon's family had practically *cornered* chemicals! He didn't have to live with this jerk. There were limits.

He had also learned that Colfax had left Yale after his freshman year and gone into the Marines, where he had only lasted about eight months. Probably flunked out of the Marines. Now he was back, proposing to move in with, no, move in on, Gordon Durant. Well, it wasn't going to happen.

He met Mr. Peake at Mory's at 12:30. Mr. Peake turned out to be very amiable and agreeable, but not very helpful. Yale was *democratic*, Mr. Peake seemed to be trying to communicate tacitly, if necessarily porously, DEMOCRATIC. I *know* it's democratic, Gordon Durant tried to convey back, through his frowning eyebrows, don't you think *I* know! *I'm* democratic, we're *all* democratic!

All the while, over the cream of mongole soup and the Dover sole, what they talked about was curriculum changes and construction plans, the art gallery, and Gordon's half-brother Pete, who had been in the same class as Mr. Peake at Yale. Finally, over the Boston cream pie, they reached the subject of Colfax openly. Mr. Peake explained that there were procedures for changing roommates, that it would not be good for the work or the personalities of either student to share quarters if they could not get along. "On the other hand," continued Mr. Peake, knitting his eyebrows, "he must be a very *interesting* person."

"He does? He doesn't interest me at all. Why does he have to be an interesting person?"

"Well, his I.Q. And his Range-of-Interest Index. I did some investi—I looked into his record after your call. And what I'm saying now is sort of confidential. But he has an exceptional

Interest Span Rating, and his Qualitative Concentration Ratio is in the highest five-percentile group. He also scored very well in Extra-Sensory Perception."

"Oh my God."

"Well," Mr. Peake leaned back and tossed his napkin on the table, "all of that must make for a fundamentally very *interesting* person, say what you will."

"I'll tell you, Mr.—ah—Peake. I don't really want my mind read by anybody. I don't want a tutor in residence either. I want somebody who plays a really good game of bridge, a good game of squash, and invites really attractive girls for weekends. I also would like somebody who had some kind of decent *income* and I'm not being a snob and talking about his family background or what school he went to or any of that crap, I couldn't care less about any of *that*. I'm talking about somebody who can pay half the check when we take two really attractive girls out in New York. I've got a few friends like that around here and one was set to be my roommate, but he had some bad luck. So I wish you would fix this for me. If that's not asking too much."

"Oh, no, no, I'm sure it isn't. What I started to explain on the phone this morning was the way to do it, and I'm sure it can be done. Just bring it up at the master's office in your college and I'm sure it can be arranged. And of course, out of courtesy, I'm sure you'll find some tactful way."

After lunch Gordon strolled down the street to the *Yale Daily News* building, where there was to be an extremely important meeting. He was vice-chairman of the *News*. He and the other editors assembled on the third floor of the building, where there was a board room which, because of the sober executive elegance of its paneling and its other appointments, could have made the directors of the United States Steel Corporation feel at home. At Yale, Gordon reflected with crusty satisfaction, when they did something they did it right. The chairman called the meeting to order and came straight to the point. "All right," he said without preliminaries, "Who shall we ask?"

"*Whom* shall we ask," said a voice from the end of the table.

Then they all settled down to think, and to wonder if they dared offer the names they had already thought of. Finally from the depths of a chair in the middle of the table came these words: "The Pope?"

Another silence. Finally from the chairman came the answer. "Pius? A bit overexposed, maybe? He's in that window in St. Peter's every Sunday, you know."

"What about General de Gaulle?"

"Finished."

A concurring silence followed. "I know. Let's get traditional. How about the Duke of Edinburgh?"

Several irritated faces greeted this, from the leftist sports editor, the Irish managing editor, and the anarchist editorial secretary. "All right, all right, forget it," muttered the student.

Contemplation filled the still room. Then from the bottom of the table the editorial secretary, grinning his secret, fiendish grin, said quietly, "We need somebody practical, somebody who's really contributing to America, to world peace. Let's ask Wernher von Braun."

"Who?" whispered someone uncertainly.

"The German guy who makes rockets."

"Very funny."

"Why not? He's the wave of the future. He's everything the Duke of Whatsit ain't. Right?"

Everyone detested the editorial secretary, and so nobody spoke.

Then the chairman, who was very much liked by everyone, said in his pleasant way, "Couldn't we invite Mrs. Roosevelt? To talk about the UN, for instance."

Respectful consideration followed. Then Gordon Durant said, "Yeah, but do you think a woman, even Eleanor Roosevelt—" he felt justified in using her first name, since he knew her, "is what we need? And she hasn't been the head of the United Nations. She hasn't even been the head of the American Delegation. If we're going that way, and personally I think the UN is out of it, completely out of it, then we ought to give what's-his-name, the new head of the UN, Dag Hammarskjöld a chance."

Everybody silently agreed that Dag Hammarskjöld ought to be given a chance before Eleanor Roosevelt.

The managing editor was frowning and drumming his fingers on the polished table top. "I think we're getting pretty far off the point of this. We want significance, significance for today." He took a long, significant pause and then said quietly, "Mao Tse-tung."

"Mao Tse-*tung!*"

"How would we get through to him?"

"What languages does he speak?"

"How do we get him out of China?"

"What would the University say?"

"I guess the Secret Service would give him protection."

"*Mao Tse-tung!*"

The managing editor, finally tacitly conceding that Mao Tse-tung was too much even for them to cope with, sighed and was silent.

"What about General MacArthur?"

"Two years out of date, a nobody."

"And that 'Old soldiers fade away' speech. A cornball."

"Why don't we get off political people this year," suggested someone at the bottom of the table. "Why not get, I don't know, a scientist?"

"Well, who?"

"I don't know, Dr. Spock—"

"*Dr. Spock!*" roared four furious voices in unison.

"That was a joke, son," choked the other, "I mean, there's— well—what about, let's be original, Rita Hayworth and Aly Khan?"

The room was so stunned by this proposal that at first no one knew how to react. Any attitude toward such a revolutionary suggestion might be the wrong one. They all sensed that Gordon Durant would have to decide what attitude was correct, and decide that instant.

He leaned back in his chair, elbows on the arms, and said quietly, "Too middle class."

That eliminated that. The editor who had suggested it sighed almost audibly with relief.

"Let's settle this," Gordon went on. "Time's awastin.' Let's ask John Foster Dulles and be done with it." He settled back in his chair again. "A secretary of state has enough prestige for us."

The others looked muddled and at cross-purposes: the famous Durant tactlessness, or candor.

Still, it was settled, and the board of the *Yale Daily News* formally voted that the honor of speaking at their annual banquet in the spring would be conferred upon the Secretary of State of the United States of America.

Gordon realized that there might have been some even more ego-gratifying guest speaker for the editorial board to select, but he simply couldn't sit around waiting for the name to be mentioned. He knew they would always accept anyone as much of a world figure as a secretary of state, and he also knew, based on past experience, that most world figures would accept, a knowledge which in the furthest corner of his mind inspired in him a small, secret contempt for world figures.

Whiskey! Never, never again. Leaving the *News* building, Gordon walked straight to the Payne Whitney Gymnasium and straight to the steam room there. Once installed, prone as a corpse on a slab, with the clouds of steam thickening rapidly around him, heat seeping into every joint, every pore, every aperture, he relaxed, relaxed, relaxed.

And he permitted his deeply relaxed mind to entertain only two thoughts: the Secretary of State would do; and Lou Colfax, Interest Concentration Ratio, Extra-Sensory Perception and all, wouldn't do.

The Sterling Memorial Library at Yale was only slightly less impregnable to assault than the Payne Whitney Gymnasium. Nothing in its construction suggested that it was to be used for the storing or reading of books. Like all Yale buildings, it was a fortress, but in this case, elaborately disguised as a cathedral. This triple confusion made the behavior of people within its confines very singular. Awed and stealthy, they crept along the great nave toward the high desk, instinctively

unsure whether they could actually obtain a book from this
tabernacle, fazed by all the Gothic stone and leaded windows,
bemused by an inner cloister which lacked only nuns, feeling
reverential without reason.

To it, during his freshman year, Lou Colfax had been in the
habit of withdrawing, to meditate in a little side chapel,
wonder, speculate. Eventually he had won the right, rare for
an undergraduate, to a cubicle in the stacks, and into it he
had often retreated. After his sleepless night in Gordon Durant's sitting room he fled straight to the library, like a medieval fugitive seeking sanctuary. They gave him the same cubicle he had had two years before, and with mystical relief he
stepped into the elevator, which rose through the immense
pile of books, and got off on the catwalk on the layer where
his alcove was situated. Clement Jonaz still had the next
cubicle and was in it, studying.

"Now, Louis," he began after Lou had sat down in Jonaz's
cubicle, "I want to talk to you very seriously about your
undergraduate career. What class are you now?"

"A sophomore."

"Well, I want to talk to you very seriously about your
impact here. You have got to start now to make an impact. As
long as America is what it is, Yale is going to be what it is.
Yale is a mirror in a fun house. Take a good look at yourself in
it! All that black you wear and the way you let your hair grow
rather longer than Yale likes. Why? You're not going to prove
anything here. You've got to understand that Yale is Wall
Street and the State Department and all that, Yale is, well,
Yale is American success, much more so than Harvard, Harvard is too idiosyncratic, and much more so than Princeton,
Princeton is too casual, too Southern-oriented." He lit a cigarette. "I'm what they call a leftist, I suppose good old
Senator McCarthy would say I was a subversive. Do I go
around in black with long hair here? Of course," he grinned
broadly, "I don't think *my* hair will grow very long, kinky, oh
my, yes, kinky, but if it would I wouldn't let it. Noooo. If you
can't beat 'em, join 'em. I'm their parlor leftist, their cocktail-

party Negro, and they love it. Be part of it, I say. Being a rebel is too lonely, and you don't get anywhere around here. Maybe later, I think so, probably later, I hope so, I don't know, maybe. But I say, keep your own ideas but join 'em, bore from within—"

"You are a bit of a—"

"Shut up. Bore from within. You won't even *know* what's going on here unless you get on the social ladder. In a way, you won't even go to Yale unless you do. Yale won't happen to you. So!" he leaned back in his chair, "you've got to make an impact."

"I do? What shall I do? Jump out the window? Oh, that's right, we're in the library. There aren't any."

"Start thinking very seriously about your impact. But to do that you naturally have to know what this University, what all universities are for, on the undergraduate level, I mean. The graduate level is different. What is a university for?"

"To educate the students, of course."

Clement gazed shrewdly at him. "You're too intelligent to really believe that."

"Am I? What should I believe?"

"Education and classes and assignments and examinations and," waving, "all these books piled by the millions all around us here, that's just a façade, a fake. That's just an excuse, just a way of *organizing* a few thousand aimless young men. It's like drill in the Army. You know about drill?"

Lou looked at him. "I just got out of the Marine Corps."

"Yes, of course, then you do know about drill, don't you? You realize that all those thousands of hours you spent learning to drill and then drilling were totally useless, not the slightest practical use."

Lou nodded drily.

"It's just a technique for turning men into automatons, you know that, train them to obey order after order after order— *right* face, *left* face, *about* face, all meaningless, ridiculous, of course. Studying is the drill of the university. It doesn't *mean* anything, nobody ever *learns* anything, but it's a useful way of organizing all you rabble. The university only has one *real* job. You know that."

"Yes? Well, what is it?"

"To keep you."

"Hum?"

"To keep you. They keep young men from age eighteen to age twenty-two. That's all they really do. That's all anybody wants them to do. Keep you off the streets, keep you out of the way, keep you out of your parents' hair. They keep you. It's like a kennel."

"Gosh," said Lou sardonically.

"Oh, go to hell. The trouble with you is, if something isn't perfect you won't accept it at all. That's why you look in the mirror so much. Because you think you've got a perfect movie-star face."

"Practically," he responded jokingly. But it was, in fact, no joke: Lou Colfax had a Colfax face, and in all the sorry procession of disasters and failures his relations had trailed behind them through the years and the generations, their faces as a rule had been strikingly handsome or memorably beautiful. Wasted, Lou thought himself, wasted beauty, gems of purest rays serene buried in the darkest, unfathomed sea, lost. "Anyway, I'm nearly twenty-one years old so I'll only have the Colfax looks for a few more years and then that'll be gone. You ought to see my father. *U-r-r-r-a-a-g-h!*"

"Yes," said Clement quietly, "you'll want to destroy that family advantage."

"What?"

"Nothing."

After a pause, Lou said simply, "I know what you mean." He tried to be, at whatever cost to himself, unswervingly honest. If it was based on pride, as it was, well, then, that was one good quality springing from a bad one. But, of course, all of these qualities—pride, honesty, destructiveness, to name only three of the massive clashing passions he struggled with —made living with him, and his living with himself, tempestuous on the surface, and tempestuous in the depths.

"You may be just enough of a freak," Clement went on,

eyeing him shrewdly, "to make one of the societies. I want to explain the procedure to you, how you conduct yourself on the great day, next year, when they come for you."

Lou shivered imperceptibly, at the phrase "come for you." It touched one of his fears: the police, the Gestapo, the little men with the nets, nameless thugs, these were some of the long-shadowed figures who might "come for him"; he had imagined them as a child; he still sometimes imagined them.

"What happens," Clement went on, unaware; Lou was relieved to see that Clement after all didn't notice absolutely everything, "is that you will be sitting in your room in the college at nine o'clock one Thursday evening in the spring of your junior year. You will be alone. Shoot your roommate, if necessary, to insure this."

"All right," murmured Lou, brightening.

"*Several people,* dressed in severest New York black, will wait outside your door. As the bell tower sounds the last of its nine rather depressing tolls, one of these apparitions will knock. 'Come in,' you call in a tone receptive, interested, but at the same time by no means effusive, overeager, or too ingratiating. The apparition, all in black, rigid with the importance and absurdity of his mission, comes in, and you half-rise. You are, of course, at your desk, sketching."

Lou had been idly drawing on one of the strips of paper, sketching a firm-lined, stylized saint with halo, her palms joined, robed, barefoot, standing on a snake. It had only taken a minute or so.

"Umm. You are then at your desk sketching, and you half-rise. But this emissary is not from the society you want. You sink back into your chair. 'I am from Foot and Mouth,' he declares in his crypt voice, 'do you accept?' 'No,' you answer regretfully, 'no, I decline.' And you wait them out. You just might be freak enough to be elected—to—to any of them."

"I'm not interested," Lou said in a level tone.

After a pause Clement observed, "No, I don't think you are."

In front of Lou and behind him and all around him the great core of books, four million or more of them, reached upward, a vast rectangular load of learning and imitations of learning, piled up there over the centuries like the tower in the Bible which was supposed to reach to heaven and so free men from their earthbound limitations. But instead in the end it became fragmented into a Babel, of books. There was no way of climbing up their spines to heaven. Lou had tried that.

"Are you still interested in plankton?" inquired Clement, who was genuinely interested in Lou's interests, and so unique among his acquaintances at Yale.

"Yes, but I haven't found anything conclusive yet. Same thing with algae. You see," and with his rather large and nervous hands he took a fresh piece of paper and began rapidly sketching a cross-section of the North Atlantic Ocean off Cape Cod, its currents, migration patterns, its potential for producing food. Lou was quite sure the human race would starve to death unless the oceans could be used to grow food. Clement watched and listened. "And your desalinization project?"

"Redesigned some of the features and, you know, it's perfectly practical and some version could go into operation very soon." And then he reverted to the discussion of sowing the oceans with food. Clement followed with his habitual prayerful attention. He was very intelligent and he wished to understand. But of course no one could follow Louis Colfax through all the corridors and convolutions of his mind.

Suddenly from Lou's wrist a tiny, busy buzzing erupted importantly. It was the sole feature about him which Clement really disliked. He didn't fundamentally mind the thousand irritations and even abuses Lou in his strangeness had inflicted on him, because he felt they were a necessary roughage in the growth of this peculiar but valuable plant, Lou Colfax. He didn't truly mind the time Lou drugged him. He didn't fundamentally object even to the black eye. All of that, and much, much more, was part of the roughage. But he did really object to that damned alarm wrist watch. Looking mournfully down on it, he said, "Is it time for you to drop dead or what?"

Lou snickered once. "Time for lacrosse."

"Are you still going to spend hours of your time trying to

catch a ball in a net?" inquired Clement. "Why?"

"Because the Indians did it!" answered Lou, his head cocked in his bird look.

"*Oh*," said Clement with sour, false comprehension. "Oh. Of *course*. That explains everything."

Looking pleased, Lou gathered up his algae sketches, put them in his own cubicle, and then moved rapidly away along the metal catwalk which enclosed and bisected the tower of books. He could not pass a shelf of books without scanning their titles, and now, as usual, one caught his eye and his mesmerized curiosity. Its title was *The Totalitarian Vision*. After a moment's sharp inner struggle he found he could not continue on his way without it, so he pulled the book from the shelf and buried his concentration in it. Fascinating. Still, there was lacrosse, the next lower layer of his mind reminded him. Deeper still, the controls of his legs took command, and he moved deliberately, reading, to the end of the walk, turned accurately into the steep, narrow metal stairway without lifting his eyes from the page, and proceeded level by level down the great sandwich of books, reading. At the bottom he went through a doorway and entered the vaulting library nave once again, slipped the book inside his shirt and, smiling mistily at the book-checking lady near the main door, continued out through it. He would have *liked* to check out the book, in a sense. And in another sense he did not want to check it out at all, did not want to make that concession to regulation, restriction, order. He was destructive. Right. Coming up to his battered Morgan sportscar on the side street, he put *The Totalitarian Vision*, opened to the page he had reached, on the other seat, and roared off to lacrosse.

The Yale Bowl, being two miles from the rest of the campus on the outskirts of New Haven, had been made particularly invulnerable to attack. From the outside it simply resembled a very formidable earthenwork redoubt, not unlike the Maginot line, which could hold out against most onslaughts indefinitely.

Spreading away from it were the flat, clipped, green open fields for lacrosse and soccer and other such minor sports, for

of course only varsity football was gladiatorial enough for the
great inner oval, the great Roman hemistheater of the Bowl.
Lou trailed out of the field house in his lacrosse shorts and
shirt and shoes, slipping the helmet over his head with the
metal faceguard curling out in front of his nose and attached
to a bar strapped across his chin. He carried the lacrosse stick
awkwardly in his left hand. *Ugh*, he thought to himself, *ugh*.
Still there were the faintly undulating reaches of the fields,
evocative of some sort of glory, something magical which he
could never conceivably have identified—he had made a cred-
itable start at creating a perpetual motion machine but to
explain even a small part of what such a stretch of open sports
field meant to him was totally beyond his powers. It was one
of those sparkling Connecticut September afternoons, what's
more, which meant that Lou would be secretly out of his mind
with the intoxicating promise of it until well after sunset. No
one would notice. It smelled, of course, of grass out here,
slightly moist grass, mown grass, and that smell, especially
after the Marine Corps dustbowls where he had largely spent
the last year, was almost enough to undo him. "Nice day," he
remarked to the coach.

"Yeah," answered the coach with reflex enthusiasm, before
noticing who had spoken. "Oh. You're back again. Let's see.
You're—"

"Colfax."

"Oh yeah. Well. Are you better at lacrosse?"

"No," he answered simply.

The coach squinted at him. Then *why* are you out here, his
face demanded.

Lou stared blankly back. I only wish I knew, his mind
wanted to answer, but no trace of this showed. Most of what
he felt his face never showed.

The game began. Lou was playing one of the three midfield
positions, although he knew that midfield was the hardest
position in this impossible game. There was the usual opening
scramble for the ball; it went to Lou's team. The midfield
moved down toward the other goal, passing the ball back and
forth, Lou realizing with a kind of fatalistic, surprised pleas-

ure that he could after all sometimes catch the thing. The
other side's defenseman was jabbing him with his stick, then
Lou saw one of his own team planted firmly to his left, and
moving swiftly just behind that player he "brushed off" the
defenseman and suddenly there was the goal open in front of
him—he had never scored at lacrosse in his life—and the
goalie inadequately trying to block the whole cage with his
body and stick; Lou cocked his stick, certain to score, and
then the brushed-off defenseman was next to him holding his
own stick like a baseball bat and he swung it at Lou, rico-
cheted off Lou's shoulder and hit the face guard, driving it
back into his teeth. At the same time Lou fired the ball and
scored. The defenseman, who looked like a long, undernourished wolf, loped away. Lou's tongue explored a huge-seeming
cavity in the middle of his teeth. This was it. The single hereditary advantage he had had, the one thing to make up for the
myriad curses in his blood, his Colfax looks, had just been
ruined. His two front teeth had just been knocked to pieces by
that maniac. Stalking across the field through the other indeci-
sively milling players, gripping his own stick, now, as if it too
were a baseball bat, Lou closed in on the Wolf, still loping
along the sidelines. "You've just broken my front teeth," he
pronounced in a tone which made the Wolf glance swiftly at
him, then look at the way Lou was holding his stick. "That's
right," Lou continued in the same disturbing tone of voice,
"I'm holding it like a baseball bat, the way you held it when
you busted my teeth."

"I did not!" cried the Wolf, his voice rising toward falsetto.
"You're crazy."

"*Yes*," said Lou, or rather hissed Lou, and hearing this
sound coming from the newly jagged edges of his teeth he
started for the Wolf, but by now the coach and other players
were surrounding them, and they were pulled apart, explained to, argued with, placated.

An hour later, back in his—yes, damn it, *his!*—rooms in
Pierson College, mercifully empty of Gordon Durant, Lou
went into the bathroom and closed and locked the door.
Tensely he went up to the mirror and very slowly bared his

teeth. There they were, just as regular and white and even as ever, except for the two upper front ones which were very slightly chipped. It was not, after all, a disaster. It was not, after all, the end of the world. It was not even the end of his good appearance. He would probably still be able to find a mate, to reproduce after all. His tongue had made the gap feel infinitely larger than it was. And there were, after all, caps which could be put on teeth and make them look exactly as they had been before.

He shut his mouth, he sighed. Doomsday had been deferred. And after all, why did he play a game as notoriously rough as lacrosse unless, as Clement had indicated, he really wanted to be involved in damage, injury, destruction? It wasn't as though he enjoyed it ever! And certainly he was never going to get any recognition out of it. He liked exercise, but why this exercise? He loved the playing field, the great, clipped sweep of green, but other, easier sports were played there. Why did he insist on playing a game where everyone raced around, brandished clubs menacingly at each other? ("Because the Indians did it!") Yes. The savages.

An hour later, Durant came in and went into the bedroom which by rights should be Lou's.

"Get out of my room," said Lou in a metallic tone.

Gordon gazed opaquely over his glasses at him. After an impressive pause he said, "What did you say?"

"I said get the hell out of my bedroom." Lou was very pale, his large fingers moved faintly, he was balancing on the balls of his feet.

Gordon tried to continue gazing with calm incredulity at him, but in this long, black-clad figure just perceptibly vibrating with aggressive energy facing him he saw a force he had never suspected in Lou Colfax, deeper than mere will power, a fundamental vitality. And Colfax was, after all, only asserting his rights.

"Oh," said Gordon, beginning to gather up his books and papers, "I thought you were using your cubicle in the library to study in—"

"And did you think I was going to sleep in the living room
for the rest of the semester?"

Gordon shrugged faintly.

"Those sporting prints in the living room are ugly," continued Lou, "get them out."

Gordon, moving like an automaton, took his materials and
stalked out of the bedroom; moving like a robot, Lou turned
and firmly shut the door.

That evening after dinner Lou came back to the rooms to
find that one of the four sporting prints had been removed
from the living room wall. Then, overcome by one of the
abrupt fatigues which could fall on him without warning, he
turned off the light and got into bed. The window next to the
bed opened on one of the moats, only three or four feet wide,
but nine or ten feet deep here, with a high picked fence on the
far side of it, and beyond that, the back of a fraternity house.

Some time after he had gotten into bed, Lou was roused out
of a doze by a low moaning sound. This continued to float up
out of the darkness intermittently for several minutes and
then the moaning began to form itself into a word. "Ou-ou-
ou!" it seemed to be, and then more clearly, "Lou-lou—Lou-
lou-lou," and after a while, "Colfaaaxxx" wafted hollowly on
the night air, "Lou-lou-lou . . . Colfaaaxxx" he clearly heard
floating up from somewhere below through the September
night and into his darkened bedroom. Suddenly the bedroom
door was flung open and a ball of flame was thrown into the
room and landed on the floor next to his bed.

Lou Colfax stared at it for several seconds, then with a very
controlled manner he got out of bed and, wedging a notebook
and a ruler under the ball, which was paper with something
inflammable poured on it, he threw it out the window into the
moat.

Silence followed; or was there an undercurrent of whisper-
ing somewhere around him in the night? He leaned his arms
on the windowsill and looked out and down, and although he
could see nothing human he said into the darkness, "What
children! Silly brats! Go to hell! and, strangely enough, that

seemed to stop them. A suppressed snicker or two, a scraping, he thought he heard those, then nothing more. Nothing more except his own blood reverberating in his ears. Then, after a while, he floated into the miasma world of a nightmare, not one of his usual class B variety but a really huge, vicious nightmare, and awoke from it sitting on the windowsill with his feet dangling toward the moat. Or was he still asleep *then*, and was that all part of the nightmare? And had the cries and moans been dreamt also, the hooting of his name, the fireball?

The next morning he pulled on a pair of khaki pants hacked off above the knee and lowered himself into the moat in the classic manner, by tying bedsheets together, and securing them to the radiator. He lowered himself hand-under-hand down the red brick face of the outside wall and was nearing the grass at the bottom of the moat when Richard Anders leaned out of the window above his own and said, "And good morning to *you!*"

"Good morning!" cried Lou, letting go of the sheet in his surprise and landing in the grass in his bare feet. "I—ha— dropped my—*toothbrush* out the window and it—landed down here someplace."

He despised to lie. It rubbed so abrasively against that pillar of pride at the center of him. Still, this time, this desperate time, in shorts at the bottom of a moat, he would have to allow himself to do it.

Richard Anders smiled down at him. "Do you want to borrow mine?" he finally inquired.

"I'll find it." There did seem to be bits of charred paper on the grass, or were they bits of burned leaves which had drifted there, or soot from a chimney?

"You sure were noisy last night," said the voice from the second story.

He stopped and looked up. "I was?"

"That yelling out the window—"

"Oh, was I—yeah, um, few drinks too many, I guess." His rigid commandment against lying was by now in shreds. "I forget exactly what I was yelling."

"So do I," said Richard, preoccupied with something else

now. Then he smiled blankly again. "Sure you don't want to take a turn on my toothbrush?"

"Oh no. I'm fine. Go on—go on about your business."

About your business! Lou Colfax went rigid as stone at hearing himself say that, all his muscles locking in a supreme attempt to block the slightest visible sign of his bottomless embarrassment. He could not believe that this antediluvian, old-lady's phrase had escaped from him. It was Aunt Fanny's favorite, and it had been lurking at the bottom of his mind, waiting for the most inappropriate moment—barefoot at dawn at the bottom of a moat!—to spring out and inflict, once again, the curse of the Colfaxes.

Richard Anders, however, had withdrawn from the window and perhaps not even heard the words, or at least he pretended not to have. Lou did not know Richard Anders very well, but he was still rather certain that he was good-natured, one of the old-fashioned natures. Unless, of course, Richard had been part of the moaning-and-fireball plot.

If there had been a moaning-and-fireball plot.

The scraps and bits at the bottom of the moat were inconclusive, so he decided to climb back to his room. He looked up for the sheet and saw that it was well out of reach and then realized that he was trapped.

"Richard," he called out, and waited. Nothing. "Richard! Ah —Richard *Anders.*" Silence, except for the echo his cry was raising up and down the walls of the college and the walls of the fraternity houses on the other side of the moat. "*Richard!*" he yelled again, very loudly. Still only echoes followed. Then a face appeared at another window, and then several more new faces, and then chuckles and remarks and more faces and mounting amusement and exchanges of observations which truly rose to hilarity when somebody noticed that sheet, hanging down toward him but not hanging down far enough, and then Gordon Durant's face appeared at his window registering first amazement and then amusement and then contempt, and then two campus policemen came with a ladder, and as he was climbing up it he received an ovation of derision, and then he was in his bedroom, the perfect fool.

II

Lou had had almost no sleep for two nights. The feeling of light-headedness this caused was familiar, and so was the gathering sense of unreality, as though he himself were made of paste and the world around him of cellophane. It was all familiar from his first infernal days in the Marine Corps, when there had never been a chance to sleep either, and where he had, of course, been the official butt of the company, forced to wear a bucket over his head for hours every day, called always and by everyone simply "Shit," the drill instructor's name for him. He realized at once that the aim in Marine Corps Boot Camp was to break down his previous personality and put in its place a human machine conditioned for combat. On his last days in the Marine Corps he realized that half their program had succeeded admirably: his personality lay in pieces all around him. But neither they nor he had succeeded in putting it together again as a machine for combat, or anything else.

The voices in the night, the fireball, the moat fiasco, all brought the insomniac humiliations of his first Marine days surging dismally back.

Not that the Marine Corps was responsible entirely for what he now was. There was Charlotte; there was his family; there was himself.

The next day seemed to pass uneventfully. Gordon Durant attended his economics class, played squash in the afternoon, and stopped at the master's office to begin the process of removing Lou from his rooms. The soundless machinery to bring this about slid into motion. Gordon had dinner at the Fence Club.

Lou Colfax went to his Greek class, his astronomy class, and his oceanography class, and offered his usual inept performance on the lacrosse field in the afternoon. The previous weather had held and the game was bathed for him in a ripe September shine, as promising as love, as transitory as love.

He had dinner alone in a cafeteria on Chapel Street. There were few experiences in life which Lou detested and feared more than having dinner alone. Dusk and then darkness settled over the city and the University. Wearing his black slacks and big black sweater, a tall figure, he moved quickly up lamp-lit York Street toward his college. An evening wind was mussing the crowded leaves on the trees, study-lamp light shone from the rooms in Jonathan Edwards College as he stole past it, feeling strange, outcast, fugitive. He went hurriedly along the walk to the entrance, through the arch, down the courtyard to the Slave Quarters, and his rooms. He was still feeling strange.

Gordon Durant, glasses set purposefully on his reddish, large yet inquisitive nose, was seated in the armchair next to the fireplace, reading. He was wearing his Hong Kong dressing gown and his leather bedroom slippers, and he was clearly possessed with a sense that his life at this moment was as it should be.

Lou came quickly through the door, cried "How're *you!*" very cheerfully, sat down on the couch across the room, hunched forward, elbows on knees, hands clasped, looking a singular combination of woebegone and lively.

Gordon gazed at him over his glasses. "I'm well," he finally said.

"Well, that *is* good."

Lou continued to look at him expectantly, and finally Gordon said, "And you?"

"Not so hot. Sleep. I—uh—have to have eight and a half hours or else you know things happen to me," his low-pitched, confiding voice went rapidly on, hands clasping and unclasping, "I guess you might say I get a little *nervous*—"

"I can see you do."

"—and I haven't been able to sleep very well here yet, there were some *noises* or something—"

He stopped but still gazed at Gordon, who retained his expression of laconic half-interest.

"Last night I heard some noises, that's why you found me down in the moat, I was looking for something connected with the noises."

"The noises probably came from the fraternity houses. What'd you think you'd find at the bottom of the moat? Water?"

"I don't know," Lou answered with candid humility, thus making Gordon a little uncomfortable. Haughty and earthy, crude and cultured, Gordon Durant had his own private set of reactions. Lou Colfax was simply too complicated for them. That was fundamentally why he didn't want to associate with him. "Tell me about your ancestry," said Lou suddenly, proving that point conclusively.

"My *what?*"

"Ancestry. Your descent. Family tree."

After studying him, Gordon answered roughly, "You can look it up in the library," and stared purposefully back at his book, sighing.

"I have, to tell you the truth."

Gordon looked slowly up again.

"A very very interesting family tree," Lou went on intently. "*Very* interesting. Yes indeed. Ambassadors and senators and board chairmen, *turf* lords, philanthropists, I don't know what all. Who was Mr. L. R. Muller?"

After a long pause Gordon found himself answering, "My grandfather."

"What did *he* do?"

"He was a tobacco dealer in Winston-Salem, North Carolina," he answered grimly.

"Not too much money on that side of the family."

"No money at all. Are you finished with my family tree, because if you are I—"

"Muller, Muller? Ah good, a good Nordic. A very good Nordic name. Are you Nordic?"

"No. I'm a Republican," said Gordon, training a dangerous Durant glare at him. "I'm reading. I've arranged other—arrangements about this room—"

Absorbing that information, which he realized he somehow already knew, Lou Colfax cut in, "You do have *certain* Nordic elements in your skull structure."

Gordon, louder: "So I'm asking you to use that room in there until you move out."

His sense of estrangement, which had been ever-increasing throughout the past forty-eight hours, at those words became intolerable. He was going to have to retaliate. He had now become destructive. Right. He had just been reading *The Totalitarian Vision* and he had, of course, his photographic memory to help him.

"Very Nordic," went on Lou reflectively, leaning back and studying Gordon's skull across the room. "In Europe, you know," his low-pitched, penetrating voice went on, "there are six racial types—the Nordic, the Phalic, the Western, the Dinaric, the Eastern, and the East Baltic." They stared at each other for a while. "You must be Phalic. A perfect Nordic skull has the proportions of length to breadth of four to three. You don't quite make that with your skull, alas. Then. Well, the Nordic nose is *small*, it is *set high*. The skin is white, rosy white, *delicate*. You don't quite make it in the skin department. I'm not making this up. You, Mr. Muller, are of the Phalic race. Sorry. Second best, Mr. Muller, second best. Pity. Yes! Let's see. Your face is broader, your hair is coarser. But your soul qualities, your soul qualities, Herr Muller, are *similar* to the Nordic. That's why I know you and I will be such great, life-long friends."

Gordon had his own kind of philosophical balance. "My
Nordic soul is going to kick your—"

"Ah-h-h! Good! Very good. Violence. V-e-e-r-r-y good.
Maybe you are a true Nordic after all. Maybe you are a World
Historical Individual, equal to the vastest demands of life,
able to *dominate* them! Blood and soil, blood and soil. Maybe
you truly understand the *Führerprinzip* after all. Do you?
The—ah—*Führerprinzip?* Two and two make five if the
leader says so? Do you?"

"You really are sick."

"No, no. *They're* sick. You, Herr Muller, and I, we are
World Historical Individuals, we are well, well! But you're
right, in a sense. There *is* sickness everywhere. The great
stream of race must be protected from it. Like congenital
weak-mindedness and schizophrenia, like lunacy and hereditary epilepsy, St. Vitus dance, congenital dislocation of the
hip, clubfoot, harelip, wolf's mouth." Suddenly he became
serious, reflective, himself. "Why were the Nazis afraid of
that, wolf's mouth? The animal inside the human. That's it.
Terrified them." His mind engaged, he had to be serious. "It's
what they were themselves." Always underlying his craziest
flights there was this flooring of sanity, reality. It gave him
what hope he had for himself.

Gordon Durant just momentarily wavered in his attitude of
disgusted hostility, and then thought better of it.

Instantly noting this, Lou plunged back. "We Nordics, Herr
Muller, are descended from the Norsemen. That's what our
ancestors were, cousin. Brother. Twin. Me. They were very
good folk, very sound folk. They knew husbandry, and cattle-
raising, and sea-faring. Yes. They built impressive monuments
to *their dead.* They dwelled in high, gabled wooden houses
furnished with beds and *implements.* They clothed themselves
in linen and twill and knew how to tan the finest leather." By
now he was using his full Prussian accent. "Zair artiztik zenz
vus highly dewelopt. It zhowed itzelv in zair *beautivul vea-
ponz, zee dagger,* und zee *battle-ax!*"

"Have you finished?"

"Nein, I haf not, Herr Ortsgruppenleiter."

But then he found that he had. There was a short silence in the sitting room, as there was in the September night outside, and Gordon idly contemplated this long black wraith before him, dark glasses, dark brown hair falling in all directions, hesitating, rattled, almost visibly vibrating from nerves, nostrils dilating like a race-horses's; he reminded Gordon suddenly of animals on his family's stud farm, for he was exactly like certain thoroughbreds in that he was overbred, too high-strung to function properly, a mass of nervous impulses barely held together by a desperate will, too finely distilled, a being the French would call *fin de race,* the end of his line, unbreedable.

"Wake up, Louis," called Clement Jonaz into Lou's bedroom the next morning at eight o'clock, thereby stunning him awake. Immediately concealing his dazed condition—to let anyone else notice weakness in him might be risky, he felt—he sat up in bed and said calmly, "Oh hi. Hello. What's new?"

"I was just passing by and I saw your roommate, the Student Prince, stalking away into the dawn and so I thought I'd come in and see how you were."

"And we came too," said Richard Anders brightly, sticking his head into the bedroom and indicating Brooks Randell behind him.

"You wanted to see how I was?" Lou said drily. "Now you know. I was sleeping for about the first time since I got here. Never mind."

By reputation a loner, Lou eagerly valued the company of those few people he knew well, and even more important, those few people who knew him well.

Brooks Randell, rather short and blond, plump but alert, sauntered into the room. "We thought maybe you'd be having your breakfast moat exercise."

Lou got out of bed, laughing nervously. He stood up, a tall, lean figure in jockey shorts, with a strong body but an attenuated one, as though nature had taken an athlete's body and stretched it three or four inches too much.

He yawned at himself in the dresser mirror. Lou was aware that he did not even yawn the way other people did, that there was a peculiar extra tautness to his yawn.

"Let's have some coffee," he said. There was a hot plate in the living room. He made some instant coffee for them, found some not-yet-stale doughnuts, and then he climbed back into his bed.

"This is the stupidist way I've ever started a Tuesday morning," remarked Brooks, following Lou into his room. "What am I doing here?"

"Sit down there by the desk," said Lou cordially. "How are things with you? How do you stand with the draft?"

"Don't talk about it," Brooks muttered. "Korea! Ugh! What the hell are we doing over *there!*"

Richard came in and sat on the floor. Clement stationed himself on the windowsill.

Lou was having almost his first happy moment since returning to Yale. He knew that he had a male streak of narcissism and a male streak of infantilism in his nature. That was why he loved to sit in bed in the morning with friends around him, feeling like a little boy being the center of attention, and also like a young king, the King of France, at his ceremonial morning levée at Versailles, respectfully attended by the assembled courtiers.

"You're looking better this morning," observed Brooks. "Less sickly."

"He never looked sickly," said Richard.

"Well, pale."

"I'm getting adjusted to this environment again," said Lou thoughtfully. "I'm like a tree. If you transplant me I shed my leaves for a while. Then they start to grow again." And then he gave them several of his theories about plant life and evolution, and then naturally moved on to the sea and the fertility of "abyss water" if it could be brought to the surface and the Benthic Boundary and how the tides if understood could explain the origin of the moon and so preclude the necessity of going there and how the ocean floor held a complete history of the development of earth, carefully

pressed and preserved there under water: all of this came out
very fast and casually, lest they should be put off by his
erudition; but these three students were not put off, not at all,
but after a while they had to leave and Lou sat still in the
bed, aware that they had listened to him attentively, that he
was not the complete laughingstock of Pierson College after
all, that there was far more to him than being foolish. He had
known this all along, of course, and Clement had known it,
and now Brooks and Richard knew it too.

Gordon Durant didn't know it.

Lou was always a good and sometimes a phenomenal student. If only he wouldn't forget to go to some course in
economics or something week after week, his academic record
would have been distinguished. If only he would remember.
But Lou always forgot, lost, one course each term.

This term it might be Introductory Geology.

It was not a science which interested him. He was interested in water, currents, oceans, troughs, fish, algae, the tidal
pull of the moon, the world-encircling currents, the fabulous
curl of surf. Why did it happen? That the ocean should roll
itself over its own undertow, arch and build and then crash
and run out and finally recede: the configuration of a breaking surf mesmerized him by its uniqueness, strangeness,
beauty, power, vitality, uncontrollability.

But Introductory Geology? *Rocks?*

Nevertheless he decided to try, and so he presented himself
for the lecture that morning. There were approximately five
hundred students on the ground floor and in the balcony of
the lecture hall. They slid into their deskchairs and began to
sip coffee from cardboard cups, read the *New York Times* or
the *Herald Tribune,* or to resume sleep. It was nine o'clock.

Almost everyone slumped, American-style, except Lou.
Knowledge deserved respect, even geology, until proved otherwise. The lecture, illustrated with slides, began, delivered
by a small and nervous man who looked smaller because of
the vastness of the auditorium, and more nervous because of

the size, virility, and famous impatience of the student body.

Two attitudes dominated student reaction to teachers: impatience and torpor. Lou Colfax, nervously sketching cross-sections of human skulls in his notebook ("If you die before me," he once told a girl he may have been in love with, "I'll dig you up in a few years, put your skull over my face and *see* through your eye sockets—real togetherness." "Ugh! You *ghoul!*"), heard the lecturer mention volcanoes and his attention snapped to the podium. Behind the small black figure of the lecturer was projected a very large and very majestic view of Mount Fujiyama, its flanks rising with the great inevitability of a work of art to the upper snows and finally to the climactic crater; it was thrilling, he reflected, this massive sweep of nature, this volcano, the greatest fountain conceivable, a mystical link to the core—

"—a great big pimple on the face of the earth," his hearing registered from the podium.

A GREAT BIG PIMPLE! A GREAT BIG PIMPLE!

A memory preempted his outraged mind. The previous December, stationed as a Marine in Hawaii, he had gone up Mauna Loa Volcano to the very lip of the Halemaumau fire pit. It was growing dark as he approached it and a reddish, hellish glow radiated from the crater into the sky; he walked up to the little, rickety viewing platform very near the edge of the crater; the earth around it was fissured, imperceptibly separating itself from solid ground before plunging, some day, into the vast pit below.

Hugely nervous but unstoppably attracted, Private Louis Colfax took his place on the wooden platform among five other speechless viewers. And finally, when someone did speak, it was in the hushed tones of those on the scene of a coronation or a hanging. Lou gazed fixedly down into the pit perhaps three hundred feet below as the wave of heat from it hit all along the front of his body while the chilly night air still clung to his back.

On the floor of the pit, rolling yellow lava slowly moved outwards from the center, inching across an older, solider black lava field webbed with golden streams. Near the center of the floor fountains of new lava shot up from time to time a hundred feet or more within the great crater to create this golden flow, and the noise of these eruptions, distant yet roaring, was the most unearthly sound imaginable, disembodied, unrelated.

How crazy, he suddenly realized perched over this uncanny uproar, to think that a volcano sounds unearthly. It was the essence of earth being flung up before his eyes, golden, liquid rock. The creation of the universe was continuing before his eyes.

He stood, unspeakably thrilled, and at last suddenly realized the underlying reason for his excitement.

This was the ultimate, uncontrollable force on earth. No fence could stop it, no wall, no channel. No will could stop it, no bomb. No one could pass any laws against its flow. It could not be decreased or deflected or interfered with in any way. It blew out of the center of the earth with its unknowable roar, its voice reverberating the chaos of the inner earth, and it spoke with the unanswerable voice: it asked no questions; it spoke chaos; no contradiction or even comment was possible; it spoke creation; it brooked no interference; all the science in the world and all the power of the atom waited helplessly before it, all government and all thought waited helplessly before it to see what it would do, where it would go, when, if ever, it would pause.

A beast in the menagerie of earth, it obscurely thrilled Lou Colfax.

". . . sometimes the pimple gets squeezed inside and then —pop!—out comes the—ah—lava."

Slowly, almost regretfully, Lou closed his notebook on his skull sketches, stood up, picked his way across the legs strewn like badly piled logs in front of his row of seats, reached the aisle, and walked out of Introductory Geology. A *pimple!*

Lou left Strathcona Hall and walked swiftly back across this hodge-podge, this medley, the University campus. It happened to be a perfect September morning in Connecticut, that is, a perfect morning. Its fresh hopefulness filled him with unfocused resoluteness, faceless gods, purposeless drive. He felt unearthly; he felt he was going to explode.

Entering his sitting room in Pierson College he found Gordon Durant burning the Soviet flag in the fireplace. Glancing up from this undertaking Gordon looked as close to being disconcerted as it was possible for him to do. "I've got somebody coming to see me," he explained gruffly, "so I had to get rid of this joke of yours."

The Soviet flag had indeed been a joke, but the burning of it wasn't.

"What are you going to burn next?" Lou inquired quietly. "My clothes?"

After a pause Gordon replied brusquely, "It's a thought. Do you have any besides those black pants and that goddam black sweater?"

Quite emphatically Lou replied, "No," and stood looking at him.

"I have some old things you might use—" Gordon began urbanely.

"Go to hell. Take that property of mine out of the fire."

After gazing at him for a moment Gordon said, "Are you serious? I won't have that thing in the place where I live."

Thereupon Lou picked up the first piece of Durant property at hand, which happened to be a Charvet sports jacket, and threw it on top of the flaming flag.

Gordon tried to lunge simultaneously for Lou and for the jacket and tripped clumsily between the two, swearing. Then Lou, not from fear of Gordon but fear of his own temper, went into isolation. On the far side of the fireplace was the bathroom; Lou disappeared into it and locked the door.

There followed an interval of commotion and some yelling from the living room, but after a short time silence fell. Then Lou thought he heard someone enter the sitting room from outside, heard a woman's voice call, "Gordon! Where are you, Gordon?" Heard heels move around the room, heard them pause on the other side of the bathroom door, and then heard tapping on the door. "Gordon, darling, are you in there?" Silence. The handle of the door was tried. Locked. "You *are* in there! Say something, my love. It's Norma—" Frozen silence from the bathroom. "Aren't you *alone* in there? Really, Gordon, and in the *morning!*" Her voice was low-pitched, penetrating, and very beguiling. She spoke with some kind of pronounced accent, a Mediterranean accent. Who in hell *was* she? ("I've got somebody coming to see me." *Who?*)

Calling on his talent for mimicry, he said in a Gordon growl: "Out in a minute. Wait in the Common Room."

"No, darling, I am going to wait exactly here."

Balked silence from the bathroom.

"You never listen to me. Now you listen, nothing else for you to do. Marvelous. Now I am happy. No, I am miserable now, and you must try to help me. Will you help me?"

Pristine silence.

"Because—who else can, I ask you? Augustus? Of course not. How can he, on his *honeymoon*, after all? And with the alimony trouble—I didn't *want* to sue him, but, darling, the lawyer I have, well, why do I pay him except to take his advice? Augustus is angry, of course he is angry, naturally, and so everyone stays away from me out of fear of him. I have no friends, no life now, darling I have no lover at all, it's *terrible*, I am becoming like a nun almost—will you believe this? Like a *virgin* again. I want to kill myself every morning for the first half an hour, until after coffee, and then my *longings*—"

Lou began desperately flushing the toilet, turning on the faucets full blast, turning on the shower. The bathroom rather rapidly began to fill up with steam. Who was this crazy woman? How was he going to get her out of the room so that he could escape? Why hadn't he identified himself at once instead of doing that mad imitation of Durant? But he knew it was not in his nature to have behaved, in this situation, in any other way.

He risked turning down the water, first the hot water so that the steam and the heat of the little bathroom would diminish to endurable levels, and then, hearing nothing outside, he turned off the water entirely. Perfect silence reigned in the living room.

He unlocked the door and stepped carefully out. A lady sat

on the couch gazing with a level stare at him, and Gordon Durant stood beside the embers of the fireplace, slowly fishing at his sports jacket with a poker.

The woman seated on the couch had shapely long legs, lithe and tanned. At first he couldn't really see anything else about her. Then he saw that she had blond hair falling to her shoulders, big eyes—*furious* big eyes—that she must be in her middle thirties, fascinating-looking; her hands were clenched, separately, on her thighs. Then she stood up. She was slim and rather tall. She wore some kind of light green dress. "Who are you?" she inquired in a low, dangerous growl, her lips curving. She had a fairly wide mouth. Definite Mediterranean accent. Silence. "*Answer* me!" she yelled. "Who the hell are you!" She moved toward him.

"I'm nobody," he was disgusted to hear himself quickly mutter.

"Who did you say he was?" she said scornfully, turning toward Gordon.

"He just told you."

"Listening to my confidential things, you sneak, you little— you goddam little *twerp!* Why the hell didn't you *say* Gordon wasn't here! Imitating his voice! You—you lousy *racketeer!*" Lou could sense that cascades of devastating epithets in Italian or Spanish or whatever her language was hung on the brink of exploding into the room. He watched entranced as she strode up and down the room like a caged panther, and although he suspected that, despite her rage, she was watching him watching her and faintly pleased by his admiration, he didn't care. He also sensed that she found him attractive, had responded despite herself to the Colfax good looks.

His overwhelming curiosity about her banished his embarrassment and alarm, and he asked, in all simple directness, "Who are you?"

Instantly she stopped striding, took a long look, full of some sort of significance, at him, staring directly into his eyes, her hands unclenched, she giggled very faintly, tossed back her hair, and finally answered. "Me? I am nobody too, I think."

She came over to him, moving more calmly now. "I believe I trapped you in there. You didn't know what to do. You were trapped. You didn't know how to get this crazy woman away from the door, so you try the imitation." She threw back her head and laughed loudly. "Then what did you do in there?"

"I just sat there thinking."

Her mood flashed change again. "So. That's where you think, that's what happens in there. Students think *there.* I believe it, when I hear the shit that comes out of them these days." She laughed loudly again, and ran her hand lightly along the side of his face.

Turning to, or rather on, Gordon Durant, she said, "Don't just stand there stirring your jacket, introduce us to each other."

"Colfax, Mrs. Taloumi Durant."

"Your sister?" he inquired with continuing simplicity.

Don't ask me any direct questions, Gordon's scowl answered.

"Oh darling," Mrs. Taloumi Durant said to Gordon in her vibrant voice, "don't be so *bombastic.* Is that the word I want? Ah, no. I mean—don't be so *pompous.* Yes. Pompous. Don't be so pompous, darling."

He rattled the poker moodily. Her eyes lighted with amusement, she asked, "Isn't your jacket done yet?"

"You may think it's funny," he answered heavily, "but I'm living in the same quarters with this—" His grimace supplied the missing word.

"And not being friendly at all." She turned her large eyes on Louis Colfax. "Do I look like his sister to you?"

"No."

"You are right." She sat down decisively where she had been before, pulled a package of Gauloise cigarettes out of a large pocketbook, and lit one, squinting across the smoke of it up at him. Lou noticed that she liked to squint this way: there was something masculine about it that she obscurely enjoyed in herself. "I'm his ex-stepmother! What do you think of that!" Her voice was so hypnotic in its penetrating pitch, its ener-

getic sensuousness, that the meaning of the words only slowly
filtered through it into Lou's consciousness. Finally he replied,
"I've never met an ex-stepmother before."

She laughed abruptly at that. "You hear that!" she demanded of Gordon. "He's honest, he's direct!" Turning to Lou,
"I think you are one American I might understand, and you
are one American who might understand me." Gordon Durant's mortification at this compliment paid to Louis Colfax
almost visibly disturbed the room. "Keep quiet, Gordon, you
don't understand *nothing!* You resemble your father too
much." To Lou: "Do you know why his father divorce me?"
Lou's face registered a thunderstruck negative. "Because I am
too *permissive!* Yes. *Yeeesss!* YES. *Too permissive!* You believe
that? *Do* you?"

Lou nodded hurriedly, lest she bite him.

All female once more, she spread a wide smile over him. "I
think you *do* understand me. *That's* why you fight with this
pig, my ex-stepson, no. Of *course* it is. He can't understand
nothing. It *runs* with the family."

"Runs in the family," Lou murmured.

"*Yes.* His *father,* when I let him go out without me at night,
let him stay out all night if he want, *I* don't care, he is a man
with a man's life to live, his father thinks I don't *love* him any
more, thinks I *never* loved him, or else I would fight and
scream and cry and be the little spoiled American wife when
he stay out all night."

"That was only a small part of it," Gordon Durant felt
himself forced to comment. "And I wish you wouldn't discuss
family business here."

"He already knows everything. I tell him everything while
he was in the bathroom. Women like me," she went on,
squinting into the fire, blowing smoke meditatively toward it,
"don't know what we want, I think. With a man who makes
very little money we say, 'You can't support me as you should.
You are a failure.' With a man like Gordon's father, who has
much money, we say, 'You only have money. You neglect
everything for money. You are a failure.' We are all bitches, I
think. What do you think?"

"I think," Lou heard himself answering, "it is just a roundabout way of saying the man doesn't interest you, disapproving about the money is just a way of saying it."

She gazed fixedly at him, and for a moment he thought she was going to kiss him. "How you know so much?"

He was silent. He thought of a girl named Charlotte, and as usual the thought of her ruined him.

"Colfax is full of shit if you don't mind my saying so come on Norma I'm taking you to lunch so long Colfax," Gordon said evenly without breathing or pause.

She got up. "I always obey this terrible family. I don't know why. It's not because of their money." She touched Lou's cheek again. "Don't let him *intimidate* you. You understand many things. You have—ach, I don't know the word in English—well, *gifts*, yes. I think you have gifts."

The two estranged roommates, equally discomfited by this unexpected compliment, stood wordless. Then Gordon more or less dragged her out the door.

Lou, tall, lean, and solitary in his black clothes, stared into the mixed tatters in the fireplace.

She had made him feel infinitely better about himself for a moment. It was a feeling which might have lasted, with luck, for about five minutes, if Charlotte hadn't been invoked.

He would never see Mrs. Taloumi Durant again, of course. Gordon would see to that. Did he really have something to offer anyone? Or wasn't he Mr. Nobody, certified as such by the Marine Corps, Yale—his family . . . Charlotte. . . .

He probed among the embers with the poker, and found a scrap of the flag. He fished it out.

"Somebody will master perpetual motion one of these days," Lou murmured to himself as he sketched a modification of his perpetual motion project at two the following morning. Richard Anders and Brooks Randell slumped at opposite ends of the couch, mulling.

This approach to perpetual motion had seemed for a time Lou's most promising attack on the problem, because it was based, not on machinery at all, but upon two ceaseless and eternal forces of nature, osmosis and precipitation. He had decided at the outset of this hobby that perpetual motion could only be achieved by linking the motion directly to natural forces, naturally. Part of his fascination with Mauna Loa Volcano had been because of this, quickly expiring because volcanoes so obviously were born, lived, and died.

"How does your perpetual motion machine work?" Richard asked, keeping his face very straight indeed and his tone serious. Lou shot one swift but infinitely weary glance at him, the weariness of someone who had been baited by others from earliest childhood because his interests were so singular. He had never known *anyone's* batting average or anything else about baseball, but he had known all there was to know about Piccard's bathyscaphe. That had not helped his popularity at all. Richard Anders, aware of this particular vulnerability and genuinely curious about Lou's experiments, therefore presented this question with the greatest care.

Noting this seriousness, touched, slightly unnerved by encountering this kindness here, or anywhere, Lou answered softly, "It's based on osmosis. You have a pool of water with a porous pole in the middle, and the water rises by osmosis up the pole, spreads naturally through a porous disc at the top, is turned to rain in a kind of involved way—that's where it looks like the whole theory breaks down—falls back into the pool, rises by osmosis up the pole again and so on, a continuing circle of moving water, perpetual because it's based on natural forces." He looked down again at his sketches. "It's not going to work because of the rain part, and I think the whole conception was too simplistic at the start anyway."

Richard doubted that. Nothing about Lou Colfax was simplistic. "Let's take a road trip," Lou said suddenly, staring at them.

"All right," said Brooks Randell, "where shall we go?"

"To my house," Lou answered. He made his Frankenstein face. "It's been empty for over a year," and throwing back his head released his extremely faithful version of the laugh of a homicidal maniac. From Gordon Durant's bedroom, feet could be heard hitting the floor heavily, the door opened, and Durant appeared in his French silk pajamas, fists on hips.

"What the *screw* was that! Colfax, this is the end. You're under arrest. I'm making a citizen's arrest. I'm dead serious. You two freaks are witnesses. I'm bringing charges."

Overcome by many feelings, Lou could only stand immobilized. He had made a complete nuisance and fool of himself again, outraging once again this new incarnation, the ex-stepson of Mrs. Taloumi Durant.

Richard Anders had the talent and the personal aura of a peacemaker. He knew how to placate even an enraged member of the Durant family.

A quarter of an hour later, Lou, Richard, and Brooks were hurtling out of New Haven in Lou's Morgan toward backcountry Connecticut, and the Black House.

The house did not exist in Lou's mind except in relation to Charlotte Mills.

He had always disliked that name so much, even in the months when no one seemed to exist in the world except Charlotte Mills, even then he had disliked her name. Perhaps it had been a label—Poison, Keep Out of the Reach of Children—which he should have noticed and heeded, instead of drinking every last drop and licking his fingers afterward. Charlotte Mills. What an ugly name it always was.

"The Black House" wasn't exactly the most beguiling name in the world either. Still, these two, Charlotte and the house, had been absolutely everything beautiful and lovable to him during the only months of his life which had ever mattered, ever been lived. He had not dared even to consider revisiting the house until two o'clock on this particular morning, on the most sudden of impulses, with these two good-natured acquaintances, daring to revisit it now, in tense circumstances, because he hoped to evade its power this way, catch it off guard and prosaic, find its shimmering spell gone, its power broken, find that it had become once again just his crazy old Aunt Alice's slatternly old house, just a place to go on weekends and be bored in, and not, as it used to be with Charlotte, the boiling core of the universe.

III

Lou forced the little English car—it had always reminded him desperately of Charlotte, this frail, terribly fast, springless, risky little English car—over the roads, and it brought them rattling through the stunned, empty streets of the town, past the Green, along through the tunnel of old trees on Main Street, to the narrow side road, the gravel road branching off that, the dirt road branching off that, and finally the old track leading bumpily upward to the Black House itself, still forlornly there, more slatternly-looking than ever, standing in the clearing alone, with a bone-deep Colfax aloneness, mad with Aunt Alice's madness, virtually the only thing his family ever had and doubtless ever would bequeath to him, rickety, frail, haunted.

It was not black on the outside, but a dull, dark green, high-gabled, a sagging porch on three sides with a roof supported by thin poles, sitting in its unkempt clearing alone.

It was truly isolated, because Aunt Alice could not afford it otherwise, and because she profoundly wished it not to be otherwise. No telephone lines led to it. No sewer led away from it. No electricity linked it to the grids of New England, no water mains to a reservoir anywhere.

It was an old house, some people said eighty years old, some said much older than that.

The Morgan came bumping up to it; its headlights raked the front porch and dark windows, the louvered double doors, a desolate "glider" on the front porch, two large and innumerable small flower pots with dead stalks in them. There was an old sense of emptiness everywhere, but not a sense of abandonment; the Black House looked as though it was holding fast to something in its interior, a secret or a treasure or a memory. There was no feeling of an abandonment about it; just an overpowering feeling of isolation, of holding fast to some bleak inner fact.

They climbed out of the car rather wearily, for like all road trips which start in impulse and hilarity, this one had degenerated by the time the goal was reached into weariness, discomfort, and regret. The clean, or almost clean, sheets of their beds in Pierson College were recollected by Richard and Brooks, and the latter began to say, "Maybe we can have a quick look around and then drive back—" when Lou Colfax interrupted:

"This house is haunted, of course. *Some* people are afraid to spend the night here, I mean, you know, girls," and that settled that.

They crossed the rickety porch, and Lou inserted the old key in the old lock. It turned and he stepped into the black room, reached to the left, finding there the kerosene lamp where it should be, struck a match and lighted it, and a certain amount of wavery illumination spread over the room.

"Be it ever so humble," Brooks said, "there's no place like a shack."

Lou stood holding the kerosene lamp at the center of its perimeter of rather uncertain light.

The house was exactly as it had been. Apparently it was too glum and shabby-looking for even tramps or teen-agers to break into. It was exactly, exactly as it had been.

Lou stood immobile with the lamp, not knowing whether he was exactly as he had been then, or not, but deeply fearing that he was, that he was the human shred Charlotte had walked out on here. The blood which flowed from the slice he made in his stomach must still stain the floor over there.

Looking more than ever like an overbred race-horse, unbreedable, he stood still for a second longer, and then stepped forward yelling comically, "Haunted! Spooks everywhere! Be v-e-e-e-r-r-r-y careful, beware, beware," and the three of them moved to the center of the room.

The walls were the dull black Lou had painted them when he inherited the house two years before. On the left wall, Aunt Alice's will, which she had written there, was still faintly visible beneath the paint.

But on the opposite wall, which had always been completely bare, someone had written something in large white letters. Someone had also stuck something, a snapshot, onto the wall beneath the writing.

Seeing Lou's face as he beheld this, Brooks said hurriedly, "What the hell is that?"

"It's not in Aunt Alice's handwriting," replied Lou with a faint laugh.

They moved up to it.

"Dear Lou," it read in a legible chalk script, "Welcome home! This is a photo of Mark. Love, Charlotte," and the rather blurred snapshot beneath showed her holding a blanket with an infant in it. She had also dated the message: "Tuesday."

Richard and Brooks looked at Lou. Brooks said, "Which one of your crazy relatives is Charlotte?" Lou glared at the words and the picture. "Which one is she?" Brooks repeated.

Lou continued to glare for a while and then he muttered, "She was a girl friend of mine once."

"So the little baby is—" Brooks suddenly saw a really ripe situation loom up; a giggle began to rise in him, "is the little tyke—?"

"Keep your mouth shut," Lou said evenly. "Of course not. Who knows, she must be married by now. When was she *here?*" he demanded in a more intense voice. " 'Tuesday.' That's Charlotte. *What* Tuesday? Last week? Last year?"

"Sort of an unusual girl friend. Leaves a note for you on the wall!"

"She knew about Aunt Alice's will. It was a joke. This is a joke. There isn't any baby, she bought a doll or something. This is a joke." He turned to stare at Brooks.

After thinking that over and studying Lou's face, Brooks said, "It isn't even funny." There was a silence. "She went to an awful lot of trouble." Brooks paused again and his well-proportioned mind reexamined the available evidence. "What if it is a real baby? It looks kind of real to me."

"What if it is? I haven't seen her since before the Marine Corps. She's married by now." He turned away to contemplate the darkness, "or else she got knocked up." His mouth would only form these last words very clumsily.

Brooks continued to look inquiringly at him. Then he echoed, "or else she got knocked up."

Lou came unleashed. "Who asked stupid you any questions!" he shouted.

"Talk about overreacting," said Brooks in a wondering voice. "Take it easy, Louis. Excuse *me*. It's none of my business," he added with a sidelong glance at Lou. "After all, it's none of my business."

"Tuesday!" snarled Lou quietly to himself. "Tuesday."

He sat down on an automobile seat, which served as a couch, under the message on the wall. In the feeble light the oval black table in the center of the room didn't look as plain as it really was, the two straight-backed wooden chairs next to it, the automobile seat against the opposite wall, the worn, round, hooked rug, the splintered wooden floor, painted black; Aunt Alice's *objet d'art*, a huge glass case containing a many-branched imitation tree on the limbs of which dozens of real stuffed birds perched, musty, frayed, some of them decayed and spilling their stuffing—a swallow and a woodpecker and an owl and a redbird and a sandpiper, a peacock, a sea gull, a thrush, a hummingbird, a finch, a lark, a redshafted flicker, a bird of paradise, an albatross, a bobolink, a Blackburnian warbler, a jaybird, and many others.

"I think it's illegal to kill and stuff birds like that," observed Richard, to change the subject.

"I'm sure it is," said Lou warmly, grateful for the change. "Aunt Alice wouldn't have wanted anything strictly normal and legal. Also, she hated birds. A cat-lover, remember?"

The two doors in the rear wall led to the two bedrooms, and a third door in the rear left corner led to a kind of shed attached to the house which served as Aunt Alice's kitchen, and a fourth door in the right rear corner led to another shed, the privy. There was a trap door in the ceiling of the main room which gave access to a capacious, sloping attic.

Brooks and Richard discovered two cots in the left bedroom and fell into them, clothes still on, and in the fatigue of post-road-trip depression, they were quickly asleep.

Lou went into the other bedroom, where there was a big, old-fashioned double bed with a great tubular brass headboard, a high, forbidding chest of drawers, a frivolous little dressing table, a valuable armoire, purple draperies, pink wallpaper, a red rug: Aunt Alice's boudoir. There were also three small chairs covered in chintz.

Lou slowly got out of his black sweater, black slacks, his T-shirt, loafers, and got into the sheetless bed.

After a long time Charlotte came out of the wall and talked with him about the condition of the house, its lack of amenities, and said, "I was here on Tuesday," in her clear English way, "Tuesday, Tuesday." She told him he didn't look well and then went on to other subjects, and in dealing with her Lou got out of bed and went into the main room where Richard found him there circling the table slowly, still asleep, and led him back to the bedroom.

Charlotte liked Aunt Alice's bedroom at once, the first time she saw it. "It's dolly," she said.

"It's what? Dotty?"

"It's that too, love, but it's also dolly. It makes me feel I would have liked your Aunt Alice. Pity I never met her. When did you say she died?"

"Last year. She wouldn't have liked you."

"Whyever not?" she asked with mock indignation.

"She used to say small women couldn't be trusted."

"You did say she was paranoid. I forgot."

"I think mad people have a lot of insight sometimes."

"Then you think I'm not to be trusted too?"

After a pause, he said, "Yes."

She scrutinized her delicate face in the mirror of the dressing table. "You may be right. I believe you *are* right. Don't trust me."

"Don't worry, I won't. I'm just like my aunt."

"Paranoid?"

"Tremendously. Isn't everybody?"

"*I'm* not. I trust absolutely everybody implicitly *and* explicitly. Hell, I even trust you."

"Then you really *are* crazy."

"How can you bear to leave this dolly house and go live in that college?"

"I live in a place called Dirty Durfee Hall on the Old Campus. It's the worst place they have there, and it's ten times as comfortable as this."

"Still you like it here. I can tell."

After a silence he said, "I love it here, it's true. I don't know why. Aunt Alice was *so* crazy, it makes me feel, I don't know," then he finished apologetically, "better about myself."

"Do you really think you're dotty? Tell me, so I'll be prepared, with the proper injection or whatever."

Lou contemplated autumn through the bedroom window. "What do you think?" he finally asked carefully.

"I don't know," Charlotte answered forthrightly. "I've known you all of . . . seventy-two hours, so how could I be expected to know. You don't *seem* batty exactly. More highstrung, and, I don't know, unusual. Original, that's it. You're what the Italians call *un originale,* I think."

Brooks and Richard woke up first and instead of disturbing Lou, who was at last profoundly asleep after his sleep-

walking, they examined the kitchen shed, found that the gas
ring was working, and deduced that, if supplied with the raw
materials, a breakfast could be prepared there. Richard found
the keys to the Morgan in the ignition, Lou always leaving
keys in locks since that's where they fitted best.

As Richard was returning from town with the breakfast
supplies he saw a woman walking along the dirt road toward
the Black House. She was rather tall and heavy, perhaps fifty
years old. She wore a long, closely fitted bright green dress
reaching well below the knee, and she carried a large hat. Her
wavy hair was bleached bright blond. Richard thought her a
flashy old bag until he stopped alongside her because she
flagged him down, and noticed that her face and head were
delicately modeled, too small for her body, vulnerable.

"Hi there!" she called out in a warm and resounding voice.
"You're going to Louie's house. Oh good!"

She got into the car. "Hi there," she persisted. "I'm Louie's
Aunt Lydia. Of course I'm not an aunt at all, I'm his father's
first cousin but it's easier just to say aunt since I'm, well,
almost old enough to be his aunt. Who're you? I saw the car
outside the house this morning when I went by to get my mail
and thought I'd just sort of stop in. Is that house liveable? I
have all the cats up home, all eleven that survived, that is. You
know about Alice's seventeen cats? Louie made me take them,
sent me money out of the check he got in the Marines—or was
it the Coast Guard?—so that I'd get them proper food. Wasn't
that a sweet thing to do? Still, five or six died off and one
thing and another. . . . Here we are! My, it looks bad. Alice
never *was* a housekeeper. Louie, Louie!"

Lou once again was wrenched out of one of his deep,
almost desperate sleeps. Louie! No one on earth ever called
him that detestable version of his first name except "Aunt"
Lydia, the failed television performer. Oh, brother!

Breakfast was set on the battered oval table in the front
room: orange juice, fried eggs, Canadian bacon, cinnamon
rolls, and lots of coffee and milk. Both Brooks and Richard
belonged to the big-breakfast minority at Yale.

Lydia spread herself in the armchair, the two friends sat on

straight-back chairs, and Lou, wrapped in a raincoat which
served as a bathrobe for him here, sat opposite Lydia, eating
with his usual ravenous speed. He never gained any weight.

"Louie, you look terrible," she began cheerfully, "just like
the house. Terrible." He continued eating; so did she. "I've
already had breakfast. I don't think the Marines did a thing
for you. How did you like it? I was in South Carolina once,
lovely, all those old plantations and places and those old trees
with the moss hanging on them. Messy people, those Southern
people. I'll bet you're glad to be back." Here she uncharacter-
istically paused and looked at him for a response. His mouth
full, Lou affirmatively brightened his eyes and flexed his ears.
"Oh, fine. This house is a disgrace. When do you want the cats
back? I think there's about ten or eleven left. They're happier
here."

Lou swallowed in a gulp. "Eleven!" He stared with a pained
expression at her. "Eleven! What happened?"

"What do you mean, 'What happened?' "

"To the other six? What happened, which ones are . . .
gone?" He stared in suspense at her.

"How do I know which ones are gone? Maybe it's only five.
How do I know? They come in, they go out, they get in fights
and get all scarred, they have kittens—"

"Oh. You have *replacements.*" Lou brightened. "How many
kittens are there?"

"Oh, I drowned the kittens," she said, not looking at him,
her brusque cheerfulness ringing false. "Couldn't have any
more cats underfoot."

Lou held absolutely still for several seconds as the waves of
dejection and fury at this went through him, and then without
looking at Lydia he continued mechanically to eat. Noticing
all this, she resumed in full good humor: "You're the limit,
Louie! Never coming up here to see anybody. When was the
last time you saw your father?"

"A while ago."

"Isn't that the limit? And here you are right here in Wetherford and you haven't even seen your own father."

"We got here at three o'clock this morning—"

"And him sitting morning till night, all alone, watching TV. What kind of son is that? Well, you're just like all the rest of the family. Selfish as sharks. Selfish as sharks." She took in the two listeners with her bright blue eyes, smiling her inscrutable smile. Richard decided she looked rather like a peroxide Virginia Woolf. "I used to be on TV. Did you ever happen to view my show? It originated in Hartford, but we reached New Haven."

"I don't know," said Richard. "What kind of show was it?"

"You don't know," she repeated in a drawling tone, giving him a cat-like glance, and then, quickly friendly again, went on. "Homemaker type, mostly. We called it, *Stitches in Time* at first, but the producer said that went over the heads of the audience, that title, so then we just called it, *Homemaker's Day. That* didn't go over anybody's head. I sang. Oh just a little, at first, "Tea for Two" and numbers like that, and did some cooking and dress patterns and interviews and, well, it lasted for a while, not too bad, thirteen weeks. Somebody else's doing it now. So Louie's father sits there staring at TV morning to night." She sat silent for several seconds and then suddenly remarked in an entirely new tone of voice, "Funny, you three students sneaking up here in the middle of the night like this. Almost like you were running away. Peculiar. Very odd. But then Louie always did pick odd ones for friends." She seemed to be ruminating aloud. "Birds of a feather . . ."

Lou was glaring at her, trying to hypnotize her out of the destructive mood which had just seized her. All the women in his family seemed to have it, a mindless urge to say something insulting to inoffensive strangers such as Brooks and Richard. Damn her and all of them; he should never have come back here, stepped back into their negation of a world.

"Aunt Lydia," he said quietly, "they're neither one of them a bit odd, at least by . . . uh . . . our standards. Richard's very active in Dwight Hall, which means he's very sound, and Brooks is very sound too. They only seem odd to you because, well, you're very preoccupied with oddness always, aren't you?" He would just let her chew on that.

She beheld him. "Left the Coast Guard awfully fast, didn't

you? Before your term was up. Odd. *Oh.* But my lands," her face changed, merriment returned to her blue eyes, "what *awful* breakfast-table talk. I used to say on my program, 'Girls, never let the men get serious at breakfast. The whole day will be *infected*.' I always told them that and I had letters from all over thanking me for the advice. What do you study?" she asked Brooks, bright eyes trained on him.

"Economics is my major—"

"Not *home* economics, I bet—or is it?" she added in an edgy voice. Then all amiability again, "Now there I could help you out, if you were a girl and it was home economics. But the other kind, the money kind, I'm not too good at, and neither is Louie for that matter and neither is his father or any of the family." She took a swallow of black coffee. "Louie tell you about the family?"

Lou observed her moving toward destructiveness again. "Aunt Lydia, they wouldn't be interested in that. Maybe you and I should go up to your place and get the cats."

She beamed at him for a while, and then her bright eyes lifted their gaze above his head and onto the black wall with the white message written on it. It was inconceivable that she had not noticed it before. Lou realized that she had stored it, as a squirrel would an acorn, for a needy moment. Now that moment had arrived: she was about to be asked to leave.

"How's Mark!" she suddenly yelled. "How's little Mark? Isn't Charlotte something, *writing* it on the wall just like poor Alice wrote her last will and testament. Past and future, past and future. Isn't it funny? Right here on opposite walls of the Black House." Lou was staring transfixed at her. "Little Mark, so cute." Her face, all one big smile, beamed across at him. "Always so, I don't know, touching for an old bag like me to—" her voice began to trail off, "see the—ah—family go on . . . ah . . . hmmm," and she pursed her thin lips and let her unfocused gaze wander.

Lou carefully extracted a cigarette from a pack on the table and equally carefully lighted it. He inhaled and then blew out the smoke. He hated smoking and almost never smoked. Through the exhaled smoke he looked across at Lydia Colfax and said as calmly as he could, "I haven't seen that baby."

"You *haven't!*" Lydia looked theatrically thunderstruck. "Is *that* so! I declare!"

"No, I haven't." He paused, and then continued with the same leaden calmness, "Did you see Charlotte when she was here?" Lydia nodded happily, like a little girl. "When was that?"

Lydia rolled her eyes upward, back and forth across the black ceiling of the room, and finally let them swing down again onto Lou's face. "I calculate it was about eight months after you left for the Coast Guard."

"Marines," corrected Richard tersely.

"About eight months after you two broke up, if I have my dates right."

Lou found himself grinding out the once-puffed cigarette in his coffee saucer, his self-control cracking, "And—uh—you saw this—baby of hers, I guess?"

"Oh yes." Silence.

By great self-control, Lou prevented himself from reaching for another cigarette. Hunching forward in his chair, chin down, he looked up at her and said, "Was her husband with her?"

After a thoughtful silence, she answered hesitantly, "No, he didn't come."

Perfectly concealing the fact that learning that she had a husband was both a huge relief and a final despair, Lou managed an almost jaunty smile and said, "I guess she wanted me to know she was married and happy—it was that Broadway producer she married, I guess—" he barely glanced at Lydia as he awaited this final blow from her; she nodded very slightly; destroyed, he went on almost jauntily, "I guess she wanted me to know she was married and that they had this—this little boy. That's why she—" he waved at the wall behind him.

Lydia knit various parts of her face, and then she said as though clearing her throat, "She didn't say about that. Just wanted the baby to come here, to see this house. That's what she wanted. She wanted the baby to be in this house." She

swallowed a gulp of coffee. "Well now, what about those cats?
They want to be back here," her eyes shone brightly again,
"back home, back, you know, where they belong. All living
creatures want to be where they belong, that right?"

Early in October Lou had brought Charlotte up to the
Black House for a second visit. Turning into the dirt road
leading to it they saw a small child, perhaps three years old,
sitting alone by the side of the road. Lou jerked the car to a
stop and was out of it and bending over the child in moments.
Charlotte followed. It was a little girl, and Lou picked her up
as though she were made of crystal, and talking very quietly
and simply to her, he eventually gathered that she belonged
to a family living not far from his house. They drove there,
Lou making comic noises for the child all the way. At the door
of the house the mother, who had many children, thanked
them but did not seem surprised that the little girl had wandered off.

"What kind of a mother is that?" Lou demanded, back in
the car. "She could have gotten run over! *I* might have run
over her!" and he began fumbling around the dashboard to
see if there were any cigarettes.

Later on, at the house, to get his mind off it, Charlotte said,
"For a freshman at Yale you spend an enormous amount of
time in this peculiar little house in the wood."

"Don't you like it?"

"I love it. Why wouldn't I? Whatever you might think, I'm
at heart domestic. Do you believe that?"

"No, not a word." He did believe it, knew it to be true. But
he did not want it to be true. So he repeated, "Not at all."

"I mean, if we just started from the beginning we could
make this a half-decent-looking place in a year or two. What I
wouldn't give for some decent-looking curtains on those windows." She pointed toward the front of the house. They were
lying on a blanket in the clearing in the afternoon sun, an
autumnal rustle of wind in the changing leaves, the flares of
yellow and red and shadings and surprises unearthly in their

splendor, the wood scents and smoke hints drifting by, autumn changing the face of the world, everything in motion.

"Who ever heard of a domestic actress," he persisted. "Do you think Bernhardt was domestic?"

"She was French," replied Charlotte with finality.

"Well . . ." conceding her point, "do you suppose Katharine Hepburn is domestic?"

"I believe she's a very good cook, and I know for a fact she has a dog. You have to be sort of domestic to keep a dog." She put her small, shapely hand in his hand, which was larger than seemed likely and full of nervous strength. "But that's all beside the point. The point is: do I have a face, a real face?" She studied him as he lay beside her on the blanket, "or don't I?"

He studied her in return. Impudently pretty, green-eyed, lots of dark brown hair, a small and shapely body, a little undernourished, a little over-agile, a dancer's body; but she had asked about her face; he returned his attention to it: high-bridged little nose, wide-set eyes, rather wide and sensual mouth, good cheekbones; clear, delicate jaw line. Yes, she had a face, all right.

"No, you don't have one," he answered, "not at all." She punched him. Seemingly immune to pain, he went on discerningly. "I could give you a face. Let me have all your creams and pencils and liners and sprays and all that. I could give you a face."

"First you want to select my clothes, now you want to do my face. What kind of a boy are you?"

"I love you too much, like a man *and* like a woman," he said shortly. "I think I'm a lesbian."

"Oh good grief. Get her."

"I'm serious. After all, you have your masculine side."

"I *don't!*"

He loved the way she said that, emphasizing the 'don't' in the British fashion; it sounded kind of pugnacious, Rule Britannia. "Just the way you said that is as butch as hell. Besides, all the leading actresses are dykes."

"Katharine Hepburn is *not* a dyke."

"Most of the others are. Just the amount of drive it takes to
be a success as an actress, the generalship a career like that
takes, means you've got to have lots of male hormones."

She drew in her breath sharply. "Louis, I am a woman."

"Oh my *God!*" He buried his face in the blanket. "Wheeew!
What movie did you get *that* line out of, and that *reading.* 'I
am a woman.' Eaoughf!"

"You're horrible."

Had he hurt her? He had always nervously gone too far in
every situation in his life. Petrified at that thought, he controlled his face and voice and after a silence filled by the faint
hissing of the leaves, he said carefully, "You have the most
wonderful and the sexiest voice in America." Husky but British, strident but tender, her voice was that to him.

"Louis, are you having me on?"

"Especially when you use Limey expressions like 'having
me on.' But sometimes an American accent starts to creep in.
Don't let it, darrrling."

"After all, I've been here for three years," she said, her
accent unobtrusively edging Mayfair-ward.

"But thank the Lord you still say 'after' to rhyme with
'crofter' and 'been' to rhyme with 'seen,' so all I'm saying is,
don't change."

"All right." She settled against him.

"And then there's some kind of anarchy in you, the way you
walk, a *snap* in your walk, something risky, and that's a good
sign. You *might* make it as an actress."

"They love me at the Yale Drama School."

"I hate Yale University."

"Don't say that. It isn't true."

"It is true. It isn't Yale, it's a university as such that I hate.
It's all so, I don't know, *artificial,* and everybody's hypocriti-
cal, and how you have to 'prepare a face to meet the faces that
you meet' and, I don't know, conversation at lunch, Jesus, and
the clubs you're supposed to join unless you're, you know, a
big rebel and then you're *not* supposed to join them. It's just
conformity either way, as far as I can see."

"You were made for a university. You're a brilliant student, you love to study, to do research, to delve into things."

"I know I do but it's everything else I hate, and the teachers don't seem that good, most of them." He paused. "It isn't hard enough."

She screamed stagily. "You *are* dotty."

He turned his head to frown at her. "Do you really think I am?"

"Yes," she said impudently.

He took a deep breath, rather hopelessly. "Ah well," he began, fumbling.

Had he believed her? Horrified, she waited for a half-minute to pass and then said carefully, "You're very *original*. You're an enormously original person. Of course you aren't crazy—"

"Practically all my family is."

"Well *you're* not. You're just very very unusual and," she suddenly feared she might start crying, "that's why I—I'm so fond of you."

They had met on the Old Campus at Yale during Lou's second week there. He had run away from, been expelled from, or left by mutual agreement three private and two public schools, but his scholastic record was so full of promise that the University had nevertheless admitted him. He was assigned to a single room in Dirty Durfee, and he more or less went about acquiring his text books and attending his first classes, but in an aura of bloodless unreality.

At that time he could not believe Yale and he could not believe himself: neither one truly existed. There was no color in New Haven; there was no real air there; his skin seemed to be drying out; his mind endlessly repeated to him ideas it had already ground to powder.

During his second week at Yale he saw a girl crossing the Old Campus, and the snap in her walk, the impudence of her face, the forthrightness of her glance promised some possibility of relief. Lou was always overcome with shyness in the presence of anyone he felt attracted to or in the presence of anyone who felt attracted to him, so he shot by her without a further glance and devoted the next week to discovering who she was. Charlotte Mills; student in the Drama School; English.

He laid a trap for her as he would have in the woods for a badger or a possum, the next evening. She usually had dinner in another section of the immense Freshman Commons from his, and Lou loitered outside the door she would have to leave by, and when she came out he managed to force himself to go up alongside her and begin to speak to her in German.

She stopped and stared at him, and continued to stare as he interspersed a heavily accented English word now and then. Finally he moved cautiously into full Prussian-style English and at last she did laugh, as he had risked everything on her doing, and they walked away from the Freshman Commons together, and after that life for Lou at Yale was easier.

He simply could not get interested in any of the extracurricular life there; he did not seem to be boyish enough for it, or else he was too boyish. Nor was he interested in the time-killers: bull sessions, beer sessions, football games, TV, shooting pool, movies, or blind dates. He hesitated about political activism. These were his Yale joys: Charlotte, oceanography, Greek, lacrosse. Suddenly it seemed enough, more than enough.

He could not meet a girl at the discreetly sponsored "mixers" with Vassar girls and such held at Yale. He was incapable of functioning there. Instead, waylaying and charming Charlotte Mills in the half-light of evening as she left the Freshman Commons was something he knew how, liked, loved, to do.

He drove her to the Black House the third evening of their acquaintance, and that is where he was going to inveigle her to spend every possible hour with him, every hour he could spare from Yale, from his fascination with oceanography, Greek and lacrosse there, and she could spare from her curiously dogged efforts to become an actress. "What's curious about it?" she tried to explain. "I was born upper-middle-class English. Genteel and all that. I wanted to escape from it. And, I wanted to be *noticed*. I still want to be noticed."

"I noticed you right off."

"I know, darling, but I was already embarked on this way of being noticed before I knew there was a you. Now I want both."

"You're greedy."

"Mmmmm."

They established what Charlotte called "a private world," and Lou called "a sexual seminar," in the Black House, one hour from New Haven. There Lou could lift from himself the intolerable onus of being a "college student." These were, to him, the two most repulsive words in English. He didn't know why he felt that way. Perhaps it was the apprentice sound of them, their callowness.

In the kitchen shed at the Black House he continued his chemistry experiments, and the one explosion he caused was not really serious and Charlotte was simultaneously horrified and thrilled by it. It was in that combined state that he hoped to keep her.

And he resolved that she would never lay eyes on any member of his family.

"I think I'm going out of my mind," Lou said lightly to Charlotte a few days later as they sat shelling peas on the front porch of the Black House. Lou had a theory about the inferiority of pre-shelled peas and all other prepared and processed foods, and that Charlotte went along with it, thereby condemning herself to hours of shelling and skinning and de-boning and de-feathering, was a towering proof to them both that her feeling for him was authentically love.

"Going dotty, are you? Pity." She went on busily shelling into the pan between her sandaled feet. "That's not the thing to happen to the head of the house."

"Sometimes I feel, my, well, my hold on reality seems to be getting kind of *weak*."

Charlotte went on with what she was doing, more carefully, and carefully she didn't look at him. "Do you think you ought to do anything about it?" she then said.

"Do what?"

"I thought everyone in America rushed to psychoanalysts at the very first sign of a complex."

"Not if you're poor."

"They have them at Yale. Free, I believe."

Lou took a deep breath. "I feel too . . . autonomous to spill everything to a psychiatrist. We're a very autonomous family."

She stopped shelling. "Do you know that's the very first time you ever mentioned your family."

Hurriedly he said, "There's hardly anything to say about them. There's really just me. Is that enough?"

Resuming her work, Charlotte said guardedly, "Some people say certain drugs clear up their personalities, give them insights that help wonderfully. What do you think?"

"What do *you* think?"

"I asked you."

After a pause he said with quiet sincerity, "I think I might go completely crazy and never come back. That's what I really think," and he looked very sharply at her to see her reaction.

"God," she said tentatively.

"What?"

"God," she repeated. "Have you ever thought about God?"

"God," he exclaimed wonderingly, as though she had mentioned Peter Pumpkin. "Didn't I ever tell you that when I went into the Marine Corps there was a form asking my religion, and I wrote pagan?"

"No," she said. "You didn't tell me that."

"I had to be truthful. My trouble with the Corps started right then, I guess."

"Yes, I would guess it would."

"They couldn't put 'pagan' on the dog tag and so on."

"I see. Yes."

"No chaplain assigned to us pagans, and all."

"Mmmmm."

"But the only religious feeling I have, the only true religious feeling, is pagan. Always tell the truth." Then he hurriedly mumbled, "Would you like to read what I wrote about it?" and almost seemed to blush a little. Charlotte had not thought her bizarre scientist capable of blushing.

"Yes, very much."

He went into the Black House and came out carrying a
black-bound notebook, and opened it to a page where there
were two paragraphs written in his flowing, excitable handwriting:

I worship nature, and people, and most of all people in
nature. I love trees which are going to survive, fog on the
surf, birds screaming and settling by the thousands in trees
overnight on their way south. I revere grass. The meaning
of life is the season of spring, naturally, and the meaning of
death is winter, and then comes the Resurrection, my Resurrection, spring again.

"Well, that's just the myth of Persephone," said Charlotte.
"Exactly," said Lou, pleased. "I wrote that when I was
twelve. I didn't learn about the Persephone story until later.
When I did, I began to see that I was a pagan. Read the other
paragraph."

Confiteor

I believe in Physical Desire, the Power Almighty, Creator of
Heaven and Earth, and in Love, its only son, Our Lord,
which was conceived by man, born of man, suffered under
man, was crucified by man, died and was buried. But it
rises again every day and sitteth at the right hand of every
man, and from thence rules the world.

"When did you write that?" asked Charlotte.
"I was a little older. Not much. I believe that more than
ever now."
"So do I," she said faintly.
A little later that day Lou went off, saying that he had to
visit "a sick friend, an old lady." It was only as he was driving
past the Green toward his home that he realized that in that
wording he had told a lie, after all: by calling his mother his
friend.
He stopped in front of the little white house amid all the

shrubbery on the side street. There were barely noticeable traces of shabbiness here and there. It was very unlike his father, the Building Inspector, to let his home become the least bit shabby.

Mr. Colfax, tall, portly, fifty-six, old to be the father of a nineteen-year-old, stood pulling on a pipe on the little front porch, wearing his Saturday outfit, blue dungaree pants, canvas zipper jacket, red hunting cap.

"That motor makes a lot of noise outside the house of a sick woman," he said loudly as soon as Lou had cut off the engine. "Next time park around the corner. Come on foot."

Lou nodded without speaking, came up onto the porch and said, "How's Mother today?"

After a stiff little silence Mr. Colfax answered, "Not at all well," with a strange resentment. Lou suddenly realized that she was dying. "Don't say anything about anything that's going to upset her. I don't give a damn what this week's problem is. Understand?"

Lou said he understood, went in, up to his mother's shadowed bedroom. She was frailer and more tentative than ever, crushed first by her father and then her husband and now cancer. They talked very quietly of inconsequentials. The mortal illness had returned to her face the ghost of her girlish look, which Lou had never seen. She must have been awfully pretty once, he reflected, awfully pretty once.

She wanted to talk. It was one of the very few conversations that approached intimacy he ever had with her. "You were such a good baby, the best baby that ever was. You never fussed. You always seemed to be contented and happy. Such a good baby always, the best baby that ever was."

In a little while he left the room and he never saw her alive again.

"You've made too many mistakes," his father said, on the porch. "If you get kicked out of Yale, join the Marines. Are you mixed up with a girl?" he demanded, in a Colfax flash of intuition.

"No," said Lou stonily.

"You started all that much too early. That's one thing that's wrong with you. All that's wasting time. If you are, and I think you are, don't bring her around here and upset your mother. You've made too many mistakes."

After Lou left to visit this sick friend, Charlotte finished shelling the peas, then changed into black tights to do her dance practice. She no longer had ambitions to be a ballerina but she felt herself just old-fashioned enough, just British enough, to believe that an actress had to have a trained body, a trained voice, a trained everything. When her fellow students talked about "spontaneity" and said, "I don't feel it" about some line of dialogue, she was quietly disgusted. You don't always feel it, she muttered to herself, but you just learn to get the hell up and do it anyway.

She was doing some squats, as graceless but as strengthening as could be, when a voice yelled, "Hi there! Hi there!" from the lawn, the front door flew open and a large older woman, very incongruously dressed in a bright yellow dress, sailed in, exclaiming cheerily, "Where's Louie? Hi there! I'm Lydia Colfax. Who're you? My, that looks strenuous. Goodness. Who're you?"

"I'm Charlotte," she almost rudely let it go at that, thought better of it, after all the woman looked pleasant enough, and so she added, "Mills, a friend of—Lou's. You're a relation."

"You're English. Our ancestors came from England."

"*Did* they!" said Charlotte intently, moving toward the oval table in the middle of the room and indicating a chair for Lydia, who, however, had already slid into it. Lou had been opaque on the subject of his family. To her questions had come the answer: "They're out of it. There's just me. Is that enough?"

"I'm on TV, that's why I never have any time to visit. Have you been up here before? No, of course not, no woman would let this place stay such a mess."

"I've been here many times. Lou and I use it for work and for our—"

"Is that so? Do you? My, you're pretty, aren't you. Maybe I could use you on my program. . . ."

Charlotte's feelings were thrown into confusion; all of them had been flowing strongly away from this erratic woman, and now suddenly she was offering her a job. "I'm not a dancer," she began uncertainly. "I just do that for training. I'm an actress."

"Well, we don't use actresses," said Lydia, heartily, instantly resolving Charlotte's conflict.

"I never appear on TV," said Charlotte coolly, which God knew was true.

She was thinking about ways to get rid of the woman so she could go on with her exercises, when she remembered the reference to the Colfax family. And after all, she herself was the first relative Charlotte had ever seen. "I was just stopping to make some coffee," she said. "I hope you don't mind 'instant.' You said the Colfax family came from England."

"Yeeesss," said Lydia, eyes sparkling. "I'll say we did. 'Good riddance to bad rubbish' they must have said in Merrie England when we left. But Louie must have told you about us, didn't he? How peculiar. Well, Colfax and peculiar are just two ways of saying the same thing. I'll tell you that much myself. Poor Cousin Bill and all. Just black, dear, and no sugar. What funny cups. Alice had strange taste in everything . . . chinaware . . . nephews. . . ."

"Miss Colfax—"

"Lydia, dear, Lydia, state-wide I'm Lydia, and in western Massachusetts and upper-state New York too, I'm Lydia to everybody."

"Well—um—Lydia, you see, Lou and I have so much to talk about, studies and *research* and things, that we actually haven't talked about his relations at all. Who was Alice?"

Lydia's slightly protruding blue eyes roamed brightly over her for a moment and then planting her hands on the table she heaved around and stared at the black wall behind her. "See that? That's who Alice is."

"See what—a wall—?"

She took Charlotte over to the wall and with her finger

traced Alice's last will and testament, still discernible if the
light was right beneath the black paint Lou had put over it.
"Of course," murmured Charlotte, "he did say an aunt had left
him the house."

"And he never showed you this will? The talk of Wetherford? Peculiar."

"On the wall. She must have been crazy," Charlotte mused.

Lydia's big, sparkling eyes enjoyed the expression on Charlotte's face. "Some people thought she was."

"Well," amended Charlotte, already defensive about the
Colfaxes, even to one of their number, "I think it's grand that
way, tell the world, emblazon it on a hoarding—billboard, if
it's important enough, scribble it all over the wall! She must
have been a marvelous woman."

Lydia chuckled to herself, then looked with wayward
amusement at Charlotte, her eyes reflecting some tricky interior satisfaction. "You do, do you?"

Raising her chin, she looked back. "Yes."

"How serious are you and Louie, anyway?"

After a silence, Charlotte answered, "We have a very serious relationship."

"Oh dear, the words you young people use these days. I
don't know if a 'very serious relationship' means you're writing
a book together or whether he's got you pregnant," and the
eyes worked over her.

The chin stayed raised. "He has not 'got me pregnant,'
because something else about us young people is that girls
don't 'get pregnant' any more unless they want to. But," the
chin coming down a quarter of an inch, "we just might find
we wanted to have a child. It's possible."

"You mean get married and—"

"Oh, we might want that paper from the Registry Office or
whatever it is. We might not. As pagans we—"

"As *what?*"

"As pagans we don't really need that. More coffee?"

"I'll say. I might even have a shot of something, if it's all the
same with you. Pagans!" she echoed under her breath. "What
next?"

"Lou's father and mother, when did they die? He seems so sad about them, you know, being alone in the world."

Now Lydia really raked her with those bulging blue eyes, bright as Christmas-tree balls. "Well, I don't know what he said or didn't say, but the grandfather and grandmother of that pagan baby you're going to have *were* living about a mile and a half from here last time I heard, which was about suppertime yesterday."

Charlotte was an actress. Her face handled this information by complex adjustments which emerged finally as an expression of pleased serenity. "A shot of what?" she asked pleasantly.

"Huh?"

"We haven't anything except some whisky. Will that be all right?"

Less brightly, more analytically, Lydia's eyes studied her. "Yes, some whisky would do fine. What kind of whisky?"

"I mean, Scotch whisky."

"That'll do fine. Where is Louie, anyway?"

"He—" she hesitated, then went calmly on, "went to visit a sick friend, he said."

"That would be his mother."

Charlotte smiled carefully.

"Doesn't *tell* you much, does he?" Lydia blurted.

Charlotte poured the whisky into a shot glass, filled it to the brim, spilling nothing, and placed it before Lydia. Then she said, "Louis is the most valuable person I ever met. That makes him different from others. I knows he tells me everything that—" it had all gone so well, so far, "everything that I need, that is between us. Who was 'poor Cousin Bill'?"

"Who?" The sparkle gone from her eyes, Lydia stared, and then said, "My, you do listen, don't you?"

"I try to."

Slightly daunted in spite of all the humiliations she had inflicted on this girl, Lydia leaned back in her chair and said, "Well, Cousin Bill is forty-two or more years old. Do you know how people tell you who he is, how they identify him? They say, 'Bill Colfax, you know, the *basketball* player!'"

Forty-two or more years old if he's a day. The basketball
player. I think he still gets into a few games at the 'Y' in
Hartford on Saturday afternoons once in a while. That's who
Cousin Bill is."

"Forty-two. Or more. Yes, I do see."

"Karen, we've got a—"

"Charlotte."

"Yes. I was going to say we've got a lot of pretty strange
people in this family you want to marry into—ah, I mean, this
family you're going to have a pagan baby with."

"Tell me more about them."

"Oh, I've got to get back home. Now that you're here I want
to get those damn *cats* back over here. He tell you about the
cats?"

"Oh yes."

Lydia studied her through narrowed eyes, then said, "Anyway, you'll meet the whole damn family at the funeral, if you
and Louie are still planning pagan babies then and if he
doesn't keep that a secret too, his mother dying. Well, just for
a preview of coming attractions, there's Marguerite, our great
lady—dipsomaniac, manic-depressive, spinster. She calls her
drinking bouts 'migraine headaches.' Everybody knows why
her head is aching. Then we've got the great Philip Colfax
Clinger. You've heard of Philip Colfax Clinger, he's our celebrity, or he was our celebrity, until I took to the airwaves. You
never heard of Philip Colfax Clinger?"

"I'm afraid people in the theater never read about anything
except show business."

"Politician. National politician, didn't quite make it nation-
ally, then he didn't quite make it state-wide, then he sort of
lost it locally. I guess all those lost elections have brought out
the *Colfax* in him. He ran for President last time—President of
the United States—the Anti-Fluoridation candidate. You
know, against that chemical they're putting in the water to
keep people from getting cavities in their teeth. It's poison,
deadly, according to Cousin Philip, rots the brain, a political
trick to keep the populace down. What I think he really thinks

is that he got beaten in all those elections because they put fluoride in his water. So that's the great Philip Colfax Clinger. Well," and here her voice dropped to a new abysmal tone, "and then there's George."

Charlotte suppressed a flinch. "Miss—I—Lydia, maybe you'd just as well not tell me about George today."

Lydia cocked an eye at her. "Kind of getting to you, isn't it? Now you see why Louie didn't tell you."

Lydia helped herself to one more nip of Scotch and got up. "Fill it back up with water," she said, handing back the bottle. "Louie'll never notice. He's in a world of his own, like the whole family. Am I right?"

"Oh, why, I don't know, I don't think so, no."

Lydia flashed a last, broad, conspiratorial smile and then, to Charlotte's concealed horror, suddenly dropped a little-girl curtsey in the doorway, and left.

Charlotte returned to the oval table and sat carefully down. Dance exercises were out of the question. She eyed the whisky. She had never cared for whisky. Then she remembered the Benzedrine in her purse and took one.

Perhaps it was all a lie, Lydia a deranged neighbor no relation at all to Lou, and all the others, Bill and Marguerite and above all, *George*, figments. Perhaps Lou really had no family at all, as he had implied to her. But if he had, if it was all true, if Lydia was a close relative, that was that. She didn't care in the least. Louis himself was what mattered.

He came back about noon: tall, fair-skinned, dark brown hair, all in black, walking in with brisk grace, nervous, big smile, jittery, intelligent, incorrigible, basically desperate— Louis. "Sit down, you look upset," she said quietly.

"Are you *drunk!*" he demanded in his resonant voice, half-laughing, half-disbelieving. "Sitting alone in a room with a half-empty bottle of Scotch! In the morning! What is this?"

"I've not touched a drop. You know that's not my bit." She paused for several beats. "It was 'Cousin Lydia' who did the drinking."

Hesitating on his way into the chair opposite her, a half-guilty, half-suppressed, found-out smile broke over his face, and then he sat down, gave her a look full of discernment and said casually, "Oh."

"Yes. Cousin Lydia called."

"Did she?"

"How is your mother?"

Barely pausing, he answered matter-of-factly, "Pretty sick. Very sick. Well," he spread his hands and gazed at her unhappily, "she's dying."

"Lou, why didn't you tell me about your family, especially when they're in this very town. Am I such a flibbertigibbet I can't be trusted at all?"

"Flibbertigibbet. That's a wonderful word. I think you *are* a flibbertigibbet."

"Be serious. I don't think you've ever taken me seriously for a second."

"Boy, are you wrong. Boy."

"Well then, why on earth didn't you tell me? Were you going to keep your own mother's death a secret from me?"

He sighed, sat back, flung a scrap of paper he had been kneading with his fingers on the table. "I was afraid you would be afraid if you knew. Afraid of us. Afraid of me." He looked suddenly up at her. "Well, are you?"

She took a deep breath. "I thought you understood. I'm in love with you. I thought you understood what that was like. If you told me your father was the Mad Hatter and your mother was Lady Macbeth, I'd—I think I'd love you more, because I'd feel you needed me even more than I'd realized."

He looked into her eyes, then down to the table, then back at her again. Finally he said a little unsteadily, "Do you mean it?"

He looked like a very young boy, utterly sincere, discovering trust at last, not having dared believe in its existence before.

For a moment Charlotte felt ancient. The drug was working on her perceptions. She saw him. She could hardly bear to see what she saw.

He was sitting across the oval table from her in the

straight-backed chair and now, to occupy his hands while his feelings digested what had been said, he thoughtlessly spread out the paper he had been handling. There was a pencil. He began to make a diagram of a cross-section of something. Then as he hesitated, reflecting, he looked up and gazed not at her but straight through her, seeking his mind's vision.

He was much more handsome than was good for him. She suddenly saw that; she wondered if he knew it. He knew so much and so little. His rather wide-set dark brown eyes, full eyebrows, long lashes, rather high forehead concealed beneath falling, dark brown shiny hair; straight, well-formed nose, wide, sensual mouth, face structure modeled for sculpture. And straight white teeth, and well-shaped close to the head ears.

And it was the teeth and the ears that obscurely fascinated and even annoyed Charlotte. Why had nature bothered to go *that* far! Couldn't she at least have made him a little jug-eared, slightly buck-toothed! No. Even the teeth, even the ears.

Pulled over this ideal formation was tissue-paper skin, vulnerable to everything. And there was a sense, at the corners of the eyes, at the ears, of an infant grown up but remaining in these odd corners as frail, undeveloped, as an infant, tiny last dots of frail infancy. All his life Lou was going to have this streak of newly born in him, startled, pristine, astonished, threatened. Charlotte stared fixedly and longed to protect him forever, as a mother would, be a tigress for him, cover him with an impenetrable love.

"If there's something the matter with my face," he said in his—that too—beautiful man's voice, "stop staring and tell me. I know I haven't slept too well lately."

"Your face is all right," she said faintly.

Mrs. Colfax died the following week. She left a will bequeathing her few rings and family mementoes to this and that relative, and to Lou she left her Bible and all her other books, and five hundred dollars. It was all the money she had to leave, and Lou realized that she must have set it carefully aside over a period of years in order to be able to leave him something of material value. It must have meant a distinct sacrifice for her to accumulate this sum, and he was inexpressibly touched. It was so typical of her to conceal her feelings for him behind money, and to give it from the grave.

The Colfax family had been rich in the nineteenth century by interior New England standards; they had had a textile mill and an interest in railroading, and then there had been large houses and grand tours of Europe, and they even kept show-horses. But textiles and railroading both eventually withered in New England, but the Colfaxes had anticipated their decline by an inner family fatigue, through two generations of squandering uncles and bad-investment aunts and improvident cousins, so that in Wetherford for the last twenty-five years the word had been that they "hadn't a bean" anymore, any of them. This was not quite true. Money of that bulk flowing through the family left deposits stuck here and there, a small residue of blue-chip stocks, a little cache of government bonds, an old trust fund that continued to dribble money. At important family events this money would come unstuck and to the rescue. It was sending Lou to Yale, it had helped him buy the Morgan.

With monumental reluctance, Lou agreed at last to let Charlotte attend the funeral with him. "God knows what you'll make of them all," he muttered.

"Think about your mother, not me."

"I am." He looked fixedly at her. "You are my mother."

She started. She wished she had taken a pill.

They were standing in the little downstairs hall of his parents' house, with its lemon-colored floor, a floor which had always depressed him so much, shiny, and inexpensive and pathetic. Here his father, Louis the Terrible, had stamped out his rages, in this little lemon-colored floor, instead of in the great granite corridors of the Kremlin.

Down the little staircase, too big for it, his father came, wearing a gray suit, black tie, and a clouded scowl on his face. Some other men, pallbearers, followed with the casket containing his mother. Lou could not imagine why it had to be so big and heavy for a small woman, nor how it could ever be manipulated down the cramped staircase. Charlotte, in a dark blue suit and hat, was introduced by Lou in a mutter to his father as he paused in front of them. Mr. Colfax didn't seem to hear.

Somehow the casket was maneuvered to the ground floor and they all followed it to the hearse. Lou and Charlotte got into the hired limousine behind it with his father, and with Aunt Marguerite, who had waited for them in the car.

"She always wanted to go unnoticed," said Marguerite at once, clutching Mr. Colfax's hand, "always self-effacing, sweet. And now, leading the procession in that great—tank ahead of us," she sighed a little sigh. Mr. Colfax's clouded scowl did not clear.

Lou and Charlotte sat upright on the edges of the jump seats in front of them. As the car moved off Lou turned and murmured, "Aunt Marguerite, this is Charlotte Mills."

Marguerite's weary blue eyes settled charitably upon her. "My dear," she murmured vaguely. Charlotte returned a pinched smile.

As the procession moved through the autumnal streets of Wetherford, beneath the arching, ruby-red or russet or mud-colored leaves, Marguerite, whose odor of medicine and face powder was stronger than the musty odor of the limousine, began to cry silently. Now and then she would look up piteously at the two rigid figures in front of her. Finally she leaned forward, touched Lou on the shoulder, and said, "Do you carry a handkerchief?"

Lou fumbled nervously about his clothes and then answered, "No." Charlotte felt compelled to search her purse and offer her handkerchief to Marguerite.

"I was so—disconcerted this morning I forgot, forgot to bring a handkerchief, imagine, forgot to bring a handkerchief to a funeral, think of it, forgot to bring a handkerchief to the funeral of a relative, did you ever, forgot to bring a handkerchief to the funeral of a *loved* relative, honestly, forgot to bring a handkerchief—"

"Aunt Marguerite," said Lou quietly, "is there going to be a wake?"

Something steely happened to her face, some flexing of urges and resistances, and then the face, patrician, still vaguely beautiful, composed itself and she said quietly, "I believe so, yes. It's wise psychologically, isn't it? It's wise."

"Where?"

"At your house."

Charlotte just audibly gasped.

Then Lou said, "I hope there's enough liquor at—Dad's house."

Marguerite's face became even more composed. "I believe there is," she said calmly. "Yes, I believe so."

By the time they reached the church Charlotte had in spite of herself become favorably impressed with Aunt Marguerite who, despite some little peculiarities, seemed composed, a lady, with a version of the Colfax beauty still visible in her face, and even possessing a certain wisdom.

Inside, the church was white-walled, spacious, with large-paned windows of clear glass, and only a ponderous pulpit to break the almost stark simplicity of the room. A large group of mourners, Charlotte presumed most of them Colfaxes, were seated toward the middle of the church. As she slowly followed Lou's mother's body up the aisle, she felt, from what she could glimpse of them, that they looked a very appropriately dressed, dignified, and handsome group. If herself, a stranger trailing in as one of the chief mourners directly behind the casket, didn't shake their composure at all, she presumed it ran rather deep.

Lou had refused to attend the funeral unless she sat beside him. Mr. Colfax had emerged from his reverie long enough to insist that Lou sit with him, and so Charlotte found herself with father and son in the front row.

The service was as simple as the church. But then came the eulogy, delivered by the Reverend Colfax Carter Henriques. In his black cassock and white surplice he rose into the pulpit and contemplated them below.

Charlotte contemplated him. Something wide-set about the
eyes behind the enlarging lenses of his glasses, a certain
distinction to the forehead, derived from what she was coming to think of as the Colfax Face. The rest was going to jowls
and mottled cheeks and uncertain mouth, sparse hair and
corpulence. His voice as he began had a curious tinny resonance. It startled, almost alarmed her. Why? She glanced at
Lou. His clear profile was turned intently upward, calmly.
What she heard when the minister spoke was unnervingly like
Lou's voice, but tinny, gut-less, as though spoken by Lou
down an old, rusted drain pipe.

The Reverend Henriques spoke in sudden, rushed bunches
of words interspersed with pregnant silences. His eyes darted
sharply, suspiciously here and there. He moved about, his
hands came up, down, his arms were flung wide, and then he
would stand stock still, staring down at them. He was trying,
and only partially succeeding, in being a spellbinder.

"We're going to miss her and miss her a lot." Long pause,
then in a rush, "Women like that seem to be disappearing
from our midst . . . from our midst . . . . We look around us
and what do we find but the whole general breakdown of
moral tone not to mention law and order . . . . "

"Old people have been saying that for five thousand years
at least," Lou whispered evenly to Charlotte. As chief mourners their pew was a little separate from the others, and with
Mr. Colfax in his trance, she presumed no one else could hear
him.

"Constance Colfax stood for forbearance—she did her duty,
played her responsible part never protesting her lot . . . . "

"Never did, God help her."

"She prayed! She worked! She was perhaps what Jesus calls
long-suffering and for such is the Kingdom of Heaven . . . . "

"And hell on earth."

"Louis—"

" . . . and let me just say this to you today . . . .
there is a heaven. . . ." glaring menacingly at them, the Reverend Henriques took his longest pause of all; from a profes-

sional standpoint, Charlotte had to admire his theatrical daring.

He remained so silent so long she began to think it was not theatrical daring but a speech impediment, when suddenly he burst out, "Some of these new Divinity School products well God forgive them for their doubts and lies compromising Christian truths until nothing is left anymore . . . .

"Questioning basic Christian truths," an interminable silence; at long last, "they dare to question basic Christian truths from the housetops and still call themselves ministers of the gospel they are blaspheming dragging their doubts into the open instead of living with them in silence . . . . "

"Like you."

"Be quiet."

" . . . wrecking the house of God through their intellectual pride . . . . this generation in and out of the church is bent on destroying the past. . . . . . ."

"Yes."

"Unwilling to accept anything on faith and so doomed to be left with nothing except their doubts and their puerile intellectual pride . . . . corrupters of youth are at work everywhere. . . . "

The sermon seemed to be going to last forever. Lou's nervous interruptions, his way of holding the shock of his mother's death at bay and, like so many of his desperate devices, vulnerable to the worst misinterpretations, subsided under the bombast and silences of the Reverend Henriques' harangue. Now Charlotte realized why he had insisted she sit beside him; without her physical presence here, he might not have been able to control himself. His was the kind of temperament that irresistibly feels it is going to laugh hysterically at funerals, jump off the tops of buildings, fall into furnaces, drop babies. He could not help himself. But she could help him.

"Whew," he breathed, when the Reverend Henriques at long last descended from the pulpit.

On the other side of Mr. Colfax, forgotten by Charlotte, Marguerite grimly pulled on her gloves.

.   .   .   .

"Wakes aren't a Congregational tradition," Lou said to Charlotte, "but they're a Colfax tradition. Any excuse for a drink."

"I think your Aunt Marguerite was right. They're good psychologically."

"Do you?"

Colfaxes swirled around them in the cramped kitchen, reaching, talking, laughing, jostling. Ice trays and bottles and glasses and plates of crackers and celery passed from hand to hand. It was all extremely hurried, just as the funeral, except for the eulogy, had been.

Dispose of her! Out of the way, into the ground, out of sight, out of mind. Get a drink! Onward, onward. Lingering over somebody's death is old-fashioned, Victorian, Puritanical, as out-of-date as poor Colfax Carter Henriques and his quaint sermons. Attacking divinity schools! Get the ice trays, open the bottles, get some bourbon, Scotch, gin into your system, mix it with what's left of last night's sleeping pill, this morning's wake-up pill, and the special tranquilizer reserved for occasions like funerals, and proceed to get good and drunk.

Charlotte watched the rapid disintegration of the composure she had thought she'd seen in the church. It had been all surface and ice-thin. They were, with a couple of horrendous exceptions, good-looking people and they did dress well, at least for this occasion. But they could not hold a line, could not contain themselves, could not complete a style of behavior, did not, finally, give a damn, it seemed to her, being nudged and edged this way and that by them in the kitchen. Philip Colfax Clinger, as tall, broad-shouldered, florid-faced, silver-haired, and fatuous as a politician could be, shook her hand, a total stranger, with the heartiest cordiality, asked her when she was coming to see him, and shoved on. A cadaverous figure loping back and forth on the back porch she conjectured to be Bill the basketball player. A deadly pale man looking absolutely petrified in a corner she thought might be George. She looked quickly away from him, and concentrated on not looking in his direction again. It took all of her willpower.

Lou's father stumped into the kitchen, the clouded scowl still sitting on his face. He took a quick swallow of straight Scotch from his glass. Mr. Colfax was ordinarily one of the rare, abstemious Colfaxes. He stared into the busy space of the kitchen for a while, and then his face cleared, his eyes brightened and he suddenly saw Charlotte.

"So you're this boy's girl friend, are you?" he demanded with a strange grin. She had seen people in a state of profound emotional shock before, and knew that the depth of their sorrow sometimes took the form of a kind of glassy gaiety. Mr. Colfax was passing into this state; she was touched to see it; tyrant or not, he had loved his wife.

"I—suppose—" Charlotte's voice suddenly failed; she smiled desperately.

"You're next!" His strange smile and the light in his eyes were leveled at her. "You're next. Did you hear Henriques' sermon?"

"Yes," she managed.

"You're next, all of you. Tearing down everything," he said cheerfully. "What sort of kids will *you* have, you people who're tearing down everything, I wonder." He included in this observation his son, who had been memorizing the name plate on the refrigerator.

"Oh, we're just friends," she attempted.

"I won't support you," Mr. Colfax continued heartily. "This big kid here is on his own. About time. Twenty-two years old—"

"Nineteen," Charlotte was amazed to hear herself contradict.

"Go ahead and *multiply* but don't look at me!" When he smiled so widely he suddenly acquired the Colfax handsomeness. "Don't look at me! Give 'em an education, I say. That's it. You're a pretty sort of girl. I told him not to get involved with girls—"

"But after all, Dad," Lou said. "I am twenty-two."

A shrewd glance passed from father to son. "Maybe you'll make a go of it," Mr. Colfax then went on cheerfully. "We did!"

"The hell you did," Lou murmured, but Charlotte felt, seeing this stunned false cheerfulness, that in some way or other they must have.

"*We* did, so who knows!"

"Where's Louis!" Aunt Marguerite rasped, lurching into their group. "Where's Louis!" Her hair was beginning to come a little unfixed, and her hand gripped her tumbler of vodka like a claw.

She stood in front of him, and with her free hand, she slapped him very hard across the face.

A red glow slowly emerged on his tissue-paper skin but he didn't move.

"Mock your mother at her funeral!" she yelled. "Make jokes to that little tart in God's house with your dead mother lying ten feet away!" She started to hit him again. Lou seized her wrist and pinned it to her side. "You unnatural little freak! I'll teach you—" Several relatives were pulling her away. "I'll teach you to mock that saint! Making jokes with that little tart!" They got her to the back door and across the porch and into the back yard.

Shaking, afraid she was going to be actively sick, Charlotte noticed that neither Lou, Mr. Colfax, nor anyone else there was as shocked as she was or as anyone ordinarily would be.

Scenes like this had happened in the family before, often.

Back at last at the Black House, she took off her hat and gloves and put them on the oval table. It took her some little time to get the gloves off because her hands were shaking so. Lou noticed this, of course; Lou noticed everything.

"I tried to keep you from meeting them."

"It doesn't matter. I'm glad I did."

Lou took off his jacket and black tie. Carefully he asked, "What are you thinking about?"

After a pause she answered, "Nothing."

"What are you thinking about?" he repeated.

"*I* don't care about your family, Louis. I told you that."

"Yeah, but then you hadn't seen them in action. You'd never seen Aunt Marguerite's right cross."

"People who can't hold their whisky are no news to me."

"Does it worry you about the future? About me?"

"I wouldn't care—"

"If my mother was Lady Macbeth and Dad was the Mad Hatter. Well, they aren't. Mother was Ophelia and Dad is Ivan the Terrible. So, doesn't that really bother you?"

"Of course not."

"Jesus, what a lousy liar. You'll never make it as an actress, darling."

"Don't get nasty just because you're unhappy."

Lou sighed and slumped down on the automobile seat against the wall. "Wouldn't you be unhappy?"

She sat down on the car seat against the opposite wall and stared at him and at the faint trace of Aunt Alice's crazy will still visible above him. "Forget them. That's the past. Think about me. I'm the future, aren't I?"

Lou's face was working and she saw that she had said, profoundly, the right thing. That gave her a totally unexpected access of courage. Therefore she suddenly said, "I want to tell you something."

He fired his super-alert look across at her.

"I'm not twenty. I lied. I'm twenty-four."

"You're not—I mean. I don't—"

"I lied telling you I was twenty because I—thought the gap might seem too much for you. I'm an old woman, six years away from *thirty!*"

"Old woman," he repeated with humorous mockery.

"I'm an aged female, and my, well, how shall I say, reproductive period is at its height and won't last all that much longer. If I had a child now, well, if I—we conceived a child now I'd be twenty-five when it was born and forty when it was fifteen. I don't believe in parents being much older than that with teen-age children, do you?"

Recollecting that his own father had been fifty-three when he was sixteen, he emphatically agreed. But what he said was, "I'll only be thirty-four."

"You are a beast."

"What's your point, anyway? I don't see your point," he lied, detesting it. "I don't care if you're forty *now*."

"I want to get cracking, darling."

"Get cracking!" he said with a chuckle.

"Get *cracking!* A child, that's what I mean. I couldn't care less about a ring. I couldn't care less about what your father said about not supporting you, us. I think it was that that really crystallized this in my head, this idea of a child, now. There really is nothing like a threat to bring out an assertion, is there? It was someone telling me I could never leave England and set up in America that made me do it. You know?"

Lou did know. It was the implicit threat of inescapable strangeness and failure in his family tree that accounted for his every effort to surmount them.

"Also," she went on, "I've been doing some checking. Bernhardt *did* have a child. Illegitimate, of course. Actually, you love children."

"I know I do," he murmured.

"A child," she repeated. "I can't stand barren women, in the theater or out of it. They're so dry, like those leaves out there in front of the house, skittering this way and that, cackling. I can't bear that, not for myself."

Desperately, Lou said, "I don't think *Katharine Hepburn* has any children."

Charlotte paused and then answered slowly, "I don't think I'm going to have a career like Katharine Hepburn's—I—I don't really think I'm that good, not really anything like that good. Acting will never take up that much space in my life. I won't last that long. I'll need something more. I'll need a child, maybe just one, but—a child," she stopped. "Will you give it to me?" She looked across the room at him.

"Of course I—naturally—"

"That's the word. Naturally."

"I'm so goddamned messed up. Such a Colfax!"

"You aren't. You're very balanced in many ways. Or else you wouldn't be spending your life entirely with me and your studies. You'd be, I don't know, playing *basketball*—"

"There's my lacrosse."

"That's just aesthetics with you, a sort of nature walk, that's why you go to the lacrosse field."

He was silent, pleased to be understood.

"You'd be going to those horrid mixers to meet Vassar girls, you'd have *beer* parties. You are pursuing your goals, and I want to pursue my goals too. I don't want my dreams to go up in smoke, to fade away. I'd love to have a really good part in a good Broadway play—or *Off*-Broadway play. I don't care, maybe just once. And a child. Maybe just once."

"All right," he said quietly.

A chord deeper than any she thought possible then struck in her. It was at once the most erotic and most idealistic seizure she had ever experienced, and beyond anything she had imagined possible, in herself or anyone else.

They wandered into the kitchen shed for glasses and drank some Scotch. It had an unexpectedly powerful effect on her.

He took her shaking hand; trembling, she got out of her clothes; light-headed, she got into Aunt Alice's bed, and as he made love to her, for the twentieth or fortieth time, she felt this act between them as wondrously new, limitlessly meaningful and so as though carried out in slow motion, that all its profound movements and their meanings and clamoring excitements might be clear, its stages so fully expressed that they could be carved in stone for—yes, for future generations.

She fell asleep. She had not slept like that before, at least not since earliest childhood. She slept as though wrapped in soft gauze, layer on layer, her body and her mind too, cushioned, overlaid, rested as she had forgotten the possibility of such rest, floated deep, and when she woke in the morning it was as though she had returned renewed from some long and marvelous journey, and that she and Wetherford and the Black House and Lou were all fresh and vivid as they had never been before, heightened in all their qualities.

Lou was not beside her in the bed. Soon she heard the Morgan drive up, and he came into the main room, which was alight with sun shining into it through the festive autumnal

leaves; magical, all of it, and she was a part of, was the center
of all of it.

Lou had never looked quite this handsome before. He
moved about the room, setting the oval table for breakfast.

Charlotte stopped in the doorway from the bedroom, wearing Alice's long blue robe, shiny brown hair around her face
and shoulders, and realized that he had never set the table
before. He did not do things like that. Some faintest ripple of
apprehension stirred in her, and the cocoon of enchantment in
which she had spent one third of one twenty-four hour cycle
in all the years of her life on earth began to unravel.

"I'll do that," she said.

"It's okay. Sit here. What kind of eggs do you want?"

"Any kind." Then she broke free into deepest happiness
again. He was acting like the very stereotype of a husband
with a newly pregnant wife on his hands. It was so touching,
and so funny, that she felt like crying. Instead, her English-
ness asserted itself this morning, and she said, "On second
thought, soft-boiled, four minutes."

He glanced at her and then went into the kitchen to boil
some water on the gas ring. "How did you sleep?" he called to
her.

"Like a—baby," she heard herself reply.

Silence from the kitchen; then she said, "I didn't even hear
you get up and go out."

More silence from the kitchen, so she then pursued casually,
"Where did you go?"

"To put flowers on mother's grave."

She drew a long breath, moved by that, wondering why she
hadn't thought of it herself.

And then, for some reason, she suddenly did not believe
him. The cocoon unraveled a little more.

"Are you feeling all right?" he asked.

The solicitous husband again, she thought, and her joy
returned. "Never better." She hesitated, and then her sense of
magical joy overflowed and she could not contain it, didn't
want to, least of all from Lou. "I believe I may be pregnant
even though, I know, that's ridiculous and silly, and I have

nothing but superstition to support it, but, all the same, I can't
help that feeling. I've never felt like this *ever* before in my life
and never will again I'm sure, perfectly sure, so just don't
laugh at me and see if I'm not right in a month or so because I
just mean that there's got to be some special explanation for
the perfectly, well, extraordinary way I happen to feel this
morning and the way I slept, floated, last night. There has to
be."

"Very well," he said quietly.

"What?"

Silence.

'Very well?' Charlotte was baffled by these two simple
words he had used because they were so completely out of
character, totally absent from his usual vocabulary; they
sounded formal, clerkish, prim almost. 'Very well?' It sounded
like an impersonation. And yet it was impossible to question
him or even ponder anything so trivial. And the unraveling
progressed.

Lou came out of the kitchen and set the eggs, with toast
and coffee, before her. The texture of the eggs, the degree of
brownness of the toast, the amount of marmalade on the plate
beside it, even the height to which the coffee had been poured
in the cup, displayed Lou's scientist's concern with precision,
order, exact calculation. His own appearance and his rooms
did not show this; these were the Given, and so they were
casual, sometimes messy; but what he *did*, what he acted
upon, created, from boiled eggs to bombs to the charting of
the seas, had to be done with this meditative, devoted care
and exactitude.

Charlotte began slowly to eat the breakfast; opposite her,
he wolfed his.

"How weird," she couldn't help saying in a wondering
voice, "to have creation inside of you. *Don't* laugh! Please,
please, don't. Let me sound as silly as I want, just once, just
this morning." She leaned toward him, her long hair falling
forward. "I've never had a morning like this and," the happiness fading a little from her voice, "I think probably I never
will have again. I'm a 'Once' person, I think. One good role,

one good baby." She looked a shade tearily at him. "One good morning like this, in my life."

"Charlotte—"

"So just let me be a slob and cry or whatever. It's not a scene you're going to see me play again."

"Charlotte—"

"I know I have this *briskness,* British briskness, British *brittleness* about me most of the time. I know you happen to *like* that, my *snap* you call it. Well . . . Louis, it's a pose, a 'defense,' my wall protecting my shyness—all English people are hopelessly shy, you know—and, no I'm not going to cry at all darling, so don't look so uncomfortable—but this one morning of my life, let me be a slob, Sentimental Sarah, because a mother isn't brisk and brittle, or shouldn't be, shouldn't be *shy* either for that matter, *should* be full of emotions and feelings and sentiments, and even—tears."

"Charlotte, listen, I—"

"Probably I *am* talking a lot of nonsense. Probably I'm not pregnant at all. What do you think?"

"Charlotte—" his face was contorted with a pleading look, unhandsome for the first time in her experience, almost unrecognizable. Suddenly she remembered the utterly changed face of Marguerite between the ride to the church and the wake afterward. She felt along her upper right arm with her left hand, as though some message in Braille were written there to reassure her. But there was no reassurance. "Charlotte, you're not pregnant, you can't be because—I, we had those drinks last night, so you didn't notice . . . it seemed better, you got all upset by my family, funerals, that witch, it seemed better so I put—my—uh—the rubber—"

Charlotte stared at him for several seconds, and then as the meaning of his words reached her and the tormented expression on his face convinced her that what he said was true, she let her eyes fall to the last of the egg on her plate, pulled the paper napkin out of her lap, crushed it, put it on the plate, got up, murmured, "Excuse me" as she had been taught to do as a little girl when leaving the table, and made her way across toward the bedroom door. "Excuse me," she murmured again,

more or less to herself. Lou got up swiftly and moved across
toward her, but Charlotte reached the bedroom, slammed shut
the door and threw Aunt Alice's powerful, paranoid lock.
Nothing short of an ax could penetrate Aunt Alice's bedroom
when locked.

Lou tried for a while to talk through the door, then began
to putter uselessly around the outside room.

Two hours later Charlotte came out. She had on the same
robe; her hair hung down as before. She was exactly the same,
except that to Lou she looked violently different, as though
she had been brutalized.

He wanted to kill himself. "More coffee?" he asked.

"Please."

"Getting a little sunnier. Cream? I know sometimes you like
it black or—"

"Mmm. Cream. One sugar. Nice day to travel."

"It sure is. Travel?"

"I mean for driving to New Haven. My class."

"Yes. Your class?"

"Improvisations."

"That's tonight?"

"Mmm. I may stay over. I think I probably will. Those
improvisations can be interminable."

"When do we leave?"

She stirred her coffee. "Well if you don't need the car I'll
just take it as I've done before, and you'll want to stay here
and help your father with the after-funeral things, there must
be loads to do."

"I don't need the car, no."

"But you do, you do," she said decisively. "I'll simply take
the train from Hartford to New Haven."

"You'll take the car."

"I'll take the train from Hartford to New Haven," she said
quietly.

Lou crossed to look out the window. "Very well," he said.
"I'll call you in your room in New Haven at midnight."

"There's no phone here, don't—"

"I'll call you from the booth on the highway, okay?"

"Why go out?"

"I'll call you, okay?"

"Okay," she said casually.

"Charlotte, listen," he began.

"No need to say anything," she said, "I understand."

"Maybe you do and maybe you don't. If you want—"

"I understand. No need."

He sighed. "Do you love me?" he asked, trying for a cheerful tone.

"Love," she said. "Love is what people do, not what they say, isn't it? It's what I do that shows that, not what I say. You have to answer your own question. So, do I love you?"

After a silence, he said, "Yes."

Charlotte took the six o'clock train to New Haven that night. She was not in her room there when he called at midnight, not in when he called at one o'clock, not in at two. He was afraid to call at three, although he was still in the outdoor telephone booth on the highway, as he was at four, five, and six.

After clearing Aunt Lydia out of the house, after persuading her to keep the cats a while longer, for he could not always be at the Black House and even a cat killer like herself was better than homelessness, Lou went to see his father.

Mr. Colfax had had the most famous temper in the entire family. His was the temperament of a Stalin who had never been in the position to give an order. So he had in the last year suffered a series of strokes instead.

Richard and Brooks argued that they had to return to New Haven at once, but having made up his mind to see his father Lou was incapable of postponing the visit. Embarrassed, apologetic but unswervable, Lou left them arguing on the porch of the Black House, and drove into the center of the little old town. This morning the Green had a kind of lackadaisical animation; the Colonial mansions and the Congregational church looked a little less like relics.

He turned into a side street and stopped in front of his old

house, lost in trees and shrubbery, low-roofed, white, a little
shabbier and more unkempt than when he had last seen it.
His father would not be particularly surprised to see him.

Lou went through the wooden front gate, across the minute,
scrappy front yard, over the squeaking porch, sinking with
each step into all the feelings surrounding this house which he
had never solved.

He stepped into the modest front hall with its old Victorian
sofa and coat rack, and called out, "Dad? Father?" before
remembering that, in his last stroke, his father had been struck
dumb.

There was a scraping in the upstairs hall, and Lou grabbed
the newel post and sprang up the narrow stairway. His father
stood in a long maroon and gray bathrobe leaning forward,
his big hands clutching the top bar of his aluminum "walker."
His face was flushed and his eyes were bright. He was trying
to speak.

Lou went up and embraced him, and his father tried to
speak. They moved, Lou following, to the far end of the hall
and into a medium-sized rugless room with the sun coming in
by its three windows. Until he went into the Marines this had
been his bedroom; Mr. Colfax used it because it had a southern exposure. The furniture had been changed; it now con-
tained a rocker with a large oval table beside it, a large
television set on which this morning the sound was turned off,
and the screen showed a lady busily kneading dough and
apparently talking loquaciously. There was also a plain
wooden chair. Lou started to aid his father into the rocker,
but sensing that this would be resented he stood until Mr.
Colfax had lowered himself into it and then sat in the other
chair.

Then Lou started to talk. With his family he had until now
been as wordless as possible, all his life.

Now—*too late?*—he started to talk. "Well I should have
come sooner to see you, I know, but getting things settled at
Yale took up all my time, and I didn't figure you'd miss me
that much." His father watched him with a kind of eagerness,
his mouth moving slightly. "I've had a fairly tough time, to tell

you the truth. I've never told you the truth, the real truth, about anything before. I didn't lie either, I just didn't tell the truth. So here goes. I just wasn't cut out for the Marine Corps, and they figured that out fairly fast and so I didn't serve my full term. No, not a dishonorable discharge, I was just let out 'for the convenience of the service,' and if things ever get really drastic, the Chinese Reds start landing in San Diego or something like that, why, they'll call me back. They'll never do it for anything less, believe me! Were they glad to get rid of me. Boy."

Lou leaned forward, elbows on knees, his large hands clenching and unclenching, badly needing occupation. Usually he sketched whenever possible, the cross-section of a jet engine, or endless personal modifications of the Piccard bathyscaphe he would build and test someday, he hoped. He knew this manual restlessness was the kind other people relieved by smoking cigarettes, but he had too vivid a sense of anatomy, of the beauty and fragility of lung tissue, too clear an image of the stains smoking would splatter on it, to use cigarettes except under extreme pressure. He had chain-smoked in the Marine Corps.

"I know I never opened myself up with you before. Couldn't help it. I was too afraid of you, in case you want to know the truth. I mean the way you used to throw me around the room, this room come to think of it, slapping me around because my cats were out and I couldn't get them to come in and their yowling was keeping you awake. Everything kept you awake. If it hadn't been that, it would have been pins dropping somewhere. You didn't *trust* sleep. Or anything else. So you'd slap me around for a while. You kept it right up until that time I was sixteen and you took me on and a funny thing happened. I was stronger than you were. You felt it. And so, that was it. That was the last fight. I faked it. I let you seem to win. But you knew who won it. Remember?

"I'm just trying to make one point. You're a mistake." Lou examined his nervous hands, and then continued. "Do you hear me? I don't know whether you hear anymore. I think maybe that's gone too." His father's eager eyes stayed on him.

"And your mind, how clear is it? I hope you hear, I hope you think because maybe you can tell me what to do, maybe you have some key. Mother was a mistake too, a different kind of mistake, all nerves and submission and passiveness. A—uh—friend of mine was shocked the way I acted at mother's funeral. But how, how do you mourn the death of someone who really didn't want to live? Who never came into contact with you? Who, when any issue in your life came up, said, 'I pass' like a bridge player? So many mistakes in my family. Look at Aunt Lydia! Nothing but breakdowns, and all that about becoming a TV star—at fifty! No talent!—and my God, Aunt Marguerite hasn't really sobered up in the last thirty years. And what about good old Bill? Jesus. And what about the great Philip Colfax Clinger, that great American. What about any of them!" Here he caught himself, was still for a moment, and then slowly, sadly, added, "What about any of us?"

"I don't *want* to be a mistake. I don't want to be like you or like any of them. I'm myself, I'm nature's fresh try to make something good, something that works. I don't give a shit how pretentious it sounds: it's the truth. I'm supposed to be perfect, yes, perfect. But all my relatives are mistakes and now I'm scared to death I'm—I'm going to be one too, I've got to find a way out, I don't want to be another human flop. Can't I shake this screwed-up family off? I must. I must.

"There's another thing. There's Charlotte. I think we I think she we—uh—had have a son," he stuttered, staring for a while out the window at the fresh Connecticut morning. "What in the world am I going to do about a son. Me. College sophomore. Marine reject. She also happens to be married now to somebody else, by the way. Just a detail. Yes!" He rubbed the palms of his hands briskly together in a parody of ambition and energy. "A son." He stared out the window some more. "The next generation. Already." He continued his staring. "And me with myself not worked out, not ready, not right. I wanted it all to be perfect, for my son, my children, when they came, someday. Not all screwed-up the way you had it for me. You weren't ready to be a father. You didn't understand yourself enough to be a father. Maybe nobody does. Well, I was going to, I was going to be ready, to be right. And now, here it is! Now!

"You see I wouldn't care if it was just some girl I happened to knock up by mistake. I wouldn't think it was my son really, not really. Yes, I've had sex with quite a few girls, for quite a few years, considering I'm not quite twenty-one, but I guess that's the way it is when most other parts of your life don't work and that one *does*. That's the way it is.

"But this wasn't some other girl, this was Charlotte," he was silent for a while. "Well," he then went on more softly, "this was Charlotte, and Charlotte had a lot of power. She had power over me, my body and my mind and my everything. I had power over her too. There was a tremendous exchange going on between us all the time. We fueled each other. Not a very romantic idea, is it? It was too fundamental to be romantic. It was a matter of life and death. And look what happened. We created a new person, Charlotte and I, and if I don't function as that baby's father I lose damn near everything, don't I? And yet I'm so screwed-up. Well that's just the way it goes sometimes. And don't tell me the son isn't mine. I mean, yes, tell me, learn to speak again just for ten seconds, will you, and say, 'Son, that son isn't yours, son' or something like that and I can wash my hands of it. That's why I've been sitting here rubbing my hands together, I suddenly realize, wash my hands of it." He paused and looked at his hands. "Maybe he isn't my son." He put his hands on his knees and stared anew at the morning, contemplating it. "Maybe he isn't my son. Just because she brought him to the Black House doesn't prove anything. Maybe it's just her Limey sense of humor. One time she made one of the students in her drama class put on a lot of theatrical make-up so he'd look older, gray temples and mustache and all that, and he came with her to the Black House and said he was from MGM and wanted me to co-star in the next Elizabeth Taylor movie. Well I'm not exactly ugly and things like that do happen sometimes. Charlotte just wanted to see how I'd react. I told him I'd consider it if there were oceanography classes in Hollywood. So then they confessed. Maybe the baby isn't mine. Maybe it isn't.

"In a way that thought is much worse, much worse. Charlotte having somebody else's son, that producer's to be exact. That thought is much, much, much worse.

"Maybe he is my son though. Maybe he is. She kept saying she wanted to have a child with me and she meant it. Charlotte meant it. There was nothing silly about Charlotte. She wanted to be an actress but she never dramatized herself. She left that for the stage. In her life she knew what she wanted and she meant what she said and she knew about this power between us and she was in love with me and she wanted a child out of this power there was between us and I believe she got it, I believe she got it and what am I going to do about it, me, Louis Colfax, fool?

"You might have set me up a little better in life. I don't mean money, God knows. I mean not slap me around so much and notice God damn it that I had some talents and encourage them a little bit and not be so crazy yourself." He stared for a while at the old man, who was eagerly looking at him, baffled old man, who had loved him all the same, helpless now, never to slap again. His father had loved him, crazily, in his way, very much. "It wasn't really your fault," Lou mumbled, "because your father was a repressed homicidal maniac. I know that. And his father was some other kind of monster, no question about it, and on and on. And it'll never stop unless somebody has the will and brains to break the chain, break the chain. Who? Why me, that's who. That's who I hoped it would be. Except my God here's the next generation already, my God."

His father was looking at him with a kind of eagerness and seemingly trying to speak. A burst of vexation came out in the old man, a last bubble from that great volcanic temper; he struggled with his mouth and then hit the palm of one hand with the fist of the other. His big left hand, like Lou's but twisted, bunched-up, veined, speckled, gestured vaguely toward the table. There was a pad and pencil there. Lou got up and handed them to his father. Placing the pad carefully on his knee, gathering his hand around the pencil, Mr. Colfax began to write painstakingly. Then he handed what he had written to his son. "Be careful. Your last chance," it seemed to read. Hands rigid, Lou held this message and studied it, and then looked up at his father, who was now looking at him more calmly, almost sternly, as he used to do. Maybe he can't hear a word, Lou reflected, and maybe his mind is gone.

And maybe he can, and maybe it isn't.

He drove the Morgan back to the Black House, picked up Brooks and Richard, who were vigorously impatient to be off. As they were going out the front door Brooks looked back into the main room and said with a smirk, "Don't you want to take that snapshot with you?" Lou went out the door wordless, but crossing the porch said flatly, "Bring it"; chortling, Brooks snapped it off the wall, they got into the Morgan, and drove back to New Haven.

IV

New England has the most violent climate in the world. It hurtles from pre-tropical August to sub-arctic January and hurtles back again, forcing the foliage through the most drastic changes in nature, erupting with blooms for a brief spell, then exploding with autumnal colors, then abruptly gaunt as death and swiftly on into luxuriant bloom again.

The inhabitants of New England must go through similar desperate accommodations to this anarchic climate, alternately brown-skinned as Polynesians and sallow as monks, subject to heat prostration and pneumonia, snow-bound and heat-waved, given to fall's energy and then summery languors, responding to rustles of spring and depths of winter, naked as jaybirds and then bundled as bears, hurrying along on the heels of the seasons' changes all their lives, unresting, ever on the alert to what's next, brittle from the fatigue of forever adapting to their commanding climate.

Compared with New England's violent seasonal swings, the jungle climate is tepid and the desert's bland, Europe's banal and Asia's glum. No atoll or outpost must deal with a climate as irascible as New England's.

Lou Colfax wondered if he could do anything about it. "If

we could divert the Gulf Stream—" he began to Clement
Jonaz, sitting in the latter's cubicle in the library stacks.

"Louis, you're mad," Clement began lightly, and then noticing the despair suddenly fall over his friend's face he quickly
amended, "You're all wrong, divert the *Gulf Stream,* even you
Americans can't do that."

Lou promptly forgot these fears for his sanity in the argument. "Don't give me that 'you Americans' crap and yes we
can, eventually. We're going to have to do that and a lot more
than that with the oceans if we have any plans for the survival
of the human race. Do you have any plans for the survival of
the human race?"

"Do I—?"

"For humanity surviving. Don't tell me you've been sitting
here graphing breast-feeding patterns among the Tahitians
when you have no plans to save humanity."

"I have my plan. It's very clear. Overturn America—"

"Later, later. Now listen to me. The ocean is the largest fact
on earth, right?"

"Y-e-e-e-s-s-s."

"People are starving in many parts of the world."

"*I'll* say they are, even and especially here and—"

"Later, later. I want to tell you something."

"You always want to tell me something—"

"Later. Listen. By 1980 the underdeveloped countries of the
world will need three hundred million tons of additional grain
annually to survive. That is the combined output today of the
United States and Europe. There is nowhere to get what they
need. They will all starve." He leveled a stare on Clement for
several baleful seconds. Then he went on. "*Except* that the sea
produces *one hundred times* that figure every year!" He stared
at him some more. "But nobody *harvests* it! The sea . . . the
sea is like a huge farm, and it's all around us and we sit in the
middle starving, its crops are rotting away because nobody
tends them, harvests them. It's some kind of huge, ignored,
swaying granary. Nobody ever goes inside. All that nourish-
ment in the sea is loose there, loose, floating all around,
salvation, loose, untended, rotting. It's *the* answer. And it's

here. So what do we do. We sit here staring out into space like
some kind of idiot child, 'Daddy me want to go *b-e-e-a-u-w-
g-h-* up there!' pointing up at the *moon!* It's as sterile as those
cigarette ashes. That's all the moon is, ashes. And we want to
go up there."

"Down, boy, down. You're getting shrill."

"Later. Listen. You've heard all the bad statistics about the
population increasing faster than the food supply? I've got a
good one for you. The fish harvest is increasing faster than the
population. Our way of 'farming' the sea is like using a
wooden farrow to plow on land, but still it's producing the
only hopeful statistic we've got."

"Well Louis, I suppose that is a point."

"Thanks. Listen. If we ever efficiently *harvested* the sea
we'd solve the food problem tomorrow. And if we *cultivated*
it, *fertilized* it, well, we could have all the food everybody in
the world would ever want." Lou was doodling the cross-section of something; Clement watched it taking form. "That's
the field I might go into, aquiculture. It doesn't exist, except in
Japan, and even there they only use it to produce cultured
pearls. That's typical."

"I always thought in your heart of hearts you had your—
mercenary side. Money and all. Maybe you want to save
humanity but I notice you like your sportscar."

Lou looked quizzically across at him, then he said, "Do you
know how many hundreds of billions of dollars of oil are
under the ocean? They do a little off-shore drilling now. If I
learned how to go after the *deep* oil, well, forget it. I'd be
King Midas."

Silence. Clement looked at him. "Well?"

More silence, then Lou said, "I could do both! Save humanity, be a super-millionaire!"

"I rather doubt you could do both. Nobody ever has. One or
the other, Louis, you'll have to aim at one or the other. It's the
aim that's crucial, you can't reach any goal like that without
aiming at it years before, aiming at it now, Louis Colfax,
sophomore. You'll have to choose now, won't you?"

A longer silence, then "Yes," curtly.

"Well?"

There was no comment from Louis Colfax, sophomore.

That evening Lou was sitting at his desk in the bedroom of his suite in Pierson College reading. The book was Jules Verne's *Twenty Thousand Leagues Under the Sea* and while he was enjoying it he had to break off frequently to sketch improvements in the submarine described. Gordon Durant stalked in in his dressing gown looking for a cigarette. "Where are your cigarettes?" he said.

Lou paused, and then he said, "I like the old-fashioned courtesy you always have when you're asking for something."

Surprised by this show of spirit, Gordon became confused and as a diversion noticed the sketches. "What are these?"

Lou explained, and a look of something almost bordering on tolerance painfully worked its way toward the surface of Gordon's craggy face. "You're interested in the underseas," he commented.

"Yes, really interested. Algae trap energy, you know, and then they're eaten by fish and that makes plenty of protein and you know half the children in backward countries die before they're five years old because of lack of protein and—" Carried away by his thoughts, Lou had started to bore and alienate his listener once again, as he so often did in his enthusiasms, and knowledge. He stopped short, and flicked a glance at Gordon's face, to confirm that the inevitable expression of boredom and disgust was there. So many people were disgusted by the knowledge others possessed. Strange. Lou himself was fascinated by and grateful for the new knowledge he encountered in others when, very infrequently, that happened.

But Gordon was listening with knit brows and an expression of interest. "Yes," he said, "I knew that."

"You did?"

"Yes."

They looked at each other analytically, and then Gordon said, "May I borrow that cigarette?"

"Oh sure—it's right I think I mean—oh." He grinned as blindingly as he could. "I don't smoke."

If only he really smoked! If only he had tar-coated lungs and cancer tissue of a constant smoker! Durant had almost become human. Now Lou in his absurd "Oh sure!"—those uncontrollable nerves again!—had made himself ridiculous once more: still at the bottom of the moat looking up.

Durant raised his eyebrows, and then left the room.

For the next hour Lou suffered the tortures of the man who said he had made the *Titantic* unsinkable: he could not tolerate his own absurdity; he could not escape it. So he finally got up, half-sprinted past Gordon in his armchair in the living room, muttering, "Get a cup of *coffee!*" and went out, up the outside stairs to the room of Richard Anders. Fortunately he found Richard alone in the suite, at his desk studying.

"Excuse me, can I just talk to you for five minutes?"

"Take ten," said Richard, leaning back in his chair and taking off his shell-rimmed glasses.

"You know the college dog—"

"Thunder."

"I know he's mangy and a mutt and a few other things but I like him anyway, I like him *because* he's so mangy and such a mutt. I've been going by him outside the dining room ever since the start of the term and I noticed something. He's a real big-city loner type of dog. He's indifferent, you know, he has a real guarded look in his eyes, he's joyless, a scavenger, world-weary, seen it all. Well anyway today, I said to myself that I was going to *reach* Thunder. I thought he needed me. I *knew* he needed me. He looks like such a cynic, Thunder does, but I knew that was all on the surface. So I brought him out a piece of meat from lunch and offered it to him and he ate it, no expression, no wagging, he just ate and looked away. I petted him, praised him, I tried everything. Couldn't please him. Couldn't displease him either. I didn't have anything to do with his real problems, so he didn't waste any energy on me at all. Snubbed again. Good night," and he pounded down the stairs, through the living room of his suite, undressed, got into bed, and failed, once again, to sleep.

The next morning when he, not awoke, but came out of the
sort of stupor or coma into which eight hours of proneness in
a darkened room had sunk him, Lou gazed at the moody,
sliding gray sky over New Haven, a lowering fall day, a dead
day, and the bloodless, dry, unreal world he had escaped from
with Charlotte Mills at this season two years ago began to
descend implacably over him. He was going to get into emotional trouble; he was already in deep emotional trouble. He
did not know whether he could get out of bed. He knew that
if he spoke his voice would have lost its natural resonance,
that now it would be kind of furry, a querulous tone.

Go to the master of Pierson College for help.

Go to the university psychiatrist.

Go to the minister of your faith.

Go to hell.

He turned over and gazed in despair out the window,
across the moat, at the picked fence.

Go to your closest friend.

He did not have one.

Go to your girl friend.

He did not have one.

Go to your parents.

He did not, really, have one.

Get a dog.

Thunder . . . Lou felt he was about to lose control. He had
to do something. Self-pity, the most negative emotion of them
all, the one from which nothing good could flow, worse than
hate, jealousy, anything, he was lying in this bed wrapped in
self-pity as in a winding sheet.

That did it. Lou swiftly got out of bed, cleaned up, dressed,
got into his Morgan and drove at top speed through the
gloomy New England day to Stowe, Vermont, arriving back at
Pierson College at midnight.

"Where've you been?" asked Durant neutrally from his
armchair.

"I drove to Stowe, Vermont, and back."

"Colfax, you don't even lie well."

All the same, after thinking Louis Colfax over, Gordon went

to the master's office of Pierson the next morning and said
there was "no hurry" about the roommate change after all.

The next day was Saturday. Desperately running from that
self-pity, Lou lurched into Clement Jonaz's room.

"Let's go to the football game."

Clement slowly lowered his pen to his desk. "The *what?*"

He said it as Charlotte had; Clement had been partly
educated in England. Lou fliched at the remembered inflec-
tion. ("The *what?*" Charlotte had said incredulously. "I said,
let's go to the flicks . . . movies." "Oh, the films, the cinema."
"Don't give me that. You know what the flicks are." "I *don't!*"

"I—uh—let's go to the football game," Lou repeated a little
breathlessly. "You know, like rugby," he added with a grimace.

"Football game. I've never sat through one in my life. You
really have gone bers—you really are—strangely notional this
weekend, Louis. Whatever made you think I had time to
watch middle-class Americans acting out their world-threat-
ening aggressions against each other, preparatory to unleash-
ing them on the emerging peoples?"

"Oh shit."

"Your own need to use a club in the war-substitute you
yourself have chosen—lacrosse—just shows your own hostili-
ties are both more primitive and nearer the surface."

"I'll say they are. Shall we go to the football game?"

Clement sighed. "All right. Who's Yale expressing its blood
lust against this time?"

"As a matter of fact, I think it's Army."

"I'm not surprised, not at all. I hope you don't expect me to
yell or do any of that unison crying out."

"Just be company for me."

The bantering tone ended with that. "All right, Lou, yes,
sure."

They walked out of the Graduate School and along York
Street, past Davenport College and the entrance to Pierson
College. None of the Yale colleges was accessible one from
the other. The student had to go to the no-man's-land of the
street, then cross the moat and drawbridge to enter the neigh-

boring college; for just as the university was prepared to
withstand assault from the town, each college within the
university had been built to repel attack from all of the others.
Clement, clad in his deerstalker hat and Sherlock Holmes
cape-coat, remarked on this armed-camp aspect of Yale once
again. "When you consider who provided the money for con-
structing these bastions—Whitneys, Harknesses, Vanderbilts,
and so on—you realize that the design reflects very deeply
and accurately the psyche of the donors. The assumption of
people who make huge fortunes in your country—I'm talking
about the first generation—is of course that of a robber baron,
raiding all the surrounding country for his own profit and so
creating enemies all around him, and only safe in his own
impregnable stronghold. Ideally, if they'd been even richer
than they were, they would have provided each individual
student with his own private fortress and own individual
cannon."

They reached Fraternity Row, where the elation of a football weekend, of dressy girls, of fraternity houses which for
once had a purpose other than sheltering pool tables and bars,
had caught up the street into a gusty late October festiveness.
Cars and crowds and furs and corsages, yells and giggles and
honking and beer, through it Clement, with intellectual Marxist British Colonial composure, and Lou, with mad Colfax
envy, made their way to the Yale Bowl.

Arriving there, they trooped in, sat down, stood up for the
kickoff, and the game began. The other team was not Army
after all; it was Dartmouth.

They sat down again. Clement watched it as an exercise in
stylized aggressiveness, and had to admire it from that point
of view. "There are several ingenious actings-out of the death
wish in this ritual," he said judiciously. "And that man who's
holding the ball when each manifestation begins—"

"The center."

"Yes. The posture he must assume, legs spread, bending
down and looking *upside down* through his own legs back at
his own altar—"

"You mean the goal posts?"

"Yes. That's very significant. The devil cults of the Maubi have a similar placation posture. I won't go into all the anal erotic meanings now . . . "

"All right."

"—but they ought to be obvious."

Dartmouth scored a touchdown. Clement sat wordless and motionless through the dejection surrounding him, cogitating. The extra-point conversion was attempted, the ball centered to the holder, and the place-kicker stepped forward and kicked it between the uprights of the goal post. Clement was electrified. "Marvelous," he cried, "really marvelous. A truly successful acting-out of altar defilement. He scoops that filthy ball up from the very mud itself with his *foot* and *kicks* it into the very center of the enemy's altar. I mean the beautiful simplicity of it . . . oh, I see. Now they're getting another chance. Dartmouth kicks it up from the mud toward the other altar . . . uh-huh, doesn't work, the other army captures the trophy and starts back. I must say, there surely is a monograph here at least, if not a dissertation. Religio-Erotic Confrontation Rituals in American Football. Where is everybody going?"

"It's the half."

"The *what?*"

Again Charlotte's querulously humorous English "The *what?*" echoed inside Lou's head. Blast England and her accent, and her snapshot and her scrawls on walls.

"The half-time. The game is half over."

"Is it really?" he said gratefully.

"Yes."

What do they do in the second half. The birth trauma?"

"The same as the first."

"Must we stay?"

"No," said Lou wearily. "I guess not." Sitting passively watching the game was not nearly distracting enough for Lou, not even when listening to the Jonaz commentary.

They went out through the tunnel to the track behind the Bowl. Outside Portal Fifteen there was as usual a certain chic mingling of couples; furs, blondes, leather gloves, binoculars, fur-trimmed boots, long and bright scarves, thermos bottles and flasks. As Clement, looking like a mulatto Sherlock Holmes, and Lou, looking like a Russian anarchist, moved past this crowd, Mrs. Taloumi Durant stepped in front of them, fur hat, fur coat, blond hair, big eyes, smiling widely. "There you are! My spy. What are you doing here?"

"We're just leaving, Mrs. Durant," Lou began shyly, "because uh . . . "

"Because it is a bore. Grown up men pushing each other down like little boys!"

Clement could be heard almost to purr with pleasure at this. Lou introduced them, and each, sensing something singular, egregious, in the other, acknowledged the introduction enthusiastically. "I hate this stupid game," she said in her penetrating voice. "Where is that ex-stepson who dragged me here? Gordon!"

Durant, one of the three Yale undergraduates who still dared to wear a raccoon coat, came lumbering toward them out of the crowd in it. Eyeing him, Norma said to Lou, "Where are you going?"

"We were just going to visit a—uh—unique person here at Yale, someone very very interesting, a unique person here at Yale, someone—"

"I go with you?"

"Please!"

They wended their way through the parking lot to Norma's car, an ancient Cadillac convertible. "I bought it in Hollywood *many* years ago." She began backing and changing gears energetically.

"I didn't know you were in Hollywood!" said Lou, fascinated. Hollywood had always bored him sick, but he was not himself any more, he suddenly realized; he was fascinated because Charlotte would have been fascinated. I identify too much with her, he reflected desperately.

"I've been everyplace. Hollywood was crap, pure crap. I hate Hollywood. Los Angeles is the most ugliest city that ever was. You have been in Los Angeles? No, eh. Well, *don't go.* Which way we go?"

Lou directed her away from New Haven for a short distance and then right along Forest Road, on a wooded bluff overlooking the city. "Is this the way to . . . *that person's* house?" inquired Clement politely from the back seat, hoping by his question to learn whether Lou had an actual "unique person" in mind, or was going to lead them in circles until the car ran out of gas—which would not be unlike him—or deliver them to the doorstep of the President of the University —which would not be unlike him either.

"Isn't the Stoetzers' house this way?"

"Oh," said Clement, "yes, of course it is." The Stoetzers would be perfect, if only they were at home, just the place to take this exotic lady who had inexplicably landed in their midst.

She was talking on. "One thing I do not permit people to inflict on me is boredom. *Ennui.* That, never. I have been heart-broken, I have been robbed, I have been *beaten.* I say, okay. It is part of life. But I have *not been bored.* Never. When Durant start to bore me, I leave him and I leave his money too. If I *smell* boredom, like a—what you call that small animal with a stripe on the back?"

"A skunk?"

"Like a *skunk* creeping near me, I run away. As I do now. You are so *sweet* to take me to meet this unique person. Who is he?"

"Oh, a kind of local sage, a character. Myron Stoetzer, and Mrs. Stoetzer. He wrote a play once called *The Colors of the Rainbow.* Never could write another. So he's here at the University, he's our Sage-in-Residence."

"It's impossible not to have a wise man near," observed Norma. "Is he a priest?"

"Of course not," said Lou. "He's married."

"In Greece our priests are married sometimes."

"I didn't know you were Greek," said Lou.

"Of course I am. The only thing not Greek about me is my name. Norma is not a Greek name. But my mother loved the opera *Norma* so that is what she call me. Yes, in Greece our priests are married sometimes. It is *much* better. How can a man who is not married help and advise with the problems of marriage, of sex, and that is the root of all problems."

"He prays," said Lou experimentally, "and gets inspiration."

Norma growled something in Greek. Then she said, *"The Colors of the Rainbow? Les Couleurs de l'Arc en Ciel?* I think I know that play."

"It's quite famous."

"I am thrilled."

"They will be too. They love to meet new people."

Myron and Vilma Stoetzer looked through the window of their library and saw the unknown convertible turn through the gate into the spacious gravel spread before the door of their Greek Revival house.

"Oh my God!" she exclaimed in her liquid alto.

"Now whom have you invited?" he demanded in his slightly drawling, cultivated voice. A somewhat Hitlerian lock of black hair fell over his forehead. At sixty he had the face of a ruined boy. Vilma, with her thick brown hair cut short and her full figure, bore a marked resemblance to the Rumanian Communist leader, Ana Pauker.

A fire was burning in the grate. Books extended from floor to ceiling. The Stoetzers watched the car stop. They were being assaulted by the pangs of the overhospitable, the sudden deprivation of the one afternoon they had planned to sit alone, speechless, shoeless, and let their facial muscles rest and fall and grow flaccid. Now his began to curve by habit into that shy boyish smile, hers to resume its set look of sardonic, slightly dazed interest.

"I didn't ask anybody, I don't think," she said in her hoarse alto. "Who in the world is that in that strange hat, and cape?"

"Clement Jonaz, certainly. No one else dares wear clothes like that. You have to have mixed blood for that kind of courage."

"I suppose so," she murmured. "Well, I'm glad that's who it is. At least he's subversive. Who's the other student?"

"All in black. Like a ghoul. Of course it's—"

"Louis Colfax. Well, he's mad as a hatter, so at least it won't be dull. And whose date would that be?"

"Maybe both. *A ménage à trois.*"

"What fun!"

Somewhat cheered up, Mr. and Mrs. Stoetzer began getting out the vodka, the tomato juice, the bitters, the ice, the gin, the Scotch, the brandy. They never entertained a non-drinking student twice ("This isn't a nursery school").

Twenty minutes later the vodka and gin and Scotch had reached the blood streams of hosts and guests, and communication began.

"Is your husband a professor?" Norma asked Mrs. Stoetzer.

"Oh no. He's what they call a fellow of one of the colleges. Nothing, in other words. We just like to be in a university community. We find people are more original in university communities. And also Myron is an alumnus. People *are* more original in university communities, aren't they?" Mrs. Stoetzer pursued in the rather provoking manner she used with women, whom she almost always disliked.

"I don't know," said Norma carelessly. "I never been in a university much. I think it is naive here, very naive. Is that the same thing?"

"No, not at all," intoned Vilma.

Norma was already bored by Mrs. Stoetzer. She had sensed the hostility inside this rather ungainly woman and been bored by it. Life was too short even to return Mrs. Stoetzer's hostility. Calling across the room Norma said, "You are naive, no, you, my spy?"

Lou, sunk in one of the deep, box-shaped chairs next to the meditative fire, pulled himself up. "Yes," he answered simply. "Yes, I'm naive."

"He isn't," continued Norma, indicating Clement.

"And my husband, Oh Pythoness," inquired Mrs. Stoetzer with a stretched smile.

Glancing at her and instantly away again, Norma exclaimed to the room, "Ach, I talk too much, as always. You are a great man, sir, a great writer. Are you naive?"

From the matching chair facing Lou's, Mr. Stoetzer, after making demurring noises about his greatness, answered, "Hopelessly. No one can spend his life among college students, college boys, without in a way remaining one himself. Of course, the students are changing."

"Is it true? In what way?" Deeply interested already, Norma drew her legs in light-colored slacks under her on the couch next to Mrs. Stoetzer, to hold herself from hurrying across the room to sit at his feet. Like all erratically intelligent women of little education, Norma was enthralled by brilliant men, and felt that this must be one. Mrs. Stoetzer noticed this and her animal dislike of Norma declined a shade: Myron badly lacked feminine admiration at Yale. Lou noticed it and was hugely relieved: he had supplied the promised "unique person."

"When I was a student here, a thousand years ago," Mr. Stoetzer explained in his pleasant, if marbles-in-the-mouth, voice, "we did a certain amount of conversing in Latin. Would you believe the change in my lifetime? Now, Yale admits these winning—in every sense of the word—young men who just don't want to be bothered with anything that disciplined. They're beginning to question the need to know English grammar, let alone Latin. Present company excepted, to be sure. Clement is virtually the most brilliant student in the Graduate School and was partly educated in Britain. That saved him. Louis has his own sort of distant drummer and hears all kinds of illuminating things." Both students dutifully blinked and beamed. "But the rest? Urchins, most of them. Proper clothing is beginning to disappear, and I expect in another ten years they'll be wearing animal skins and rags, like a cross between Arab street beggars and Laplanders. Our climate here means even beggars have to have a variety of dress. We had a code of manners in my day and we were *really* naive. How was the football game?" he suddenly asked all of them.

"A bore."

"Childish."

"Couldn't sit through it."

After a silence Mr. Stoetzer went on, "I have an Intelligence Quotient—if those silly tests mean anything—I have an Intelligence Quotient of genius level, and *I* sat through every football game played at Yale all my four years, absorbed. Absorbed. It was an expression of school spirit in those days. All that's gone glimmering. Most of the other things will go too," he muttered. "It's the dean of admissions, of course who recreates Yale regularly, like some mad alchemist in his cell with his herbs and potions. More of this! Less of that! Sometimes I wonder if it'll all blow up in his face some day."

"Oh Myron don't be silly and gloomy," Mrs. Stoetzer said.

"What's a university for," put in Clement, "except to give very bright people a first-class education. Nobody has time for 'school spirit' or all those 'gentlemanly' things any more. There's too much to learn. We're . . . well, *they're* too busy. I think I'm closer to the students than you are, Myron. They're deeply sensitive, much more so than before. It's the fraternity louts who are beginning to disappear. It's the special spirits who are increasing. They're careless about dress, true. But they're becoming more interested in ideas, and eventually I think in ideals, than before. I think the dean of admissions is really quite a good chemist."

"I hope so," sighed Mr. Stoetzer vaguely.

Norma had kept her big green eyes fixed on each speaker in turn. Now she turned to Lou. "What do you think, Louis Colfax?"

"What do I think?" He had been designing a habitable underseas bubble in his mind while following the conversation. "I just, well, the Yale student body? I don't know, it's like asking me what's inside my head, what it looks like, I just can't see it, because it's me . . ."

She studied him. Then she said, "Good," decisively.

Lou didn't understand in what way his fumbling answer had been good, but he smiled brightly at her. She smiled back in a way which made him lurch inside.

"Louis," said Mr. Stoetzer from his Scotch, "is not a happy boy."

"No," mumbled Lou humbly.

"He's quicksilver," said Mrs. Stoetzer from her gin, "he's a dragonfly. There is only one of him. He's one of those serials, those cliff-hangers movie houses used to show. No one knows how it will come out, least of all Lou."

"No," he mumbled.

"He isn't of this generation," added Mr. Stoetzer, "or any other."

"Just a spook," mumbled Lou. "I wonder what time it's getting to be."

"Why do you say these things?" said Norma intently. "It is true?" ignoring Lou, the patient, she asked the Stoetzers, the diagnosticians.

"Louis is very singular," said Mr. Stoetzer meditatively. "What will happen, no one knows . . . no one knows . . . valuable mind . . . no one . . ." then recollecting himself, he said with his customary cheerfulness, "we expect great things of you, Lou," and then the Scotch flowing through his system reasserted the upper hand, "provided—"

"Provided?" pursued Norma.

"We're embarrassing the poor boy—"

"*Provided!*" she insisted, glaring. "You cannot stop now."

"He . . . well, his family, if he gets control, we all have our nerves to contend with."

"Yes," said Lou, flashing a grin, "our *nerves!* Shudder, shudder. I am *nervous*. Just ask the Marine Corps! Could I . . . some vodka . . ."

When the drinks had been refreshed, and everyone was settled again in the comfort of this grand yet intimate library, suffused as it was with the warmth of reading and wood-fire, of money and learning, of older hosts and young students, of hospitality and discernment, of fame and whisky, Norma suddenly said, "You know why I maybe am a prophetess like— this woman call me, when she said 'Oh Pythoness,' meaning Apollo's oracle, of course?" (Norma usually drank little; the vodka was busily putting her brain cells to sleep, which was why Mrs. Stoetzer had become "this woman.") "Because I feel very wide and I feel very deep and this is all that is necessary to be a prophetess. You know why? Because I feel other people's feelings, not only my own. It is so easy to be *sensitive!* To feel for yourself! To feel hurt by others, feel this, feel that, hurt feelings, reactions, complexes, all that, about *yourself!* But to feel *about others!* That is the true sensitivity, the other is just crap, useless, selfishness, every boring person and every neurotic person in the world has that! I have the other, thank God. I feel what *you* feel, I feel *your* feelings. That is why I am a prophetess. That is all that is necessary. So I know the lives of others, even their destinies sometimes." She settled her gaze on Lou. "Louis Colfax? You have, as you say, 'great hopes' for him *'provided.'* I will tell you! Listen." She laughed penetratingly. "The Pythoness will tell you! Listen." She began to sway, humming, eyes almost closed. "There is a young woman, a girl. Yes. I see one young woman. But I can't see if she is in his future or in his past. Could she be in both? I don't see that too clear. But I see one young woman. She will have *much* to do with his destiny. She may make a big mess of him. He is all vulnerable on his emotion side. I can smell it. He even think he is a little in love with me, which is adorable. He is all vulnerable there. And there his destiny will be decided. His *first* and most important destiny. Everything else is already decided. He will be some kind of very *valuable* person if he passes through what this woman does. Ach, it is true, since he is not destroyed *yet* then she *must* be in his future. Or else he has *already* survived her! Or!" Eyes suddenly open, she glared at Lou. "He will become *stronger* because of her, he will *grow* from what she put him through. It all depends. It all depends. *Provided,* as you say!" Then she laughed. "May I have one more drink? It's a lot of crap I talk, parlor game. Isn't it?"

No one answered. Conversation became general for a while, and then Norma interrupted. "Who the hell's that!" pointing through the window. "Oh, *merde*. My stupid ex-stepson!"

Gordon Durant was plodding toward the front door accompanied by three other students and four girls. Their cars, two convertibles, were left in the driveway with their doors open.

"Ah, Gordon," said Mr. Stoetzer suavely, rising. "Get more glasses, Vilma."

Gordon stormed in, explained that he had seen Norma's car in the drive en route back to the campus from the game.

"Who won?" asked Mr. Stoetzer.

"Hey Farwell," called Gordon, "who won?"

"Gee, let's see. Ginnie, who won the game?"

"Won? Uh, I think it came out a tie or something, didn't it Lucie?"

"Didn't what?"

"The game. Come out a tie or something?"

"Gosh, I don't know. I mean, there's that man behind the scoreboard that's supposed to be keeping track of the *points* and things. Billy, who won the game?"

"Dartmouth won thirty-two to nothing, and your seat cost $4.50 and I might as well throw it to the birds."

"I wish you had. In that case I—"

"Drinks!" intoned Mrs. Stoetzer over the hubbub. "Taking orders for drinks!"

The room was now just too crowded for everyone to find a seat. So people knelt, leaned, sat on armrests, leaned against the mantlepiece, perched on the tiny stepladder serving the bookshelves.

Norma suddenly cried out, "Stop! There are thirteen people in the room! Oh my God. I must leave. Thirteen. Danger, danger."

"Norma," said Gordon, "be quiet."

"It is very dangerous," she muttered.

Neither Myron nor Vilma Stoetzer would permit a cocktail party being committed in their home. Promiscuous conversation was one of the few social practices which disgusted them. More chairs were brought; a rough circle formed; an intelligent conversation leading conceivably to the enlightenment of one or more persons was encouraged and, under their practiced prodding, took form.

"We were discussing today's student," began Myron.

That unleashed all the new arrivals. Gordon decisively agreed with Mr. Stoetzer up to a point, and then decisively disagreed with him beyond that point. The other three young men had different but equally emphatic views and, although they were a little slower to express them, so did the girls.

Gordon said, "Yale is letting in too many scholarship high school people and so, what do you expect? The traditions have got to go. But! Most of the traditions are stupid anyway so, to sum up, what Yale needs is frankly the cream of the crop, people with money *and* brains, and w— they will hammer out some new traditions for you, like giving polo and hunting a real place at Yale."

Billy said, "I think Yale is pretty okay the way it is, and if outsiders would mess out, *mess out,* then it would all go on being very okay."

Farwell said, "It's all stuffy and boring and the courses haven't anything to do with what really counts today and, well, I like most of the guys but they're all stick-in-the-muds basically, and what we need is more training to go out and have a good life and succeed and . . . *contribute!*"

Three of the girls' views meshed into an overriding sense that what Yale needed was co-education.

But Ginnie said, "I think co-education is for the birds myself. I've had a co-education, I *go* to Yale, the Drama School. It's for the birds, excuse me, but that's the way I've seen it. You don't know . . ." her voice trailed off, her glance slid around to settle on Lou, who was still inwardly wrestling with Norma's prediction for him.

Clement said, "Yale is a complete anachronism. The Yale Corporation is a combination of Wall Street and Washington at its most reactionary—Senator *Taft*—the curriculum is doing to us what the Americans say the North Koreans are doing to the prisoners of war, brainwashing, they're brainwashing us here with the dogmas of capitalism with a thin overlay of bourgeois government planning, plus ancestor-worship, and the student body are good little fat-cheeked boobs who've never had an opportunity, or an impulse, to think in their lives." After a long, ironic pause he added, "Present company excepted, of course." Then he murmured, "I'm a Negro so my views can be discounted by all of you."

"Clement has a lovely Brazilian grandmother," Mrs. Stoetzer put in.

"Black as the ace of spades," said Clement. "I love her. She saved me from being like . . . the majority."

"My, aren't you hostile," said Ginnie.

Clement bowed formally.

Lou took a longer look at him than he ever had before. Inside this tall, broad-faced man, with his hooded eyes, very slightly coppery skin, with all his reserve and scholarship, was there a raging, celebrating African beating a wild tom-tom of liberation? Was it fading or getting louder? Clement sat with his arms along the armrests of his chair, impassively contemplating his surroundings.

"I don't know how you all see this in these students," put in Mrs. Stoetzer in her alto-soloist manner. "They're the most vapid group I've seen at Yale. Never say anything. Never *do* anything. I think the reason they dress badly is they haven't the energy to dress well. The Silent Generation, that they certainly are, as everybody knows. To me they're simply boring."

"The calm before the storm," murmured Clement.

"What?" asked Mrs. Stoetzer.

"Yale is becalmed," he amended, in the manner of a priest saying, "*Missa est.*"

Reassured, Mrs. Stoetzer resumed her expression of dazed, sardonic interest.

Norma leaned forward from the couch. "Louis, what do you think?"

He had been nervously digesting her prediction, resuming work on his underseas design, and continued following the conversation. As always, this complexity did not make for snappy opinion.

Lou sat up straight, conscious of the derisive stare of Gordon from across the room, Gordon who had so far this afternoon ignored his existence. "I think a lot of good points have been made, and I certainly agree with the co-education part, and I agree they ought to practically abolish the curriculum —there doesn't seem to be anything to *learn* here," he put in hurriedly, in spite of himself, for he always sought to hide his intellectual impatience, "and uh more courses in oceanogra-

phy. But there is a lot in some of the past traditions and we
don't want to throw out the baby with the bath water, and
still Clement's point about Yale being just a sort of capitalist
mirror has a lot in it, and . . . I don't know . . . there's a lot I
would do but a lot I'd like to save and there's so much . . . I
don't know . . ." Norma was smiling at him in an odd, quizzi-
cal way.

"What did you say your name was?" the girl called Ginnie
inquired, leaning across toward him from the chair Mr.
Stoetzer had occupied before. He told her. "Oh." She looked
very guiltily amused at that. "Oh."

" 'Oh' what?"

"Oh. Nothing. Just . . . I'm in the Drama School."

Lou just looked at her.

"The Drama School," she repeated.

"I knew a student in the Drama School once."

"I know you did."

"Do you ever hear from her or . . . anything about her?"

"Yes."

Lou felt himself growing almost insanely angry at the little
game this bitch was playing. He fixed the manic-depressive
Colfax glare upon her. "How is she!" he demanded in the
family Boris Karloff voice.

"She's fine," the girl replied rather shrilly. "Just fine."

"Tell me what you know about her."

"Oh well, there's not that much to tell. She's *married,* you
knew that, there's this baby, you knew about *that,* they live in
New York and she's gone back to acting, I can't really feature
Char as a mother, can you? She wants to work and I heard she
was up for something, some musical. She can sing and she's
really quite a good dancer, so who knows, she just might make
it! Wouldn't that be the end!"

"Yes," mumbled Lou, meaning it. That really would be the
end, if on top of deserting him and taking perhaps his own
son away from him she became a great success in her field,
Louis Colfax's opinion of himself would reach that absolute
zero known to physicists at which a substance becomes totally
without movement or warmth.

"That's all I know," Ginnie said, shaking her molasses-colored curls and retreating into her drink. Then she emerged again. "Char never would let me meet you. She said you were 'too dotty.' " Ginnie giggled. "I thought she was afraid of the competition. But anyway! I shared that apartment here with her when she was breaking up with you . . . the time you built that twenty-foot-long periscope or whatever it was and looked in our window!" Lou flinched inwardly at the memory of that manic period just after the night he had failed to try to have a baby with her, that manic period when they were still, sadly, madly half living together. "And the time you came to see her disguised as the janitor and almost got away with it . . ." (She was having drinks on the sofa with the producer; Lou had seen them go into the building together, raced to the Drama School where friends had disguised him "as a joke," been admitted by Charlotte to the apartment, seen the man seated easily on the sofa, wanted to kill somebody, lost control of his voice, been recognized contemptuously—but also with secret amused pleasure?—by Charlotte, ignominiously left; that was the night he had gone to the Black House and stabbed himself in the gut, and it had not worked.)

"Yes, I remember that night," he said.

"And I was still sharing the apartment with her when you know you began opening her mail and trying to tap the phone—"

"Trying! That tap worked!" His pride of invention overcame his urge to deny guilt. "How's your mother's arthritis? Did Ned pass chemistry at Poly Prep after all?"

After a shocked silence, Ginnie rallied. "Charlotte could have told you those things. Never mind! All right, it worked." They looked at each other. Then Ginnie felt moved to say, "She really did like you tremendously. I never knew why you drove her away by . . . persecuting her that way . . ."

At these words Lou felt that some day, sooner or later, the monumental mistakes of his life really would drive him to suicide. He had thought of it a great many times and attempted it that once. The reason that attempt had failed was that in his wild rage and mortification he had used the wrong

method. People who really commit suicide do it by attacking
the part of themselves which drove them to it: poison for
those tormented by their appetites; throwing themselves out
of windows or off bridges for people hating their lack of
identity; slashing wrists for those who have identity all right
and hate it and so want to drain away its very life's blood; and
for Louis Colfax, when . . . if . . . the time came, he knew
how to do it now: take a pistol and blow out his overactive,
overjealous, overambitious, overdreamy, overintelligent brains.

"She was always talking about you. 'Louis says' and 'Louis
thinks' and 'Louis' theory is.' She sort of ran away from home
and away from her country, she had a lot of nerve but she
needed some kind of stability and she thought you were so
bright you could give it to her . . . and then the periscope and
you . . . you tried . . . after the janitor bit you tried . . ."

"Yes," mumbled Lou. "Yes let's not, yes I—"

Then Norma came up, Gordon in tow, and sat down on the
arm of Lou's chair, and put her arm over his shoulders. "You
look *very* sad."

"We were talking about an old friend."

"You mean an old love. My God you are crazy as a lord.
Never talk or think about the old love. It is suicide." ("Yes,"
muttered Lou inaudibly.) "It is today and tomorrow and next
year that you must think about. If I ever look back at my past
I would turn to salt, to stone. My mistakes are there like
monsters to haunt me. But I never turn around."

"I guess you're right," Lou murmured.

"Of course she's right," said Gordon.

Norma gazed analytically up at him, her head tilted back,
blond hair tumbling around her shoulders. "Gordon," she
asked, "what do you think of the peace talks that never end
about that war in Asia?"

"Korea? What do I think? I think we give them six more
weeks and then if their side keeps stalling at the negotiation
table we forget about the armistice and those 'privileged
sanctuaries' of theirs in the North and we bomb the daylights
out of them."

"Six weeks," echoed Norma reflectively. "Why six weeks?"

"That's all the time we can let them have. Then we have to take advantage of our superior airpower."

"I see. What do you think, darling?" touching Lou on top of the head.

After a pause Lou began slowly, "Well, it's pretty complicated, isn't it? We *have* got superior airpower and all, but they *have* got six hundred million or whatever it is Chinese behind them—or do they? Who knows, maybe the people of China aren't behind them! It's like quicksand if we sink into Asia too deeply, but on the other hand if we don't defend our allies in Asia then there's the theory," he went on reflectively, "that the Communists will knock over one country after another . . . of course there are *some* good things to be said for the Communist system . . ."

Gordon snorted senatorially. "Most muddled mind I've ever heard of. Thank you, Colfax, for talking in circles and tying yourself in knots for us." He surveyed the two women for their approval.

Ginnie smiled tentatively, but Norma's analytical gaze upon Gordon now became autopsy-like. Then in her most penetrating voice she said, "You are even more full of shit than I thought before." She continued studying him. "Your head is a big piece of pig's feet, like your father's. What do you know! Who are you? Six weeks! Why not five? Why not seven? You yell—you don't know nothing. Let me tell you one thing. How old are you?" she snarled.

"Twenty-two," he answered faintly, and swallowed a large gulp of Scotch.

"A boy who is certain of his opinions in his beginning twenties as you are, his head is pig's feet. This one," her hand sweeping toward Lou almost accidentally slapped him in the face, "*He* is youth, he is valuable, he has something inside him. Let me tell you one thing. Young people—the good ones among the young people—all of them feel *here*, in their hearts, that they have some—some *great—message* to deliver. They feel all heavy, loaded with some great thing in themselves. So that is why they are like Louis Colfax, they hesitate, they are cautious, they doubt, they see many sides. Why?

Because they must know exactly *where* to deliver this great thing they have in themselves, *who* should they give it to, *what* is worthy of it, *where* to plant it! But somebody like you! You got nothing inside, just big bundles of pig's feet, so *of course* you have fast opinions, you know all the answers, you know exactly what to do because whatever you do doesn't matter, you got nothing inside to deliver, nothing to lose."

This attack in Norma's commanding voice had silenced the room. There was now a brief interlude of rattling of ice in glasses and the clearing of throats while the Stoetzers, whom everyone expected to change the subject, tacitly declined to do so. To divert attention artificially away from a confrontation like this one seemed insincere and middle-class to them: Fight It Out, was their ruling principle. Myron Stoetzer now acted on it: "I know what you mean," he said easily from his seat on the little stepladder. "Not about Gordon," he added, not too hastily, "but in general about young, cocksure people. Year after year they come through Yale, generation after generation, and here they are chairmen of the *News* and leaders of this and spokesmen for that and heroes of something else, and then they go what used to be called Out Into The World and are never heard of again, spent rockets, too-early bloomers, Little Mr. Grown-Up at twenty-one and Little Mr. Nonentity at twenty-five, and fifty, and forever." He gulped some Scotch. "There are some exceptions."

Gordon, who had never, as far as he was aware, been publicly insulted in his life before this, had passed through seven distinct, desperate emotional states: 1. Incredulity: she can't be speaking to me! 2. Panic: She is! 3. Outrage: How *dare* she? 4. Violence: I'm going to punch her in the mouth! 5. Mortification: Everybody is listening to her! 6. Counterattack: Which crushing rejoinder will destroy her best? 7. Anarchy: I'm going to knock over the coffee table! Now he reached a too-proud-to-fight stance. "Would you say I was one of the exceptions, Myron? Norma's a foreigner, so I don't take her views seriously."

"The exception, I'm sure."

"You don't, don't you?" cut in Norma. "Well, maybe you

better. It's true your money will save you from showing the world the mediocre man inside. Without the money, you would be digging ditches ten years from now. No. I am unfair. You are *not* without intelligence. You would be . . . let me see, I never ask myself this before . . . you would be, yes, how do you call people like that, *chasseur blanc,* someone who takes people on safaris in Africa to shoot beautiful animals and hang their skins on the wall, Hemingway describes them—"

"White hunters," said Mr. Stoetzer.

"Yes, that is you, if your name was Smith."

In extremity, Gordon's face became contorted, his voice uncontrollable, "Norma, just because my father ditched you—"

"Don't tell me that crap about the scorned woman and her fury worse than hell! I have no fury that your father divorce me! None. I have only fury that I stay with that pig's head so long! *That* is my fury!" She leaned toward Gordon, the firelight reflected in her full, tossed blond hair. "Do you know something, Gordon? You will be richer because of me. Do you know how much alimony I ask from your father, do you? No. He did not tell you that. I ask for none. Nothing. I ask him to pay for my lawyer in the divorce action and to send me my clothes. It is true he give me some jewelry and furs and I keep them. But I do not take any money. *Why* I take his money? I don't have any children with him, I have only myself to support, I am healthy, I will maybe marry somebody else one of these days, I take good photographs and supported myself before that way and now I do it again. *Why* would I ask him for any of his money? I am not a whore, to be paid for sleeping with him! When I marry him I think I love him, mature older man, *world traveler,* he will understand me, complicated world wanderer like me. So I marry him. And he *doesn't* understand me. *And* I understand him *too* well! *Too* well. We lose interest in each other. So it is finished. Bye-bye. No money! I want my clothes, my car from my Hollywood days, and for him to pay the lawyer. I spit on American lawyers and their fees. So there it is. You lose none of the Durant money on me! And I don't tell you these things about

young people who know too much from revenge. I tell you
. . . well, because you are so cruel to Louis Colfax that you
make an explosion inside my head and I say what is in it. I
hate cruelty. And you *are* cruel. You have the heart of a white
hunter. That is why I explain you to yourself."

Gordon had passed through four more powerful emotional
states: 1. Scorn: She's lying about the money! 2. Amazement:
She's telling the truth about the money! 3. Avarice: I'm going
to inherit my full share after all! 4. Alarm: She's still making
me look like an ass!

"Look gang," he called out in his Racquet Club voice, "let's
get cracking. She's raving on. There's nothing worse than—"

"One more thing I tell you." Norma did not raise her voice,
but it was such an instrument that the blur of Gordon's sound
disintegrated around the concentration of hers. "I say as soon
as I come in this room that Yale University is naive. I feel that
more strong than before now. You say bomb the North in the
Asia war, eh? You think *that* will end this war? Never. This
war will never end. I tell you why, my naive American. Wait.
I was born in North Greece. There is much Turkish things
there. It used to be in Turkish Empire. Both my parents were
Greek blood, but my mother was born in St. Petersburg, in
Russia. In the Russian Empire. My father was born in Alexan-
dria, in Egypt, that was in the British Empire then. Before it
was in the Turkish Empire. Everywhere around us in the East
Mediterranean we see the ruins of the great Roman Empire,
and after that the great Byzantine Empire. In Lebanon where
I go to school, that was in the French Empire when I go to
school there. So. *I know empires.* I smell them. I taste them. I
dream them. America has the biggest empire that ever been.
Korea is on the frontier of it. All Europe that is not in the
Russian Empire is in the American Empire. All Asia that is not
in the Russian or Chinese Empire is in the American Empire.
All South America is in the U.S.A. American Empire. Talk the
truth to me, don't talk myths! We invented myths, we Greeks.
We know them when we hear them. We use them to explain
difficult things to children. Stop being children! Forget myths!
Tell yourself the truth! The fighting in Korea is on the frontier

of your empire, the way the Romans were on the Danube and the Turkish people in the Balkans and the British in India and the Russians in the Caucasus and on and on and on. Of course your empire is more clever, more sophisticated. You don't fly your U.S.A. flag over Paris, over Tokyo, you don't have a U.S.A. Governor to run England. Sometimes you don't even put some soldiers in there. But your military power and your money power decide everything in the end in Tokyo and Paris and England and everyplace in your empire. Sometimes a little country wants to drop out, like Egypt, or a big country, like India, and you let it, if it not too big a risk. They will come back when the chips are down or the guns are up! And you have so much left!" She inhaled on her long cigarette and her eyes squinted. "But. Do you want to keep your prosperity, your cars, your shoes, your good food, eh? Then you must have your empire to support your prosperity. And as long as you have your empire you will have your wars on the frontiers, just like the Romans and the Turks and the British. You settle this one and soon you will have another one, in Berlin, or in Greece, or somplace else in Asia."

Clement was almost visibly shaking with pleasure. "I think that's the best thumbnail exposure of the capitalist exploitation of the underdeveloped world I've heard."

"Oh, bullshit," said Norma. "You don't think I'm a *Communist*, do you! They are *worse*. Their empire is caught in a trap, and it is *poor* besides! It is worse. I am no politics. I am a realist. I see the truth. I tell it. America is not fighting for freedom in Asia. America is fighting for America. Russia is not fighting to free the masses of the world from exploitation. Russia is fighting for Russia. The people who run countries, whether they say they are kings or Democrats or Communists, want power for themselves and propserity for *their own people* and to hell with everybody else."

"You're very cynical," said Ginnie sagely.

Norma stared at her, and then leaned across and patted her cheek warmly. "You are pretty. Be pretty. Be innocent. The boys will love you more. I am older. Two divorces. Some love affairs. I live everyplace in the world. Don't listen to me.

Dance. Be pretty." She drew slowly on her cigarette. "Ach, I
am sorry. I talk like a maniac. My head explode sometimes. I
am so so sorry. I am sorry. Gordon, darling, forgive Norma. I
am so so sorry, to make serious your happy afternoon of
American football. Will you forgive me?"

Hugely relieved that the volcano was quiescent at last,
Gordon smiled very briefly, swallowed another large gulp of
Scotch, and then shepherded his group toward the door.

Standing before the fire Ginnie said to Norma politely, "It
was very educational to meet you."

"Oh my God!" cried Norma. "I am so old now I become an
education, an institution. Oh my God. Life is finished." She
grasped Ginnie's shoulder. "Be pretty. Don't think too much,
not yet. What do you do here, what do you study? I was
talking to that woman before and didn't hear what you said.
You have an interesting face, wide. Are you studying to be an
actress?"

"Yes," said Ginnie faintly.

"Interesting. You may have possibilities."

"Are you—an actress?"

"Me? No, no, never. I said before, I am a photographer.
However, I have this voice and I was doing much dubbing in
Hollywood. My French is like a Frenchwoman's, and so I was
the voice of some big stars when they dub their films for
France. Very interesting work. You find out their speech
problems, what's wrong with their acting, how they fake when
they don't understand an emotion, hesitate or speed up or
whatever. Me, I understand *all* the emotions but I have to
speak like them to match their lip movements. Frustrating!"

Lou was standing beside her. During a bit of conversation
between Ginnie and Mrs. Stoetzer she said swiftly out of the
side of her mouth to him, "Take me away from here."

"They were charming, charming," Norma said as she drove
her car forcefully toward the center of New Haven. "But I
had to leave. I get very nervous at the scene of one of my

crimes, like attacking poor darling Gordon. I want fresh air after that!"

Clement, shivering in the back seat, said swiftly, "You're getting plenty of that now."

"Ha! It's good for you. Or maybe your Negro blood doesn't like it—"

"Please!" exclaimed Lou. "Don't get him on that!"

"What do we do now?" asked Norma.

"Straight ahead, you're doing fine," answered Lou.

"Is this the best route there?" inquired Clement, probing for Lou's plans again.

"Yes."

"How do you *spell* the name of this place?" persisted Clement drily. "I've always wondered."

"S-m-i-t-h-s," replied Lou immediately.

"What do you two talk about? Where do we go?" said Norma. "I want to see the naive American college boys, how they play. Where is all the confusion?"

Lou glanced back at Clement. "Fraternity Circle."

"You hate where you take me now," said Norma.

"Yes."

"No," said Lou. "It's fun in a way if you don't think about yourself or anything, isn't it, Clem?"

"It's the propertied classes doing their dance of death."

Like all big student partying at American universities, the spirit along Fraternity Row that night was beer-cellar Germanic. An ocean of beer flowed beneath and around and sometimes over everything, bad unison singing croaked in the air, in the glare and haze of smoky basement bars reddish faces beheld each other, male backs and female behinds were slapped, stairs were fallen down, glasses were hurled through windows, a mish-mash mingling, purposelessly hilarious, engulfed everyone.

"Incredible," said Norma as they entered the stone cavern, oak tables strewn about the stone floors, students and their girls sitting around and on the tables, gray smoke, spilled beer. "It's like a Greek *taverna* at four o'clock in the morning.

They are too far ahead of us. We never catch up."

But they did. Clement rid himself of his cape-coat and
deerstalker hat, removed Norma's mink ("*Paris Match* Magazine, not Durant, got me that!") and Lou's long black raincoat, escorted them out of the cellar to a large room upstairs
with deep couches and a fireplace, settled them in a couch in
a dark corner out of the tide of moving bodies, procured three
powerful martinis from the bar in an upper alcove, and encouraged them to drink. "If only they had *ouzo*," sighed
Norma regretfully.

"What's ouzo?" inquired Lou.

"Don't ask," she answered, and suddenly kissed him not on
but near the mouth.

Long and lithe and blond, older and more magnetic, Norma
in her silver blouse and ivory-colored slacks had already
attracted attention; this display of affection for Louis Colfax, a
spooky non-member of the fraternity, hurtled him to sudden
prestige.

Lou took a swallow of his martini and, added to the drinking at the Stoetzers', he was suddenly released. He did not
drink every often ("Colfaxes dominate the alcoholic wards in
our part of Connecticut") but when he did, a certain precise
amount would open the gates of his personality wide. He put
both arms around Norma and kissed her on the mouth. "I just
wanted to do that all day," he said in a bubbling, grinning
way. "You don't mind, do you?"

"Mind affection? Me?"

"I didn't think you would mind."

On seeing this, a flash of consternation had shot through the
students milling near them. They studiously looked away from
Louis Colfax, the show-off. Lou was totally unaware of them.
But gradually several lone students and several couples sidled
up, drawn by this blond woman with so much vitality visible
in all her gestures and glances, and Norma yelled something
friendly to each of them, and a vivacious circle formed around
her, Lou and Clement. Norma was creating cheerfulness ("I
do penance for making this afternoon so serious!").

Suddenly Gordon loomed behind the circle formed in front

of Norma's couch, staring down. "Darling—" she began; he
didn't hear her, didn't move. He seemed to begin following
the debate Norma had instituted between Clement Jonaz and
a student about which cultures considered it polite to belch.
In the middle of the discussion Gordon suddenly belched,
enormously. Norma's eyes flashed to him, then she said to
Lou, "He is drunk! He cannot drink. He becomes insane. And
he is drunk." Gordon seemed to be again following the discussion with interest.

"He looks okay to me," answered Lou.

"He is out of his mind. We must do something. What shall
we do?"

Myron and Vilma Stoetzer, the most unobtrusive and toler-
ant chaperons the Yale community afforded, were making
their way across the pulsating room toward Norma's circle.
When they reached it, Gordon turned at them and roared,
"Well! Myron One-Play, hi there!"

Myron Stoetzer stood still, arms hanging down. Mrs.
Stoetzer said, "Gordon, what do you think you're saying!"

Gordon's light blue eyes behind their horned-rimmed
glasses had a messianic light beaming from them; his broad,
ruddy face was set with risky revelations. "You have to know
one to tell one!" he roared. "Look at her! The prophetess! I
brought her here. Zuleika Dobson! Lenin in his sealed train.
You have to know one to tell one! One, right? One teeny-
weeny play, right! *The Colors of the Rainbow,* right!"

"Myron," intoned Mrs. Stoetzer. "I think the campus police—"

"Uh-oh," cried Gordon. "Gotcha! Gotcha! Bye-bye!" he
yelled at them "Bye-bye!" and with a sort of prancing step
disappeared into the crowd in the direction of the front door.

"Go and get him," Norma said to Lou.

"Me? He won't even listen to me when he's sober!"

"True. Well, well, what to do?" Then she giggled. "It was
Bismarck who said the Lord takes care of drunks and Americans and so Gordon is both and so, may the Lord take care of
him. Am I a bitch, I came with him but I do not go with him?"

"You think you'd be able to control him?"

"*Nobody* can control a drunk Durant."

"Well then let's enjoy ourselves here."

"All right. If you think it is right."

"I think it's completely right, myself."

"So do I," she then said confidently. Turning to the nearest student she asked, "Is Yale healthy for sex? This evening, all this drinking and noise, seems a *substitute* for sex. Am I right or wrong?" At that, the shouted discussion leapt energetically forward.

Somehow in the tumult Mrs. Stoetzer edged herself onto the couch next to Lou, who was now pinned between her and Norma. Myron Stoetzer hung, a rather static figure, on the outskirts of the group, glancing suddenly and seemingly at random here and there, toward the ceiling, then the floor, then a window, then the bar.

"It was vicious of Gordon," Mrs. Stoetzer, whose Scotch consumption had been heavy, was saying rapidly and hoarsely into Lou's ear. "He doesn't know what it is, to do it again. Not unable to write another *major* play, unable to write any second play at all, even to finish one more. It's like living in a vacuum after breathing champagne air once upon a time. Myron can't *breathe*. I keep him alive by artificial respiration. A gift for art or for anything is a horrible curse when it's taken away. And it can go at any time, out the window one fine morning, gone like a bird, flown away, unrecapturable. And the derelict being it leaves behind!" she sighed heavily into Lou's ear.

"Is a gift so great to have?" he said.

"What?"

"Is it so . . . rare, having a talent like that, does it matter so much, is it so precious?"

"Don't you think so?"

"I never thought about it."

"Well," said Mrs. Stoetzer steadily, "you'd better think about it."

Some time later in the evening he spotted Ginnie across the room. Mrs. Stoetzer had moved off and was now talking intensely into her husband's ear. Norma was standing in front

of the huge fireplace holding mesmerized seven undergraduates. Clement was leaning on the bar in the alcove, telling the
Negro bartender about the battle for the rights of the "Memphis Five."

Lou, drunk, made his way across to Ginnie.

"Charlotte tried to wreck me," he began, glaring at her.

"No she didn't." Ginnie was not phased by his abruptness.
"How did she?"

"Left a picture of the kid in the cabin in the woods where
we used to shac—to live." Lou could not use or even think
crude language ("shack up") in relation to himself and Charlotte, not even now when it was finished and he was sure he
hated her. "She was telling me that the kid was ours, mine,
but I couldn't have him. That producer's got him. I'm just
some little sophomore, some nobody, I don't count . . . to hell
with you, that's what she was saying. She didn't take my
money or anything if I had any or my Morgan or anything or
my birth certificate or uh anything like that or my citizenship
away . . . she just took my son because uh I guess I'm not
supposed to be up to having one . . . Lou Colfax, sophomore,
you know, too callow or something like that to be the father
of a child of the great Charlotte Mills, actress, balls, she'll
never get anywhere as an actress unless that producer sinks
all his money in it and *then* it'll be a flop because she has not
. . . got a gift, she is not gifted, she has a knack and a little
talent *maybe* but no *endowment,* she is not *endowed* . . . even
Yale is endowed . . . so . . . she's never going to get anywhere
except in some vanity production using all that producer's
pull and all his money BUT . . . in the meantime I am not the
one, me, Lou Colfax, sophomore, to be recognized and certified as the father of her kid because you know I just don't
have enough weight or something in the community or standing or whatever you call it, I'm too callow and I guess crazy
and who am I? That's the question, or her question, or mine or
somebody's . . ."

Hours passed; the fraternity emptied; the campus quieted;
Lou, Clement, and Norma, sobered up, were delving conver-
sationally into Korea and the "Memphis Five" and sex and

religion, and failed to notice that they were virtually alone. Norma suddenly said, "My head is splitting. I need a pill."

"We didn't give you any *dinner!*" Lou exclaimed. "I forgot!"

"Never mind, darling. No food. Just a pill and to lie down for a few minutes."

Lou's room in Pierson College was only a dozen yards away, but forbidden to women at this hour, with a campus policeman at the gate to enforce the regulation.

"My room . . ." murmured Lou.

"Yes," said Clement steadily.

"Forbidden . . ."

"Yes."

"Just over the back wall here."

"Ummm."

"Norma," said Lou, "what kind of shape are you in?"

"Shape? You mean my figure—"

"I mean physical condition. Can you climb over a high wall and a piked fence and a moat?"

"Of course," she said immediately with a proud frown. "I am an athlete."

"Then let's go."

They went downstairs, out the door into the backyard of the fraternity, and by piling furniture against the wall and with help from two stray students, Lou, Clement, and Norma found themselves on top of the wall moving hand over hand along the piked fence to a point opposite Lou's bedroom window. Now all that was required was to climb over the high piked fence, step across the moat, which had narrowed here into a mere symbolic obstacle, and enter his window.

"Any good cat burglar could do it," whispered Lou encouragingly. He hoped not to awaken the students in the surrounding rooms; one moat adventure seen by everyone was more than enough.

Norma was all agility, leverage, and determination. She was the first over the picked fence, and guided Clement over it. "No, don't put your foot there, or else you destroy your crotch forever on that iron point. Careful! Swing your derriere over, careful! There. Slow, slow, slide the left foot down, *slow* till you touch—there! Now—"

They moved one at a time into the darkened bedroom and on through to the brightly lighted living room.

"Here we are!" said Lou enthusiastically, rubbing his hands together. "Now! A drink! No, I mean, of course, some aspirin."

"You know," said Norma slowly, "my headache is disappeared. Prop open the front door, so we get some air in here. It did not need aspirin, but only to get out of that place and I needed a challenge, the wall, the fence, the iron points, the moat—Yale is a crazy house, no? That is why the patients are locked in like this?"

Clement replied, "Mother Yale in her wisdom has seen fit to lock the unwashed masses *out,* not so much the students in. It's like the old International Settlement in Shanghai. Reserved for the exploiters."

Norma swung around to Lou for his rejoinder. She instinctively created debates.

"Do you think that's it?" began Lou thoughtfully. He was truly undecided about most things. He saw many sides of most questions. He was that hesitant youth with something precious inside himself which he felt so valuable that he proceeded with great caution and hesitation. But Norma's praising this quality in him, which he had always been ashamed of, this hesitancy and seeing so many sides to a question, praising of all things his indecisiveness, made him more conscious of it and play it up just a shade.

For the first time in his life he saw that one of his innumerable defects was not a defect at all no matter *what* the Marine Corps thought. He saw that it was potentially valuable, appropriate, useful, right. He wanted to throw his arms around Norma. He did throw his arms around Norma. Shoot himself! He felt deliriously happy.

They sat down, found some of Gordon's Scotch, and began having a nightcap. Soon Clement would go, and perhaps Norma would stay . . .

In the middle of their conversation a clattering sound echoed from the courtyard outside, a clitter-clatter re-echoed from the Georgian walls of Pierson College.

"That sounds like—" Lou began, chuckling in disbelief, "you'd almost think that was a *horse* coming down the walk!"

"You would, wouldn't you?" agreed Norma ominously.

The clatter grew swiftly louder, came to a nervous tattoo just outside the door, and then with a neigh Gordon Durant's polo pony pranced through the door into the room, with Gordon flattened along its shoulder and neck. Halting in the center of the Moroccan carpet in front of the fireplace, with the other three people falling back into the corners, Gordon sat upright, his head just grazing the ceiling, holding the reins carefully, just in front of his waist, sitting the English saddle properly, his toes in the stirrups, heels down, riding crop unobtrusively in his left hand, and gazing through the windows at the end of the room he said in a puzzled way, "Damn those drivers. Why can't they put on their *dimmers!* Practically blinded me." He stroked the mane of the animal, who twitched and tossed his head up suddenly. Norma screamed faintly, and then gesturing with her hand at them she began shakily, "Gordon—"

The pony was clearly high-spirited. Flaring his nostrils he rolled his eyes toward Norma and began rapidly side-stepping in that direction. Gordon lurched in the other direction, but after hanging sideways momentarily, recovered his position.

"Ho, Thor, ho," commanded Gordon, patting him on the neck. "Ho, boy, ho!" Thor stood very still again. "Never gets any goddamn exercise—" Gordon ruminated, "damn stable people—"

"Tell me," began Clement in his most rational, urbane tone, "wouldn't this work, Gordon? I take the—whatever you call it —bridle, and sort of lead Thor around in a half-circle and you can go back through the door and—"

"Give him more exercise!" finished Norma shrilly.

"Why don't you get off, dismount," said Lou, managing to keep most of his mad hilarity out of his voice, "so it'll be easier getting Thor through the door."

"Got the best seat at Yale," reflected Gordon.

Thor side-stepped suddenly toward Lou. "Gordon!" all three shouted almost in unison.

The horse settled into this new position and Gordon very slowly swiveled his head from face to face to face, and then back again. "What are all of you doing in my room?" he then asked.

"Gordon, you are riding on a horse—" Norma began desperately.

Just then Thor lifted his tail and dropped a large stool on the Moroccan carpet.

Norma screamed. Thor lurched sideways again. Gordon lost his balance and very slowly regained it.

"Listen," Lou began. "I'll take the bridle and Clem, be ready in case Gordon falls off."

"He's going to fall off," said Norma.

"All right," said Clement stiffly.

Lou approached the horse in front and reached for the bridle. Thor tossed his head but Lou's movement was swift and he had hold of the bridle. Thor instinctively asserted his remaining freedom and began stomping and kicking with his hind legs. Gordon, his eyes now closed, looking bored and half-asleep, still sat the horse. Lou began slowly to turn Thor in the direction of the door.

Norma said, "Gordon will hit his head on the door!"

"I know," said Lou. "Clem, pull him off."

Clement stepped forward, put his arms around Gordon's waist, and slowly pulled him off the horse. Thor suddenly caromed his hindquarters away from Clement and knocked over a table, two lamps, and a bookcase. A picture crashed to the floor. One of the lamps broke a window.

Gordon had been eased off the horse, Clement had him beneath the shoulders, Gordon's legs were on the floor and he might be trampled at any instant. Lou plunged toward the door and Thor, now thoroughly frightened, accepted this lead and bolted out of the room. Once through the door Lou released him and Thor set off in a calmer canter to explore Pierson Courtyard. Glancing back in at the wreckage, seeing everyone uninjured, Lou cried, "I guess I'd better get the horse!" and set uncertainly off into the courtyard.

"Louis Colfax!" cried Norma. "Do you know about horses?"

"Not exactly."

Students in surrounding rooms must be either away for the weekend or *very* drunk, reflected Lou as he made his way up the silent courtyard. If somebody wakes up they'll think it's me making a Colfax of myself again instead of Gordon. But that suddenly didn't matter, because he had something valuable inside him and—and people who were afraid to make fools of themselves never made anything of themselves!

And that insight was not Norma's; that was his.

Thor was at the far end of the courtyard, near the French doors leading to the Common Room and the Dining Room. Staying in the grass to be as soundless as possible, Lou approached. Thor was nibbling shrubbery.

"Is it good?" said Lou softly. "It's good, is it? Good, hmm?"

Thor went on chewing.

"Umm, good," said Lou quietly, coming alongside Thor and, leaning forward, he nibbled at a leaf himself. Thor paused in his chewing briefly and then continued. Lou reached over and patted him softly on the shoulder, and then began stroking his mane with his right hand while with his left hand he took hold of the bridle. Since Thor didn't protest Lou then put his left foot in the stirrup and in one rather shaky motion swung onto the saddle, found the other stirrup and put his foot in it. The horse felt like a great barrel of tense muscle between his legs. Thor appeared to be in an indecisive mood; his ears rose and fell several times and he tossed his head.

Norma approached from the right. "You are on him," she said guardedly.

"At the moment, yes, I am on him."

"What are you going to do?" she asked in the same low, guarded voice.

"Take him home, I guess. Where does he go?"

"Those stables near where we saw the football. You remember? We drove past them in my car."

"I think I know where they are."

"You know how to ride?"

"I . . . don't know. I've ridden a few times, at fairs and places, you know, little ponies that go around in circles."

"Thor is a thoroughbred, and Gordon says he is really high-spirited. Gordon likes them very high-spirited."

"He does, does he?"

"Yes."

"Well," said Lou as cheerfully as he could, "here goes!" and he turned Thor toward the underpass leading to the long stone walk and on to York Street. Seeing this unobstructed avenue before him Thor lurched into a jouncing canter. Lou did not fall off. Down the long walkway they clattered and out into York Street.

There was no traffic at this hour. Thor seemed calmer and they went ahead at a trot, which Lou found much rougher than the canter, to the corner of York and Chapel. The traffic light there was still operating. "Do I stop for it or what?" Lou asked himself; but Thor in effect answered by trotting proudly through it. Lou managed to turn the horse into Chapel Street headed out of town in the direction of the Bowl and the stables.

Each time, after Lou had turned the horse, Thor would glance beadily back at him. What is he thinking? Lou asked himself. What's going on in that strange long head? I'm much fonder of animals than Gordon ever was. I've got seventeen cats. The horse suddenly sprang into a canter. "Whoa, now, now, Thor, easy, take it easy, ah pull up, pull up now Thor *Thor* THOR ooooooooooh, *wow*, yes, now, now, that's that's better, easy, take it easy, don't keep looking back at me that way. No, don't start eating that tree, people live there and that's their tree, they wouldn't like that and we've got a long way to go. That's better, now just do that walking and don't go into that trot because that's rough, that really is . . . Thor, Thor, listen to me. There's a bus coming toward us down the street. Do you see it, Thor, that bus coming toward us. We're going all the way over here on the far side of the street and we're going to pass calmly."

The bus moved up to them and the driver and one lone

passenger gaped at Lou and Thor. Somehow emboldened by
this, Lou gave a single encouraging noise out of the side of his
mouth to Thor as he had heard cowboys in movies give to Old
Paint and, instantly galvanized, Thor plunged forward
through several gaits with amazing speed and threw himself
into a full, flat-out gallop. At an intersection, desperately
swinging, Lou turned Thor off Chapel Street and its traffic
hazards and at the next intersection, desperately swinging
again, he turned him into a quiet street paralleling Chapel
and headed out of town. He had not fallen off, although he
had lost the stirrups. However, he had long legs; Thor was a
powerful but not a large animal, and Lou was able to get a
good grip around his middle with his legs.

As they pounded down the empty street Lou was not so
petrified that he hadn't a corner of his mind free to see himself
as Paul Revere rousing the town, as the Headless Horseman,
as the Pony Express. Galloping was oddly easier than any of
Thor's other gaits, easier to stay on, provided Thor didn't trip.

They tore along the street. Then Lou began to realize that
he was having an absolutely fantastic ride.

The moon, huge at harvest time, was sliding slyly in and out
of cloud banks, the autumnal trees were still and burly with
leaves as he rode through the smell of them, the clarity and
emptiness of very late at night exhilarated him, the coordinate
bunch and stretch of Thor's muscles under him, the unbelieva-
bly rapid and clear clit-clat of Thor's indestructible hooves.
The horse was happy too, Lou sensed it for certain, and with
that certainty fixed in his mind Lou's fears evaporated. They
hurtled on together.

They came to a crossroads and Lou suddenly realized that
this street ended here, a park lay dead ahead and Thor
plunged gleefully into it. Now began cross-country riding.
This was different.

Thor began to plunge down embankments, hurtle past low-
branched trees, swerving in and out through what seemed a
crazily disordered orchard, leaping a ditch here and there.
Lou now abandoned the reins and threw his arms around
Thor's long, pumping neck. Thor did not seem to want to

throw him off exactly, but only to enjoy the thrill of the park.
Lou was welcome to share this pleasure if he wished, and
could.

Some water lay ahead and Thor pulled up abruptly, trotted
up to the bank, stopped, and began to drink.

It would now be possible for Lou to dismount safely, his
neck unbroken, his duty, whatever it might have been to
Gordon's horse more than fulfilled. He could call the police
about Thor or something. But he hadn't the faintest intention
of doing any such thing. He regained the reins, found and put
his feet in the stirrups, and waited for Thor to finish drinking.

The horse was calmer now and seemed ready to be directed. The trouble was that Lou hadn't any idea where they
were. Like most Yale students, he had a conception of New
Haven consisting of East Rock and West Rock at the extremities, the Yale Bowl in the middle distance, the New Haven
Green, the Shubert Theater and the Taft Hotel at the center
with an aureole of restaurants and bars surrounding them. All
else was unknown.

A macadam road curved through the park and Lou headed
Thor along it. He felt the horse now respected him and was
willing to be guided. This road led to a large street which Lou
recognized as close to the Stoetzers' house.

They would help; they loved to help. Nothing brought out
the best in the Stoetzers faster than a student in a jam; surely
a rank amateur rider lost on an overspirited polo pony at four
o'clock in the morning qualified.

"Thor," Lou began, "we're going to visit some friends of
mine. They're crazy about animals too. They will want to be
your friend too. THOR! Don't lift up your front legs like that
my God I almost fell *off* and then where would you be? Easy
take it easy. Oh you want to trot well all right though I like
walking or even . . . canter? you feel like cantering you aren't
too tired after all are you all right uhhhhh! You're not tired at
all! Those sudden swerves you ought to tell me about those
swerves, hell, stirrups gone again here's where I get you in a
leg lock again, okay?"

They were coming up fast to the Stoetzer driveway. Lou

desperately leaned and Thor plunged into the gravel area in front of the door and slowed to a trot, moving in stylish circles, like a circus horse.

A light went on in an upstairs window, and both Stoetzers appeared at it.

". . . Canadian mountie?" Lou heard Mrs. Stoetzer suggesting.

". . . nightriders, here?" Mr. Stoetzer could be heard rumbling.

"Mr. Stoetzer, ha, it's me, Lou Colfax, and ah *Thor!* I'm well kind of lost, it all looks so different at night out here, or I mean this early in the morning and I can't find the stable for Gordon's horse!"

"Gordon's *horse!*" Mr. Stoetzer chortled. "I'll come down—" Thor was gallivanting back and forth proudly over the driveway and lawn. "Can you hold him?"

"I might. I might." He patted Thor's neck, which was warm with sweat. Somewhere in his sponge-like memory he remembered reading something—an article in the sports section of the Hartford *Courant,* as a matter of fact, it was six, no seven years ago—about horse training, which said that horses should not be stabled while sweating. Lou would have to somehow force Thor to walk the rest of the way to the stables to cool off.

The front door opened, and the Stoetzers, in incongruously old-fashioned looking night robes for such an up-to-date pair, stood rather limply in the hall light pouring past them. Lou realized they had both had a lot to drink during the preceding evening and had been sleeping it off when he had awakened them with his ridiculous predicament.

Mrs. Stoetzer inquired, "Does he want a drink of water or anything?" and Lou suddenly loved her for being so good-humored with him.

"I don't think they're supposed to drink when you have them out," answered Lou, "but I'd like something."

"A stirrup cup of brandy?" inquired Mr. Stoetzer jovially. "Or just a good canteen of hootch for the trail?"

He must be still drunk to be talking that way, thought Lou.

"I'm afraid to drink anything like that," said Lou humbly. "I don't have too much *control* up here the way it is."

"I can see you don't. Shouldn't I call up someone to bring a van for it? That looks risky to me."

"No, we're friends, Thor and me, even if he kind of forgets it once in a while. Just show me which road I take to get to the stables."

Mr. Stoetzer explained.

"Why don't you get down and lead him to the stables?" suggested Mrs. Stoetzer.

That struck Lou as a good idea, since that way the horse could cool off. He dismounted. Thor stood still. Mr. Stoetzer disappeared very briefly and returned with a bottle of Scotch and an elegant silver goblet. "Your stirrup cup, Nightrider. Quaff!"

Lou quaffed. Then he set out.

"Tally ho!" cried Mrs. Stoetzer.

"View halloo!" added Mr. Stoetzer.

In an undertone she said, "Mad as a hatter."

He replied, "Imagine breaking into that stable in the middle of the night."

"Risking Gordon's horse. That's a valuable horse." She gathered her robe around her.

"And risking his own neck."

"Oh well." Mrs. Stoetzer delicately shrugged.

Following Mr. Stoetzer's direction Lou and Thor were soon amid the huge expanses of the athletic fields around the Bowl. Here the moist grass smells, added to the effect of the stirrup cup, plunged Louis Colfax into the heart of paradise. He had never been happier in his life, and no one else had ever been happier than he was now.

"Thor, I'm going to ask Gordon to sell you to me."

Thor continued walking.

"Do you have a son, Thor?"

Thor walked on.

At the stables the door was ajar as Gordon had left it, and inside in the darkness there was the sound of two or three horses breathing and pawing. Thor's stall had been left open.

The sole remaining problem of the night was how to get Thor
into the stall. Lou felt sure that Thor would not back in,
would not go in at all unless Lou led him in head first. Once
in the stall he and Thor would be at rather close quarters. Lou
would have to get by him and out of the stall, and if Thor
became unruly during that maneuver he might kick Lou
around quite a bit.

They stood in front of the stall. Lou looked at Thor, felt his
neck. He was cooler now. Thor gazed over Lou's head at the
stall, waiting.

"Let's go," said Lou quietly, and entered the stall, leading
Thor. Then letting go of the reins, Lou moved along the side
of the horse, patting him gently, gained the door, stepped
outside, and swung it shut. There was room for Thor to turn
around in the stall and he did so, put his head over the
half-door and seemed to want to nuzzle him, or maybe that
was just Lou's imagination.

It was a very bright, ebullient dawn when Lou got back to
his rooms in the Slave Quarters. The freshest of morning lights
poured all around him, the shrubbery was etched in sunlight,
the windows shone, and Lou's own large hand, which he
brought up in front of his face, seemed charged with life, like
Michelangelo's portrayal of God the Father's hand reaching
out to transmit life into Adam's.

Lou felt dizzy at the significance of this quality of light. He
was dazzled by its overwhelming freshness and clarity; it
seemed inexpressibly beautiful to him; he wanted to yell
something and nearly did—screw everybody if they didn't like
it—but then remembered his performance at the bottom of
the moat, and although that humiliation had dwindled far and
fast, he decided against waking Pierson College up at dawn.
Instead he proceeded slowly along the flagstone walk past the
red-brick façade with its green shutters alight with morning
light; charged with every meaning those shutters were, as was
each blade of grass, each flagstone, his shoes, the overwhelmingly beautiful single tree at the end of the court, near his

rooms. It was the most eternally heavenly tree in the—

What the hell was all this? Raving over an ordinary tree at dawn. He must really be going crazy at last. But he couldn't help this tidal wave of feeling occasioned by the fresh wash of morning light over Pierson Courtyard. It was—it was, there was something—it was—birth. This morning light evoked profoundly in him a sense of the miracle of birth.

So that was it.

Head down, he walked on into his room. Gordon Durant was asleep fully clothed, with a blanket over him, a pillow under his head, in the middle of the wreckage of the living room. Norma and Clement had departed. On the mantlepiece was a note in Norma's big, excitable handwriting.

> Darling
> Gordon is too much of a stone to move.
> You are a hero.
> Norma

Lou almost wanted to cry. Probably it was just because he was so tired. He wasn't ready to be called a hero.

And what would she think tomorrow, and next week? After new impressions had crowded in on her, other people, changed emotions, a different perspective on this night, second thoughts, reconsiderations? Love and admiration and friendship were so unstable, unrealiable, shifting, untrustworthy: they were Charlotte Mills.

He hated that name. He hated all feminine forms of essentially masculine names—Charlotte for Charles, Francine for Francis, Louise for his own, Micheline, Joanna, Pauline, Georgette. *Bellaughf!* ugly, all of them, and the ugliest of all was Charlotte.

He was now very depressed, and knew that he would never sleep. He remembered some pills he had for that, but also remembered that he had used them up. Gordon Durant, human log, would not have any sleeping pills anywhere.

So Lou sat in a corner and watched Gordon snore away the early morning.

Around ten o'clock—Lou must after all have dozed off in

his chair—Gordon began restlessly rolling and after a few minutes opened his eyes, very slowly surveyed the damaged room, his own position on the floor in the middle of it, and slowly his gaze came to rest on Lou in the corner. "Where," he croaked, cleared his throat, and began again, "where can I find a registered nurse?"

Lou had to chuckle. Gordon was, of all things, comical at the core. Inside everyone in the world one sprite or another reigned: the gnome of gloom, the satyr of sex, the imp of mischief, the clown of comedy. Inside Gordon, of all people, pompous, self-important Gordon, sat with his bells and giggles, the eternal clown. "Gordon," said Lou gravely, "you're comical."

"Never mind that. Where can I find a registered nurse?"

"It's Sunday morning. Half of them are in church, and the other half are in bed."

"Blind leading the blind. Where are my glasses?"

Lou found his glasses on the mantlepiece and handed them to him.

"Oh my Christ! What happened in here? What the hell kind of party did you have!"

"Don't you remember anything?"

"I remember—I don't—I, well, I remember my God-damned ex-stepmother giving us her Greek temper act at the Stoetzers, and dinner at Mory's, I remember that we had three Green Cups."

"*Three?*"

"Three Green Cups and, let's see, didn't I see you at Zeta Psi?"

"You did. And also Norma."

"And then . . . but I don't remember the wild party you threw in here, I can tell you that!"

"I didn't throw any party. You rode your horse in here."

Gordon had begun to struggle out of the blanket. He stopped. "I did what?"

"You rode your polo pony in here and he kicked over a few things."

"You're a liar."

"I rode Thor back and put him in the third stall on the left. I left the bridle and things on because I didn't know how to take them off. I stopped at the Stoetzers to ask the way to the stables. Call them up and check."

Gordon, on one knee, stared with massive vacantness at him. Then he said quietly, "Oh no."

These were the most genuinely felt words Lou had ever heard come out of Gordon. He said, "Yes, I'm afraid so. He dropped a big pile of shit on the floor. I guess Norma and Clement cleaned it up, but that's what that stain there is."

"Oh no." He stared into space for a while. "Did I hurt Thor, ride him into anything?"

"He seems to be okay. I rode him all the way back and he was okay."

"You did?"

"It was a good ride."

"Was it?"

"Nice horse."

"Yeah." He stared some more, looking urgently uncomfortable. "Listen. Thanks. I . . . well, I guess you're not too fond of me, why should you be?"

"I like everybody, in a way."

"You haven't got any reason to like me and if you ever would it'd be a miracle. I'm not too friendly, *I* don't like anybody really, and I never expect anybody to like me. Usually they don't, unless they knew me since the age of three or something. They're *impressed* by me or," he added swiftly, "my family's money, and so I get elected to things like the vice-chairmanship of the *News*, but there's no affection lost in it anywhere along the line. What I'm trying to say is, I hope you'll sort of excuse my attitude. The thing is, all I have is the way I *impress* people and so with you here, that didn't help, it made it, I—"

"I don't make things look more *impressive*, that's for sure."

"What do you care. You've got all those things you know about, oceanography, all your interests. You don't need to worry."

"That's very funny because ninety-nine percent of the time

I—there's this girl I used to know, English. She had a funny expression, 'haven't a hope' . . . 'We haven't a hope of getting to the films on time' or something like that. Most of the time, ninety-nine percent of it, I haven't a hope for myself. And you say I don't need to worry. That's funny . . ." Also, he wanted to add but didn't, I care tremendously about *everybody's* attitude toward me, including beggars, horses, and dogs. A dirty look from anybody can set me back for days.

"You'll develop out of it," Gordon was saying in a monotone. "I don't frankly think there's that much in me *to* develop." He drew a massive breath. "Water! My God, water!" and standing up, he headed into the bathroom. Lou sat looking after him, blinking.

It was Sunday morning.

New Haven is a city of belfries, and in them are many bells, solemn or delicate or declarative or grave, which send their tones tolling across the quiescent city on Sunday mornings. They rolled over Pierson College now from here and there, sounding calm reminders to those who wanted to listen, and spreading out into the sky this echo of their worship to others for what they wanted of it, rolling by and dwindling and finally disappearing over the city, meaningless if those hearing wanted meaninglessness, speaking calmly of Sunday to others. Lou, one of the others, listened and felt calmer.

"I love Yale," he yelled to Gordon.

There was a kind of scuffle in the bathroom and then Gordon stuck his dripping head out of the doorway. "What?"

"I love Yale," repeated Lou very bravely.

This was the last crisis of their friendship. Gordon realized that if he could forgive this inane, hopelessly irrelevant and bottomlessly unfashionable remark, as ill-timed as possible, from Lou Colfax now, he could forgive anything. Lou was looking brightly across the room at him, waiting.

Gordon drew in his breath, and then said judiciously, "I'm glad you do. My grandfather built it," and withdrew into the bathroom, feeling that he had cemented that friendship for life.

"I love Yale," Lou went on aloud to himself. "You know

why I love it? Because it keeps things, preserves them, not just the Gutenberg Bible and the first book printed in America, but it, I don't know, keeps, well, *geology,* who else would? *eeoughf!* and it keeps the rules of German grammar and all the old poets . . . who else would keep Dryden? I ask you, who else will keep T. S. Eliot in a hundred years—*Four Quartets?* Brother. They take care of finished philosophers here, and they have all the oldest and newest mathematics, they even have that cozy pornography collection in the library, and they have all the latest chemical formulas and all the ones that led up to it, that's important, isn't it, to be able to find the answer not just to 'Where are we?' but 'How did we get here?' That's very very important. Yale can answer that question. That's why I love it."

Gordon was still taking an immensely long shower.

The bells continued rolling their calm reminder across the roofs of the University, and Lou suddenly felt he had to answer. He put on a black necktie over his black shirt, a tweed sports jacket, the inevitable dark glasses. Where to go to church? Battell Chapel was too much like the Congregational service at home. St. Thomas More, just across the street, had all the interminable tradition of Roman Catholicism behind it, and that appealed to Lou strongly on this Sunday morning, but unfortunately the building itself was a failed 1930's experiment in combining Georgian and contemporary architectural styles, and Lou felt the need for aged stone and statues and incense and encrusted vestments, for "the works" ecclesiastically, so of course he went to the dark, thick-walled, portentious High Episcopal Church up the street, and got it.

He followed closely as the venerable priest moved slowly through the solemn old rituals and felt calmed, calmed by the almost endless continuity these rituals represented; perhaps some detail of the ceremony flowed back to the old gods, to Apollo and the speaking spring and the laurel tree.

Outside the church Lou drifted down the street, past Saybrook College, through the Old Campus where freshmen were tossing footballs, where ladies in flowered hats were coming out of Battell Chapel, where the complex ferment of a Sunday in New Haven was rising, Sunday, no classes, unscheduled Sunday, when you had to be yourself, God help you, Sunday, that was why he had gone in search of religion, of God, or of Apollo, because it was unscheduled Sunday, when you had to be yourself.

In the middle of the following week Lou set out for downtown New Haven to visit a settlement house. Clement Jonaz was working there part-time as a volunteer and Lou wanted to see what he was doing. On the way he passed the Shubert Theater and noticed the billboard announcing the next attraction—"En Route to Broadway":

THE BEES KNEES

A Musical Comedy of the Twenties

His eye lighted here and there—"Starring Nigel Newhard"—"Directed by Roy Rich"—"Book and Lyrics by Elizabeth Ross MacDonald"—names so well-known even Lou had heard of them.

Then he noticed a special box below the title: "Introducing and Co-Starring Miss Charlotte Mills."

It was exactly like the time she had slapped him in the face.

Clement was not at the settlement house, but Lou found him back in his rooms at the Graduate School. "Well, she's here," he said without preliminaries as he came into the room.

"Who is? Margaret Truman?"

"Charlotte Mills."

Lou continued across the darkened room and sat down. Clement kept the windows permanently concealed behind blackout curtains ("I'm besieged in this country"). A maroon North African lamp of beaten copper hung by a chain in one corner, faintly illuminating it, and at Clement's desk in the other there was a fluorescent reading lamp. On a very low coffee table a red votive candle flickered in its glass holder. Used to the layout of furnishings in the room, Lou crossed without bumping into anything and sat down in the black butterfly chair across the desk from Clement.

"Back for some extra work at the Drama School?" Clement inquired with low-pitched dryness. "She could use it, if the last time I saw her—"

"Back in the lead, of a Broadway play, that's where she is. Playing the lead in a big Broadway musical."

"Well, as they say, marry a producer and anything—"

"I've got to do something."

"What?"

"I've got to do something."

"You? Why?"

"I've got to."

"*Why* do you? Excuse me, Louis, what has she got to do with you any more? You don't even like the theater."

Lou stared at him. "She's the mother of my son, and I've got rights . . . rights."

"Rights? To opening night seats or what? You don't know for certain that that's your son and even if it was, she has all the legal *rights* to it. I'll tell you what your rights are as far as Charlotte Mills starring in a play are concerned. You have a right to buy a seat and to sit in it and boo! That's it."

"I've got a right to see her, and see him."

"You have a right to ask to see her and to see him," Clement qualified.

"Will you come with me?"

"Me? Why?"

"You're calmer. I wouldn't be likely to—ah—get carried away, you know to start yelling at her or anything, if you came along, I don't think."

They went out of the Graduate School toward the Taft Hotel.

It was November. An indecisive lowering gray sky meditated over New Haven, and the first Canadian winds carelessly stripped the dead leaves from the trees and sent them skittering along the campus streets. They passed the back of the Sterling Memorial Library; Lou noticed that it presented its habitual baffling aspect of an ill-planned citadel. To be continued, its foreshortened forms and pointless patterns seemed to say. But nothing more could or would be done with the Sterling Memorial Library except to tear it down some day and try again.

They turned left at the corner and proceeded down Elm Street. Color was disappearing from New England with the last of the leaves, fading with the leaves into gutters and extinction, and the New England winter world of grays was assuming control, smoke grays, dull browns, black, periodically brightened by snowfalls which, however, quickly sank into the prevailing grayness of New Haven.

Perhaps that was why the theatrical season came into full swing in November, bringing all the artificial dazzle of costumes, the glittering illusion of stage sets, the other-world evocativeness of stage lighting to the gray crowd huddled in the darkness of the playhouse. It was a northern predeliction, the theater, and perhaps this autumnal draining away of the surrounding color was a powerful impulse for it.

Lou and Clement continued along through the November gloom in front of the Old Campus, and as Lou looked down across the New Haven Green with its three New England churches, the uncompromising assertion they made that solid down-to-earth Protestantism was here to stay, for good, that the mind and the body must be purified of their lusts and prurience, that "uprightness," hard work, and a circumspect attitude toward the world were by divine law the only acceptable way to live, while on his right the University, society in microcosm, armed to the teeth, confronted the Green and everything else in New Haven, he felt himself crossing a No-Man's-Land with Clement, his best friend, where neither

one of them, for deeply different reasons, could feel any sense
of identity with God on their left or Man on their right.
Instead Lou proceeded between them on his own special
straight-and-narrow path toward . . . toward the Taft Hotel,
toward Charlotte Mills, toward this baby, whosoever he was.

"She'd better be polite to me," he said evenly between set
teeth. His straight brown hair was falling over his forehead
above the big dark glasses, and despite them and the black
raincoat, he retained an elusive air of grace, a fugitive distinction, as though his was a family of long-exiled and impover-
ished aristocrats who hadn't quite forgotten. "She'd better be
polite. If she tries to give me the old show-business brush-off
I'm going to do something drastic."

"I believe you brought me along to keep you calm. Keep
calm. There, now I've done my duty. Tell me when you need
another booster shot. How about a drink?"

"Yes," said Lou instantly. They went into Kaysey's across
from the hotel and Lou ordered a double vodka on the rocks.
"Doesn't smell," he said. "Can't have her thinking I have to get
drunk to face her." He lit a cigarette.

"I still think it would be a grand idea if you telephoned
her."

"No. No advance warning. I want to see how she reacts
spontaneously to suddenly seeing me."

"She knows she's bound to see you here. New Haven . . ."

"Are you kidding? She thinks I'm still in the Marine Corps."

"Oh," said Clement uneasily.

Lou drained the double vodka rapidly, Clement sipped at a
glass of beer, they paid and went across the street and into the
gloomy marble rotunda of the hotel lobby. Lou put out his
cigarette on the floor and lit another one. Then he sat down
on a couch. Clement sat down beside him. "Aren't you at least
going to call her room and see if she's in?"

"Of course not. I told you. It has to be spontaneous."

"Well then," said Clement dryly, "why don't you find out
her room number and climb up the *fire escape* and come in
through the window? That would be enormously spontaneous
for you both."

"That wouldn't surprise her, coming from me."

"I suppose not."

"Not from me. I wonder if her voice has changed." Clement stared at the side of Lou's exalted-looking face. "You know, acting, all this rehearsing and singing over and over all night long, they rehearse all night long in Broadway try-outs she told me, it can make your voice fall, drop an octave, or *more*, and," Lou was now talking fast, rattling on in a machine-gun, mechanical way, "so she would sound very different. And then after all that rehearsing, she has to come back and sing to the baby, lullabies, doesn't she? Doesn't everybody have to sing lullabies to babies? Must be a terrible strain, using her voice all that much. It's a funny thing about Charlotte's voice. She's what you'd call soft-spoken usually, you know in conversation and normal discussion and on the telephone, but uh her— she's a 'belter,' she told me she found out in her voice lessons, the teacher kept saying, 'sing louder, sing louder' and it turned out that the soft-spoken little English rose had a voice like a drill instructor, Jesus, what made me think of drill instructors, D.I.'s, Parris Island, *eaougph!* Well, *I* found it out too, I never heard that voice she had except, well, the very last time I saw her," Lou's gaze shifted every few seconds back and forth between the elevators and the entrance to the lobby. "*Then* I heard it all right. Jesus. What a row. Brother."

"Louis, do you really want this girl to walk in here, proba- bly with her husband and the director of the show and eight other people surrounding her, and find you babbling on to an Afro-Brazilian in the lobby?"

"Yes," he replied. His eyes were on the arrow of the eleva- tor. It was coming down. "Jesus she—when she's really *mad* —and well I made her . . . well her voice well when I saw her the last time well she damn near blew the *roof* off the Black House that's what happened the last time we saw each other—"

Lou was waiting for Charlotte at the Black House. For the last five evenings he had telephoned her from the phone booth

on the highway and she had said, Yes, she was coming for the
night, and she had not come. For the last three mornings he
had telephoned her from the highway for an explanation and
it had always been the same: These people here have been
auditioning us . . . play possibilities . . . a part! . . . New
York! After receiving these excuses—auditioning her at midnight!—Lou would be incapable of driving to New Haven for
his own classes because what was the reason for doing anything except in cooperation with his life with Charlotte, and if
she was throwing these long shadows of doubt across their
relationship then Lou saw no reason to function at all. And
these shadows her nights of absence threw were not merely of
doubt; they had the blackness of certainty; desperation had
made him a master of detection.

So Lou would return to the Black House and do the only
thing in the world he could do in these circumstances. He set
to designing underseas vehicles. And this did indeed take him
out of himself, sever, very temporarily to be sure, the virtually
umbilical connection with Charlotte and enable him to function as an independent being. His inventiveness was independent, independent of Charlotte, independent even of his
own nature.

The vehicles, he called them names like Triton and Sala-
mander and Leviathan and Moby Dick and, for a particularly
daring and dubiously designed one, Titanic, all were marvels
of intricate and yet fundamentally simple design, it seemed to
Lou, and they filled him with a kind of eerie happiness, eerie
because it could live outside his feelings for Charlotte and
himself.

But finally this drug, if that was what it was, would wear off
and Lou would turn to real ones. Pharmaceutics was one of
his interests and in an informal way he had learned a good
deal about this field. One way and another he had acquired a
number of stimulants and depressants, sleeping pills and heart
stimulators, inhalers and sprays, and he never took any of
them according to the directions. Following directions seemed
to him quite dangerous. So he would grind the pills to powder, take part of one and cross it with a bit of another, dilute

the result with something, cross this mixture with another he had concocted after considerable study and experiment, and then swallow the result. He felt rather like Dr. Jekyll, but no Mr. Hyde emerged, exactly. Instead he put himself into a variety of heightened states, and by carefully controlling them, and spacing them, he felt that no harm, and considerable benefit, was being done. He was not "normal"; that had been true of him from conception. He could not get through life as people with less tenuous nervous systems and complex brain cells did; he had to improvise and find his own way empirically.

He looked up from his chemistry table, hearing Charlotte drive up in the Morgan. Lou was only very slightly under the influence of a mixture of rum and a drug called Orbitol. He felt in complete control of himself and more self-possessed than usual.

She strode across the neglected front of the house, across the little porch, and came in. She was wearing a tweed suit and looked much dressier than usual, looked older, with something newly successful around the edges somewhere. Lou couldn't locate it. The large, slender, oval earrings? The competent handbag hanging from her shoulder? It was her hair. Her long, bright brown hair had been cut drastically short. "It's the new Italian cut," she said shortly. She didn't ask if he liked it; he hated it.

"What are you all dressed up for?" Lou asked.

She put the handbag on the oval table in the center of this shabby room. "Work," she said.

"Hmmm? Work. These are your work clothes."

"Is there any coffee? Louis, I'd give anything to see you in some color, any color, besides black, if it's clothes you want to talk about."

In all their limitless discussions she had never alluded to his addiction to black before. He was obscurely shocked. Black was a talisman for him, public acknowledgement of his special identity, it was like wearing the Miraculous Medal or the Star of David or the "Ruptured Duck" discharge emblem, a little apologetic, a little proud: this is me, take it or leave it. It required a certain amount of courage: now Charlotte was disparaging it.

"How was your week?" he inquired formally.

"What?"

He put some water on the gas ring to boil for the coffee.

"Are you sleeping all right these nights?" he substituted.

"Yes, why?"

"Sometimes you don't."

"I'm very tired at night . . . auditions . . ."

"Mmm."

"My, but this house looks neglected."

Lou spent several seconds studying the jet of flame under the water. Then he said, "This house is just like you and me. It used to be beautiful in its own peculiar way. And now it's neglected."

Charlotte was sitting on the automobile seat next to the wall. In her city clothes she looked very uncomfortable and even uneasy there, as though she had not sat there countless times before. "Well, whose fault is that?" she said after a silence.

"If you don't know whose fault it is—"

"I have my work in New Haven. And also, when I do come here you don't seem to be all that interested in me, interested in me, how shall I put it," she finished with an attempt at a worldly laugh, "carnally."

Lou was making an absolutely microscopic study of the jets from the gas ring. "That's true," he said in his low-pitched voice, which was almost under control: thank God for rum and Orbitol.

"So I would say," she went on, "that the root of the neglect is there. Wouldn't you?"

The British query intonation of this question, so characteristic of her, had a kind of little-girl-sincere ring to it; it nearly destroyed him there beside the gas ring. (Inhale the gas! Set fire to yourself!) How was it possible that someone so lovable could make him suffer so atrociously?

Suddenly he had to put an end to this atrocious suffering,

its evil root had to be exposed, even if stating it devastated their relationship.

"So I'm neglecting you carnally," he said meditatively, his voice steady by a triumph of will and pharmaceutics. "Well, I never could enjoy leftovers."

She got up slowly from the seat. "What are you saying to me! You . . . how dare you accuse me! Leftovers! You *rat!* You—that's the most—I—"

She really is such a good actress, Lou noticed with infinite sadness, she really is.

She had crossed to him and he had turned and faced her, a newly lighted cigarette hanging from his lips.

"*That's* what you suspect! Spying on me! Eavesdropping! You insecure *sneak*. Imagining everybody's *betraying* you, you're so *inadequate* you have to imagine everybody's *betraying* you!"

The room and the house were exploding around his head; inside his head all was indescribable.

He knew that she had a sexual relationship with that producer. It was not that, ultimately, which drove him to the point he now reached. It was that she even refused him the intimacy of a confession; she lied, excluding him even from being told.

All purpose for him was now gone, all feelings bankrupt.

He pulled the cigarette from his mouth and shoved it toward her left eye.

At the last instant she turned her head and its burning tip ground into her cheek.

The outcry.

". . . well her voice, well, the last time I saw her, well, I wonder about her voice, all this rehearsing, and they often rehearse all night. And then having to sing to the baby, those lullabies, everybody has to do that."

Lou lit another cigarette and fell silent. He watched the New Englanders purposefully cross and recross the lobby. It was November and a sudden adjustment to sharp cold had been required of them. Wool scarves tried not too successfully to protect throats from the various infections of winter; thick gloves impeded hand movement but at least prevented numbness in the fingers; thick socks tried to preserve blood circulation in the feet; rubbers tried to insulate them from chills. The vulnerable human bodies of the inhabitants of New England took the usual defensive measures as they faced up to the leading edge of Arctic air now moving down upon them, prepared themselves as best they could for the long seige, the illness known as New England winter, resigned themselves to losing an appreciable measure of their vitality and health to winter, to the North as it rolled down over them once again.

Charlotte was applying her make-up with a faintly shaking hand. Her coloring was good, she believed, for movies made in color, her sea-green eyes, a kind of delicate Celtic flush to her cheeks sometimes, shining dark brown hair. But it did not register across the glaring footlights in the theater; this ruthless theater lighting washed out her coloring completely and almost washed out her features as well; she had to paint a kind of caricature of her face on the surface of the real one for the audience to see it at all. That vividness was the point of all her efforts at make-up; Mrs. Temple was reported to have reduced all her advice to Shirley before every movie "take" to that: "Sparkle, Shirley, sparkle!" Of course a sort of burlesque appearance was right for the satiric mood of *The Bees Knees*. The show laughed at the 1920's, and laughed at itself. Charlotte worked assiduously around her eyes, widening them, enlarging them; she reduced the size of her small nose still more, broadened her mouth, sharpened her cheekbones.

Her face aglow, the rest of her drab because she only prepared her face here in the Taft, she threw on a nondescript gray raincoat, and peeked into the bedroom to check on Mark. He was napping. His nurse, Miss Hinkel, was sitting in a straight-backed chair, staring, apparently content, at a television screen with the sound turned off, showing a hockey

game. They waved their fingers at each other. If there was one
category of female help Charlotte could not stand it was the
English nanny; Miss Hinkel was a nice, plain, very American
practical nurse. After all, Mark was half-American by blood
and had a right to his father's heritage.

She went out the door into the corridor heading for the
elevators. *What* was that new variation of her "shimmy" number? *What* was it?

Louis Colfax out of the blue flashed into her mind: "You
always say 'what' so emphatically," he was saying to her,
again, with his grin. "You're such a Limey."

The elevator came and she got into it. Both the elevator
operator and the other passenger, a man who looked like a
retired telephone company executive, stared at her brilliant
face as though she were some kind of whore. Damn bloody
New England! She had gotten out of Old England because it
was stuffy and rancid, only to land in New England, a blurred
copy of it; all of the Old Country's pretensions and hypocrisies
were here, but they were blurred, muted, diluted by a sea-
change into a paler, even duller reproduction. *Would* this
show even get back to New York, where she now felt so at
home, New York which had simply inundated all the bad, taut
memories, of New Haven and the Black House, flooded them
out of her feelings, flushed Louis Colfax and New England
stares and crazy aunts and tapped telephones and the fever of
betraying someone with someone else and lying about it and
acting at acting in the Yale Drama School: in New York she
had acted, done acting itself in front of an audience instead of
in front of other actors; in New York she had gotten married
instead of shacking up with someone; in New York she had
borne her baby.

Charlotte leveled her glittering green glare upon the telephone executive and he glanced apprehensively away.
"Lobby," she let drop in her most British manner to the
elevator operator. Her scared-rabbit days, she felt, were a
thing of the past, a relic left at the Drama School and the
Black House.

Very unexpectedly for Lou, who had instinctively not be-

lieved it would or could happen, Charlotte stepped out of an
elevator, her face unnaturally glowing, her green eyes purposefully fixed on the exit to the street. Quite unconcerned,
her glance then swept over the lobby, just to "check the
house" in the theatrical sense and, with a disbelief much
stronger than his, she saw the long black frame of Louis
Colfax rising from a couch.

Stepping onto her path he said, "Hello, Charlotte," in his
low-pitched voice and smiling his best smile.

In that instant Charlotte saw him: she had never, never
seen him before; now she truly saw him. He was like some
incredibly twisted, convoluted, self-strangling plant, so entan-
gled its being alive at all was a miracle, nevertheless putting
forth desperately a beautiful foliage, this wide radiant smile,
desperately, despite all handicaps, seeking the sun, seeking
survival.

"My word, it's Louis," she breathed, becoming very British,
to keep her heart from breaking over the trap he was in, his
wild aspirations to get out. "Whatever are you doing here? I
thought you were at the war."

"I came back," he said awkwardly, almost senselessly. His
brain had congealed the moment he saw her; he could not
breathe properly, his tongue seemed to have suddenly thick-
ened. "I came back," he heard himself absurdly repeat. She
looked beautiful in her stage make-up, and he didn't like it.
He disliked the unnaturalness of this beauty, as though the
make-up was a screen between her and him. But there were
now so many screens.

"Uh," he began chuckling nervously, shifting on his feet, "I
wanted to see you. Want a cigarette?" he suddenly inquired,
pulling the pack from his raincoat pocket, realizing, too late,
her last association of cigarettes with him.

Charlotte merely looked eloquently down at the cigarettes
for a moment or two, and then slowly raising her bright green
eyes to his mortified brown ones, said simply, "No, thanks."
He had had time to notice a faint irregularity in the skin of
her left cheek.

"Oh yeah," he rushed on, "congratulations on the part. Wonderful. You'll be a star."

"Oh no, who knows, anything can happen."

"Oh um this is Clement Jonaz."

They shook hands. Charlotte gave him one brief, bright smile, nailing him firmly into a respectable but minor place in the scheme of things."

"You will come to see the show, won't you. We open next Tuesday. Do come backstage and see me afterwards."

Still chuckling faintly, Lou then said, "I'd love to see the baby."

Charlotte's eyes had already been fixed on the exit. Now they started to snap back onto his face, but she was too trained an actress for that and so they made the journey back in stages, hopping from the door to a potted plant to a couch to Lou's face. "*Would* you?" she asked in her ineffable way.

"Yes. The snapshot you left up in the Black House wasn't too clear. I want to see him in the flesh."

Charlotte was silent, her eyes studying his, as though his request was so unexpected she had to analyze it in depth. Finally she said, "He's napping."

"Um-hum," said Lou, realizing she had at last made a mis-step and that he might finally score a point in this encounter, "I dare say he is." His use of Britishisms used to be a joke between them. "I didn't mean now. But sometime. Anytime."

Charlotte was suddenly furious. She didn't know exactly why. "Well, good-by!" she said, her eyes suddenly bright with coldness. Then, giving each of them a stagey smile, she proceeded swiftly across the lobby and out the entrance.

"Bitch!" growled Lou bitterly.

"I told you," said Clement as gently as he could.

"Miserable bitch."

"White Anglo-Saxon Protestants aren't good at spontaneous encounters. You have to be a 'person of color' for that."

Lou turned his dark eyes on Clement, who had never seen this particular, fixed look in them. "She's not going to get away with it. She's not going to get away with it."

So the great spontaneous meeting had been a total failure.
Lou had collapsed into the depths of Colfax foolishness
("Want a cigarette?"); Charlotte had retreated into her most
English chilliness.

Soon after that the director and the cast of *The Bees Knees*
began remarking to each other how their little star was suddenly taking hold of her role in a way she hadn't before,
bringing a concentration to rehearsals which they had been
looking for hopefully. Being the star of a Broadway musical,
her husband had told her many times, was like joining the
Army, like taking the veil, it was all she would have time for:
she must give everything to it; he would not mind being
neglected by her, that was show business; the baby had the
nurse; there was a housekeeper to maintain the apartment in
New York. Charlotte herself must sleep, breathe, eat, and
excrete *The Bees Knees.* Understand?

Charlotte hated that 'Understand?' which invariably concluded pronouncements by him which he felt of deep importance. Nevertheless she answered, "Yes, love, I understand,"
mildly enough, because she did. So the show was silly, super-
ficial, due to be forgotten in two seasons; it was also bright,
fast, rather clever and tuneful and had many of the earmarks
of a hit. A lead in a hit: how many actresses started *that* way
in the theater! The abrupt encounter with Louis Colfax,
which had stirred her up in ways she did not understand, had
given a fresh thrust to her ambitions. Among other things, a
success in this part would show *him* a thing or two! She found
the sight of New Haven troubling and distracting, but fortunately the show insured that she would never see it. She saw
the inside of the Shubert Theater; she saw the inside of her
suite in the Taft Hotel; she saw the inside of a restaurant or
two, a bar or two, and that was all she saw. For all she saw of
Yale, she might as well have been at Harvard.

Everything ached in her body from so much rehearsing, so
much dancing, but she oddly enjoyed these pains ("All
women are masochists," she, very involuntarily, recalled Lou
telling her).

Little Mark seemed to be well. Funny creature. When she

thought of him Charlotte saw her attitude as that of a typical upper-class English mother. She was not from the upper class actually, but like so many English she gave that impression almost in spite of herself (Another Colfaxism forced itself into her mind: "The English are the only *honest* phonies in the world"). A child should be reared by others, and the short period daily when he saw his parents should be blissful for the child and restful for the parents. Tears, diarrhea, minor fevers, refusals to eat, temper tantrums should be coped with by people trained and hired so to cope. The parent loved and inspired the child from a safe, dignified distance.

She had, once, with Lou, resolved to raise the child she hoped they would have by the opposite method, and if she did not have her career, and if she did have Lou, she might still have done it: bear the baby by "natural childbirth"; breast-feeding; carry him as papoose on her back everywhere, rear him to be free, natural, spontaneous; bring him up like a lion cub. She had that liberal, even radical side to her, the high-handed rebelliousness against convention which had carried her out of England to America. But that, like so much (like Lou Colfax?), had had to be sacrificed to her career. It was to that side, naturally, that Lou had so deeply appealed. But now that side had been abandoned, left with the snapshot on the wall back at the Black House. Charlotte was a New Yorker now, with a prosperous husband, a real career, and a son who was being raised like a proper rich boy, by a nurse.

She was so busy and so tired that she did not want Lou Colfax to keep popping into her mind, all grinny and bell-hung, like the clown he was. And so as a means, she felt, of exorcising him, she sat down at three o'clock in the morning after another exhausting rehearsal and dashed off a note:

Dear Louis—

I was glad to see you looking so well the other day. Sorry I was in such a rush. Rehearsals will do me in yet. In case they don't, do come to the opening Tuesday. Here are two tickets.

She hesitated over making some coy joke about bringing his new girl friend, whoever she might be, then decided not to, just signing it:

Aff
Charlotte

When Lou got the note and the tickets in his mail at Yale Station they set up a peculiar chemistry in his brain, in his stomach, in his bloodstream. He wished she hadn't sent them, for then his attitude toward her could have remained pure anger. But now the mixture was much more complex, full of chancy possibilities. He shoved the note and the tickets into the pocket of his black raincoat and headed out of Yale Station into a kind of flailing gale which was blowing across New Haven that day, and on to his class in the Diplomatic History of the First World War. In this course Lou felt he was truly being educated, that is, made to examine and analyze information and from it, by mental effort, extract illuminating conclusions. It forced his mind, his understanding to expand, and for this he was very grateful.

"Guns and Huns," as the course was known to the students, met in a small amphitheater. There were thirty-seven students. It was conducted by a rather elderly teacher, famous in his field, Professor Gilders.

In examining the origins of the first world war, the class dealt with the raw material itself, as one did in a scientific course, with the basic elements, as in chemistry, with the rocks themselves, as in—*eoaufph!*—geology. Here were the telegrams exchanged by the foreign ministers of Austria and Germany on the brink of the war. Here were the minutes of crucial French cabinet meetings. Here were the secret clauses of the fatal interlocking series of alliances which, more than anything else, actually caused this most catastrophic of wars, Lou concluded. Here is why the Czar felt he had to mobilize, and here is why that was the last fatal step. Here was Imperial Germany, aggressive and expansionist certainly, but Lou was finding his way to the conclusion that it was not Germany which was most responsible for the outbreak of the war.

Amazing. "Everyone knew" that Germany's invasion of Belgium "caused" the war. Not true, Lou concluded, on the basis of the fundamental evidence. This sort of discovery was what he thought a college education was all about. Which country had been most responsible for the outbreak of war? Germany's ally, Austria-Hungary, his study concluded. She was the weakest major power in Europe, an ancient state decomposing there at the center of the continent, and her very weakness made her recklessly aggressive and provocative, dragging Russia, Germany, France, and Britain, in that order, into the First World War.

Lou entered the little amphitheater that morning, Charlotte's conciliatory note burning such a hole in his raincoat pocket he half-expected the room to be suffused with rubber smells.

It was 9:04 A.M. "Guns and Huns" was a rather "shoe" course, so that there were fewer dungarees and more gray flannel pants in evidence. (Lou had tried to avoid ever learning what "shoe" meant at Yale, knowing instinctively it would depress him, and when he learned, it did: "shoe" referred to a certain kind of white sports shoe which, when properly dirty, symbolized the socially elite. Lou was immune to caring about social gradations, his mind couldn't function that way, and he was amused to notice that white shoes themselves began to lose caste as the "wrong" people began to wear them, the "right" people quickly throwing theirs away in favor of dark brown Italian loafers or cordovans. Lou had ostentatiously given Clement a pair of white shoes for one of his birthdays.)

He sat down, opened his notebook, and began as usual to sketch. For the last couple of days he had been doing three-dimensional geometric designs, for some reason, shafts diminishing into the distance, arrangements of planes in restricted spaces. Today he opened his notebook and immediately saw what these designs were: they depicted the inside of a theater, sight lines, lighting patterns, sets arranged on a stage. So that was it.

This was the one course Lou and Gordon had in common and Gordon now came in. He wore gray flannel pants, a

tweed sports jacket with the elbows rakishly reinforced with
leather pads, and dark brown loafers. He took the seat next to
Lou, to which he had moved in stages during the term from
the one farthest away from him.

"Do you know what the word 'Reich' means, Gordie?" he
asked immediately without preliminaries.

Used to him by now, Gordon answered casually, "Yes, I
suppose I do, kind of. It means, well, realm, nation, the
German state."

"Wrong. It means reach, the German Reach. Reaching toward the East and West, outwards."

"Typical. Damn Boche. Well, if there's one thing this course
settled it's that Germany started the war."

Lou went on sketching for a while. Then he said, "You're
wrong. The alliances started the war, and Austria-Hungary
triggered the alliances."

"Well," shifting away from argument; Gordon had learned
Lou was almost undefeatable in argument, "Whoever started
it caused the end of civilization. There hasn't been any civilization anywhere since. All the gentlemen disappeared with
that war and we've had nothing but peasants and slobs and
fanatics running the world ever since, except Roosevelt who
was a maverick, and Churchill, but they wouldn't let *him* in
power until that tradesman Chamberlain had already fumbled
into war with that lower-middle-class lunatic, Hitler. And who
have *we* had? Truman! And now Eisenhower! Army staff
officer, junior grade, running the world! Well, God help us, I
say," and he snapped open his copy of the New York *Herald
Tribune* and began very dubiously scanning the front page.

Boy are you lucky, Gordon, Lou wanted to say, not for
being rich but for being so squared away in your head. No
doubts!

And then he remembered what Norma Durant had said
about the supreme value of doubts in young people, and at
that lifting recollection, the frail net which had always broken
under him at such moments, letting him drop into depression,
into despair about himself, miraculously held, proved for the

first time tensile, springy, sent him rebounding up again, with the first tentative beginnings of pride in himself stirring somewhere in the endless chambers of his mind.

Charlotte! The note from her grew hotter and hotter in his pocket, ever closer to some kind of spontaneous combustion. Why couldn't she leave him alone to hate her!

And why couldn't *he* leave *her* alone? He was the one who had sought her out.

No, not true; she was the one who had come back to the Black House, stuck the challenging snapshot on the wall.

There was unfinished business between them. Neither could leave the other alone: something more had to happen before each of them, before their relationship, could come to rest.

Mr. Gilders came in and took his place at the lectern in the center of the small amphitheater. The students didn't stir from their semi-somnolent postures, except for two eager sophomores in the front row. The others, virtually their whole lifetimes having been devoted to one teacher after another appearing before them, year after year, never moved. Professor Gilders was popular, but he was just another link in that incredibly long chain. Lou, thinking of this, rapidly calculated that so far in his life he had attended 10,086 classes.

Professor Gilders was discussing the personality of Czar Nicholas II of Russia this morning. First he dealt with and rejected the Marxist dogma that historical forces alone shaped history, and personality was of no importance.

Lou thought: *That means Eisenhower and John Foster Dulles are shaping history. Gosh, John Foster Dulles? Shaping history?*

"The first fifteen years of Nicholas the Second's reign were a study in vacillation. He had, one might say, an obsessive inability to make up his mind. Often when he made some governmental decision one of his uncles would come into his office and pound on the desk, and Nicholas would then reverse the decision. And then the minister who had recommended the decision would come into his office, more ceremoniously to be sure, but succeed in getting the decision reinstated. Then the uncle would come back in. On one decision Nicholas reversed himself a hundred and thirty-seven times."

Lou thought: *Even I'm not that bad. Even Norma says by the time you're thirty you ought to have made up your mind pretty much and stand for something.*

"The Empress on the other hand had extremely definite views on almost everything. The twin foundations of her certainty were a mystical version of the Russian Orthodox religion, and her family. When the Emperor's vacillations changed under the pressure of the war into a virtual disintegration of his personality, she took over the power in a very definite way."

I don't expect ever to be henpecked. There aren't any henpecked Colfaxes. The one aberration we don't have. The Empress was kind of good looking. Nicholas the Second, Autocrat of all the Russias, unlace my corset, will you? In the 1920's women got out of those corsets. The 1920's. The Bees Knees. She's rehearsing now. No, not at 9:20 in the morning. Sleeping. Who's feeding the baby? Who's feeding the baby! Some room clerk!

"The Empress didn't merely love her son in the normal maternal fashion. The blood disease he suffered from, hemophilia, caused him terrible pain many times and nearly killed him on several occasions. He had inherited this disease through her, and she knew this. So she came to dedicate herself to his survival, and then to the survival of all the czarist prerogatives which he would inherit, all the political power, to the preservation of Russia's medieval autocracy, in the twentieth century."

How much does she really care for that boy? And I mean really. I've never even seen her with him. The maternal type? I never would have thought so. Still, I suppose you can never tell, in advance.

"The one person in Russia who met her need for mystical religion best and who also apparently really could assist the boy in recovering from hemophilic attacks, perhaps by means of hypnotic suggestion, was of course the religious wanderer who went by the name of The Dissolute, Rasputin. The Empress of course could not be expected to say, 'The Dissolute is coming to dinner, Nicholas.' She called him Father Gregory. Rasputin began life in a Siberian village, and after having seduced many of the girls became very religious and went for a time into a monastery and—"

Wow! Seduced all the girls. Went into a monastery! What a combination! That's what I want, I think, isn't it? A monastery . . . peace . . . endless time to think, to draw plans, to study the oceans, to discover some truth that hadn't been known before, that I could add to the accumulation of truths . . . but the girls, the village girls, to seduce the girls . . .

"All the official classes in Russia quickly came to detest Rasputin and his influence."

Naturally. They would. Envy, envy.

"I'm not suggesting that the characteristics of these personalities alone shaped Russian history of the period, of course. Obviously not. But I am suggesting that an interaction of the personal and impersonal was taking place, and that Russia cannot be understood if either one or the other is ignored or not given sufficient weight. The blood disease of one boy has to be considered alongside the growing material expectations of the peasant class, and the belated industrial revolution then taking place."

"Sir?" Gordon Durant had lifted a hand.

"Yes?"

"Sir, all those leaders of that time, that period. They were all what you might call 'gentlemen,' weren't they?"

After considering this question gravely for several moments, Mr. Gilders said, "Yes, with a very few exceptions, all the leaders were born what you call gentlemen, and the exceptions attained that status before they attained political power."

"Don't you think that in spite of letting the First World War break out they did a better job on the whole than the peasants and slobs and fanatics who have been running the world since?"

A few titters and one belly laugh greeted this.

Mr. Gilders in full gravity considered this second question. Then he said, "Well, the assumptions of your questions are very broad and vague, and my answer would have to be very broad and highly subjective. But if you would like my—we're discussing the influence of personality on Russia this morning —if you would like my strictly personal evaluation of the personalities who governed Europe before World War I as compared to those after it, I would say that the evil caused by the 'gentlemen' sprang mainly from their ignorance or stupidity, while the evil caused by these later leaders was often done very deliberately, as a matter of policy."

"Thank you," said Gordon firmly. And in an aside to Lou which only half the class heard, he growled, "The Century of the Common Man for you—peasants, slobs and fanatics."

After this class Lou had agreed to meet Clement Jonaz at George and Harry's Grill for coffee. This was part of Clement's policy of keeping in close touch with Lou during this week. Clement sensed that his friend was entering another crisis. He had to be advised, listened to, unobtrusively watched. Lou brought Gordon, who was not in the least embarrassed that at his last encounter with Clement he had been indoors, on horseback, and blind drunk. Any gentleman might have done the same thing.

"We learned something in class this morning," Gordon began as soon as coffee had been brought to their table.

"Really? What was that?" inquired Clement in his habitual courteous manner.

"That the world has been run by peasants, slobs and fanatics ever since the First World War."

"Ever since the beginning of time, I would say," murmured Clement.

"No, you're wrong there," continued Gordon. "Before the First World War gentlemen ran the world and they at least *meant* well, they had—"

"Meant well for whom?"

"Well, for—for society in general. They—"

"For the top five percent, you mean."

"For everybody. Everybody knew his place—"

"I've forgotten my place and plan to go on doing so." Courtesy had its limits.

"Is that so?" said Gordon easily.

Lou put in hurriedly, "You're an intellectual, Clem, so your place is outside, criticizing, isn't it?"

Clement turned his hooded eyes on Lou. Then he said, "For the moment. For the moment."

"And where will it be *after* the moment?" asked Gordon.

Clement paused. *The Meeting of East and West* by F. S. C. Northrop of the Yale Law School was one of the influential books on the campus. "All of you think the great conflict in the world is between the East and the West, between the communist countries and what you call the 'free democracies' of the West. But that isn't so. The real coming world conflict is between the North and the South, that is, between the white and the colored peoples. Your side is tremendously outnumbered and surrounded by our side. The white Americans and the Europeans and the Russians and a few other white enclaves scattered around the world, against the rest of us. Whom do you think will win?"

"I think you're talking a lot of hogwash," said Gordon in his downright Durant manner.

"Yes," said Clement with quiet regretfulness, in his inscrutably understanding way. "Yes, I suppose you do. More's the pity." Then he went on quietly. "It's not just that those old frauds you call 'gentlemen' are finished, but so are those peasants and slobs and fanatics you referred to, those white criminals who've been running the world since the 1920's. It's all over but the shouting—and the killing," he added softly, in his regretful way, "yes, that party is just about over."

"Not as long as the North controls most of the guns and the planes and the bombs, and the atomic bomb, and the hydrogen bomb, it isn't over, and won't be. Not that I agree with this North versus South hogwash of yours."

"Oh it isn't mine," protested Clement. "I don't claim that distinction for myself. *I* didn't have this insight. I merely recognize it as true, and I wait patiently for the rest of the world to recognize it too. They will, before very long, they will. So I . . . we wait." He looked almost monastic, sitting with his hands in his lap, having finished his coffee, wearing an inconspicuously checked shirt, black knit tie, dark gray flannel suit, his shoulders slightly forward, the prayerful look his wide face sometimes acquired now visible on it, on the faintly coppery-colored features; sitting there he embodied one monastic attitude: I possess the truth and so I can wait with infinite patience for its fulfillment, which is inevitable.

Gordon resented this kind of personal authority which Clement radiated because he had never seen it before, and never suspected that a rival to his kind of authority existed in the world, or at least at Yale. Therefore he felt a visceral resentment. "I guess you have to think you're going to come out on top some day. Everybody needs his opiate, the only bright thing Lenin ever said."

Clement passed over the misquotation in silence. "Oh *that's* not my opiate. When I want an opiate, well, when I want an opiate," he gazed innocently across at Gordon, "I take opium."

"I see," said Gordon. "Yes, I see. Well! Times *are* changing at Yale, aren't they. What I like about having you for a roommate, Lou, is that I find out about sides of Yale I never —" then in a suave undertone, "never in a million years, would have come into contact with. Yes, I think I can safely say, never."

"Nor I," said Clement courteously.

"Mmmmm. Well! See you round the campus!" and Gordon was up and away.

"He's so much more attractive," murmured Clement speculatively, "dead drunk, and mounted. Or even sprawled unconscious on the floor, then a certain humanity suffuses him. But cold sober, in the morning like this, well, he comes as a nasty shock. I frankly didn't think there were any survivors, in the pure state, as immaculately reactionary as that."

"Gordon says people like himself quietly own this country and always have and always will. They never get their names in the paper, he says, never run for any office, naturally. They just own the country, before the elections and after the elections."

"I think you've heard too much from Gordon Durant," said Clement. "It's time you heard the other side of the story. What are your politics, by the way?"

"We have always been Democrats, because Wetherford, Connecticut, where we come from, is rock-ribbed Republican."

"Of course," said Clement.

"But my own political opinions? Well, they are kind of in a state of flux right now."

"I see. I'm taking you to a meeting of the John Reed Club tonight."

"The what? If that is one of those underground secret societies, I can't use it."

"It is not a social club, not at all. Don't you know who John Reed was?"

Lou's memory was selectively photographic, and now he remembered seeing the name in the syllabus for Professor Gilder's course. "He was involved in the First World War," Lou improvised. "He served on the Italian front during the retreat from Caparetto—"

"Oh shut up. John Reed was a young Harvard graduate, a journalist, who went to Russia during the Revolution and wrote a book called *Ten Days That Shook the World*. He died there and was buried in the Kremlin Wall." Clement paused. "Something about *that* has always intrigued me most about him. What can that really mean: buried in the Kremlin Wall?" He sighed; one more speculation to be checked out once the great North versus South war was won by the South, and the yellows and browns and blacks rode triumphantly into defeated Moscow, after accepting the surrender of the United States Marine Corps in the suburbs. "Well," he went on, "Reed was one of the earliest American champions of the Bolsheviks, of communism. The John Reed Club here is formed in his spirit."

"Gosh. Wait till Joe McCarthy hears about that."

"Yale will defend to the death the right to have dissenters in her midst, or very nearly to the death. Besides, there are so few of us, maybe a hundred. We can't cause any trouble. Not yet we can't."

The John Reed Club met in a well-lighted lecture auditorium in Strathcona Hall. Lou had assumed they met among steampipes by candlelight in one of the subterranean passages which wound beneath the Yale campus. It was not until they entered this pleasant, banal auditorium that he emerged from one of his periodic trances to recognize with a sense of comic shock that his geology class met in this room. It made him want to laugh; he liked this juxtaposition, it confirmed in his mind that Yale was playing her civilized and civilizing role to the hilt; it even cast geology in a slightly more favorable light, just as it downgraded all the tormented theorizing of communism, so mental, so theoretical, so tenuous when confronted with geology's rock and dirt.

There were about forty students, six of them girls, in the auditorium, and most of them seemed to be graduate students. There were several Orientals, two Negroes, and the rest seemed almost equally divided between urban radicals and Great Plains radicals. The discussion began—it was to be a "roundup" discussion of all the major issues confronting the club this year—and it gradually became clear that the one unifying attitude of this very disparate group, the one which united Cantonese with Clevelander, Trotskyite with Boston Brahmin, Minnesota agrarian reformer and Bronx anarchist, neurasthenic girl nihilist and four-square Iowan humanitarian, was a profound generalized disenchantment with everything that came under the heading of The American Way.

"We hardly have a Communist Party in the United States, with the leaders in jail, informers everywhere—maybe *I'm* infiltrating the John Reed Club right now! We've got no money, we Communists, nobody votes for us" . . . . "Communism is a science whose principles are internationally valid, and its time is coming here too". . . . "But what good are fellow travelers after all?". . . . "If you take the Hiss case, if you consider what Whittaker Chambers started out as, and

the House Un-American Activities Committee" . . . . "The
liberals will never be any help. Liberalism is Adlai Stevenson.
I ask you, what good is Adlai Stevenson to anybody?" . . . .
"Mao Tse-tung is doing a lot to improve Chinese agriculture.
But whether he's any use to the world movement . . ."
. . . ."The United States always has a great depression after a
great war, as we all know. The great depression after the
Second World War is due in approximately eighteen months,
and with it will come the rising of the American masses
everywhere against Wall Street". . . . "This country's on the
greatest witch hunt in its history, and we're the witches". . . .
"I think, if you ask me, Joe McCarthy is finished. He can only
live by attacking the administration for being 'soft on communism.' And now there is a *Republican* administration. He's got
to attack his own party. Who'll support him?". . . . "All the
Yahoos everywhere, that's who" . . . . "What about the Memphis Five and the Hollywood Ten and the New Orleans
Twelve?" . . . . "Most people in this miserable country just
want their two cars in their two-car garages and to hell with
starvation in Asia." . . . . "In Asia! There's starvation in America, and they don't give a damn about that!" . . . . "Yale is just
like America. All your typical student in this University wants
is a nice secure job in a nice big corporation, a nice house in a
nice suburb, and a generous pension plan! They're apathetic
about absolutely everything else. Talk about a Silent Generation! This is it." . . . . "I'll tell you what's wrong with this
generation. It's bored stiff. It's bored with its own ambitions
for the nice secure job, and it's bored with the big business it
wants to work for and it's bored with the shopping centers it's
going to shop in, and it's bored with the golf courses it's going
to use. It's got nothing to do. Nobody asks it to do anything.
Nothing's happening!" . . . . "The Korean War, oh, pardon *me*,
the Korean *Conflict* has finally reached an armistice, but it'll
all break out again."

Walking back to their rooms through the bone-chilling dark
Clement asked, "Well, what did you think of it?"

"They have some good points, some good points, about

ignoring starvation and self-satisfied people and all. But, I
don't know, America has made it possible for a *larger percent-
age* of its people to have a chance in life than any other
society ever has, hasn't it, and, I don't know, I wouldn't tear it
down myself, would you?"

Clement didn't answer.

The next morning Lou woke up—he was sleeping somewhat better these days—feeling ice cold. His body felt frozen,
rigid. Outside November swept capricious winds back and
forth between the Fence Club and Zeta Psi, throwing the last
dirty, tag-end leaves of autumn here and there. His bedroom
windows were open a little but the room was not cold enough
to account for his frozen state.

It was just another of his symptoms. Migraine headaches,
hot flashes, cold chills, temporary deafness, nausea, nasal
bleeding, vertigo, double vision, tremors, compulsive sneez-
ing, out-of-the-way allergies were only some of the inventory
of complaints from which he had suffered. Usually they were
too elusive, too fugitive to take to a doctor for help. By the
time the doctor's office was reached the vertigo would have
become a blinding headache, the fever transformed into a
dizzy attack. Lou's byword was for not only the Physician but
the Patient to Heal Thyself. So he lay motionless for a while in
his frozen condition and then by wiggling his extremities he
got a certain sluggish circulation going, enough so that he
could get out of bed, stagger to the bathroom, and stand
under a very hot shower for forty-five minutes.

Then he felt absolutely wonderful. Marvelously renewed
and refreshed, he began to whistle; he whistled "Shall We
Dance?" which sounded "smashing" as, well, as Charlotte
would have said, in the echoing bathroom. Not even her
shadow could check his soaring spirits this morning, and he
defiantly whistled "A Foggy Day in London Town," and then
whistling couldn't express how he felt fully enough and he
began to sing. Lou's baritone was very good. He had all the
physical gifts, balefully undermined. He sang his own version
of Cole Porter's (Yale '13) "You're the Top," dedicating it that
morning, damn her, to Charlotte Mills:

"You're the dregs,
You're the slums of Pisa
You're the legs
Of the Mona Lisa
You're the coughing fits from the gritty city air,
You're a forest fire,
A children's choir,
You're underwear!

"You're the dregs,
You're—   "

"Colfax!"
Durant.

"—Korean brandy,
You're the dregs,
You're that Orphan's Sandy
You're the endless screech of a city streetcar's rails,
You're a folk song singer,
A football ringer,
You're Woolworth sales!
You're the dregs,
You're—   "

"*Colfax!*"
Durant again. He turned down the shower a bit. "Yes? **Did**
somebody call me?"
"*Get the screw out of the shower! I'm waiting!*"
"Oh. Hmm."
Even Gordon Durant rampant and roaring in his Morning
Voice could not take the edge off Lou's euphoria.
Putting himself together on such mornings was ritualistic.
Back in his bedroom he took a long time to dry himself, a long
time to dress, and then—for every movement must be as
logical and calculated as a bomb run over an enemy target on
such days, to avoid disaster—he went to his desk and tore
yesterday's page off the calendar, revealing today's page,
Tuesday, November 21, 1953. Charlotte's opening night.
Charlotte's opening—a flood of sexual words and scenes

began filling up his mind at these words. He had an endless
supply of both and he always had had. Revived by the long
hot shower, visions of her body freed by these two words
surged through him, as unleashed as demanded by Eros, one
of the gods he worshipped most; he saw Charlotte from above
and below and around him and himself inside Charlotte and
then she faded into a more abstract, ideal woman's body and
the turmoil of warmth and heat pounded in his body, something pulsated in his throat, in his body. . . . the village girls
. . . he had to release it he had to release it he had to release
it he had to and he did release it then.

Whew!

On to geology. Last night's meeting had reminded him of its
existence and that he had better put in an appearance instead
of merely cramming for the tests and passing them with the
highest grades. One of his recurrent nightmares was of arriving, in cap and gown, on the stage to receive his degree from
Yale, before thousands of spectators including Charlotte, the
baby (but with an adult's capacity for scorn), every last living
and several dead Colfaxes packed shoulder to shoulder, waiting to receive his degree magna cum laude, and then the
President of Yale suddenly looked into his face and said, "You
can't graduate, you forgot your course in Blank, you never
attended a class or took a test in Blank, you forgot it existed,
you flunk, you are expelled and you are a failure for life.
Good-by."

After geology, as meaningless to Lou as ever since the land
was being studied without relation to the seas, which was like
studying one face of a coin; after coffee with Clement, after
his class in European history, almost equally meaningless and
for the same reason: how could it be profitably studied in
isolation from the history of the surrounding continents? Lou
recognized that a course had to have limits, could not be
all-encompassing. But he strongly suspected that the limits
imposed in these courses were the wrong limits, imposed
because the geology and history faculties had had these limits
imposed on *them* as they collected their advanced degrees in
these fields, so that now they had a vested interest in perpetu-

ating these outmoded limits, were too lazy to recast knowledge in the light of today's wider accumulations, persisted in
maintaining these increasingly clumsy and artificial bounda-
ries. That was what Lou thought. But who cared what a
student thought about courses?

Lou had lunch in Pierson Dining Room with Myron
Stoetzer, whom he ran into there. Like the dining rooms of all
the colleges at Yale, Pierson's had a definite style, even elegance, with its graceful black tables and chairs, immensely
high white walls broken by big curving windows, with its
chandeliers, a fireplace, all of it inspired no doubt by the
Oxford and Cambridge prototypes, with their privileged High
Tables, sherry and port, the Dons, the pipes, the silver.

But this was America, this was 1953, and the students who
graced, or as Myron said, disgraced the Pierson Dining Room
were every year looking more incongruous in this courtly
setting. When Myron saw someone in dungarees and moccasins come shambling in, he thought of him as a barbarian
nomad stumbling into civilization, he and his horde coming in
waves, each wave a little bigger than the last until, one of
these years, they would completely sweep away Yale as he
knew it, sweep away everything that Mory's and "Caesar"
Lohman, keeper of the precise formula which produced the
color Yale Blue, stood for: a network of relationships extend-
ing from St. Paul's School and Andover and the others,
through Yale College (but not the Sheffield Scientific School
or the Graduate Schools, which were for outsiders) and on to
Wall Street and the State Department and the Senate, a web
of cordial connections and associations with a shared background, shared assumptions, shared mutual understanding
because the calm power of Yale College had made it so; songs
were preeminently a part of this Yale, and so was liquor,
and so were *neckties*, very good automobiles, weekend house-
parties in Greenwich or somebody's place in the Adirondacks,
holidays in the Caribbean, golf and tennis and riding; being
well-read mattered at this Yale, being well-informed, above
all being public-spirited mattered, making your contribution
as a leader to the community, whether the community turned

out to be a small town where you settled, or whether it was the world; the Yale man would contribute to it constructively, that was the overriding spirit of Myron Stoetzer's Yale. And now he saw it sinking under the gathering tramp of moccasins, of public high schools instead of Andover, of student grinds instead of all-around young men, of, above all, students bent on self-serving instead of service.

As he was detailing all this in his low, sad, rather melodic voice to Lou over lunch, Lou was nodding and agreeing and thinking continuously of Charlotte's ordeal that evening. When Myron mentioned that Vilma was on a shopping trip to New York Lou asked him to use the other opening night ticket.

"I almost never go to the theater now," Myron said rather wistfully. "The repetitiousness of it. . . . However, I'd enjoy seeing your friend perform, and of course a play about the twenties, well, those were my salad days."

That afternoon Lou showed up for lacrosse for a change. The game was played in the mud, all the sparkle of September on the playing fields had been extinguished and this flailing November gloom had superseded it. He however enjoyed the game, the lowering sky, the mud, the whole slogging effort that everyone had to make together. This was sports too, the grim side of sports, effort and exhaustion and dirt, no spectators and no cheering and no one caring about the outcome but themselves; it was like service to some obscure god, done for its own sake, disregarded by everyone but you.

Back in his rooms in Pierson, he took a shower, and dressed more carefully than usual in a white shirt, black knit tie, and navy blue suit. He had dinner in the Pierson Dining Room with Gordon and Myron.

Then he and Myron set out for the theater. "They used to send me seats to every play of any consequence which opened in New Haven," Myron mused as they made their way through the chill darkness, passing between the walled moats of Branford and Jonathan Edwards, light shining cozily through the mullioned windows of the college rooms, and a

student seen across the wall and the moat and through the
window standing in the well-lighted room really did look like
the most secure, protected human being in the world. Surely
to "townies" Yale students must seem provokingly distant privileged beings peering out of their stronghold.

"They would send me tickets to the plays here and then
after the performance I'd be invited to the Green Room or
their rooms in the Taft, and they would all want to know how
to 'fix' it, 'fix' the play, as though a play were a kind of jalopy,
to be tinkered with. My advice usually was, if the play really
was 'in trouble'—that was their other phrase, 'in trouble,' like
a girl finding herself unmarried and pregnant—my advice was
usually for the playwright to go to his room and think for
twenty-four hours about what he was really trying to say in
the play, basically and really driving at, and then ask himself
how he could re-express it more directly, economically,
strongly." He puffed on his cigarette. "Sometimes they actually did this, and occasionally it helped. Of course that was in
another era. Today I presume they call in five 'play doctors'
and they all mess about with the patient. The results are
predictably tasteless and banal. There will be no serious theater on Broadway in another ten years. Can't be. The economics of it are impossible. That's why I stopped writing," he said
faintly.

Lou peered as sharply as he could at Myron's face through
the darkness but he could not see it. Myron had never so
much as breathed a reason for his long artistic silence before.
"It is?" Lou finally said neutrally.

"Yes, I think so. I needed to feel an audience waiting for my
play, and a sizable one, not some little theater group in some
loft. I'm afraid I'm too egotistical for that, too interested in the
great world, too public. I didn't want to write for a coterie. I
am a coterie, Vilma and I are *the* coterie for the Yale community. My writing was my way of reaching out to touch the
great world, and I did it, once. But then after that, the
economics of it all, producers offering me cheaper produc-
tions, things like that, I became rather muddled in my purpose, I suppose, and I became one of your, how shall I say,

steadier New Haven drinkers, yes, very steady indeed, and oh one thing and another, and Vilma and I did all that traveling once the war was over, and of course during the war itself I couldn't write, it seemed irrelevant, although I suppose that was what your generation would call a 'rationalization.' In any case my . . . talent, and I assuredly had one, got rather lost in the shuffle. Basically, it was money. Most of the greatest works of art in history were pot-boilers, you know, Shakespeare and Michelangelo and Mozart and Rubens and almost everyone else. They needed the money and so they were forced to work, and so while they were at it, why not do their best, after all, and they produced masterpieces. Well, I didn't need the money, not after I married Vilma. Breakfast cereals. That's why I never produced a real play to follow *Rainbow*. Breakfast cereals. We don't spend a tenth of her annual income. Give it to places and people. Wonderful woman, Vilma."

Lou at this point finally realized that Myron had been having one of his days of steady drinking, and while he was completely in control of both his mind and his body, a door had been opened in his soul.

"Perhaps I would have produced a real body of work without her. You knew we met at the opening night party for *The Colors of the Rainbow* in New York. She was so impressed with me. Thought I was another Bernard Shaw and she would be the devoted, *rich* companion-wife. Still, I think she's had a contented life on the whole. And I have too. It's just that I might have had another kind of life entirely, more valuable, not leaving so many areas of myself so neglected. Neglect. It's the word I hate most in the English language."

I'll never let that happen to me, Lou vowed. I can't imagine it happening. But with so many sides to him he wondered whether some of them would inevitably have to be neglected, and then his nightmare would come true. ("You forgot your course in Blank. . . . You are a failure for life.")

"You have your work cut out for you too," Myron muttered mysteriously then. "Yes, you do."

Outside the Shubert Theater there was bustle on the side-

walk, and in the lobby. *The Bees Knees* had intimations of
success lurking around it here and there, not certainties, just
possibilities. Broadway success was so rare and so overwhelmingly profitable when it happened that these mere whiffs of it
were enough to bring the hurried New York people to New
Haven for a look. They frowned through their cigarette smoke
into each other's faces now in the lobby and waited. Lou and
Myron made their way through the crowd to their seats: third
row center. Charlotte was showing Lou her influence.

His fingers and feet were tingling, so were the muscles of
his stomach, he felt light-headed, and a sense of unreality was
gathering in his mind: his usual anticipation anxieties.

Then the theater filled up with the New York people, the
keeping-abreast-of-what's-happening people from New Haven
and environs, a smattering of Yale faculty and students. Lou's
hands were like ice, his head feverish. He didn't know what
he hoped for for Charlotte. Even if they had still been together he would not have known what to hope. Success and
recognition for her? Wouldn't that have driven them apart? As
it was, would a success for her in this play throw him down
into the depths, if only in his own estimation? Would he return
to those depths he had been so slowly and painfully climbing
out of recently, because of Norma Durant, because of solving
Gordon Durant, most of all because of at last glimpsing,
coiled elusively through himself, the seam of value?

The overture began, all snappy twenties razzmatazz, with a
Charleston beat, then it broke into a ballad, back to razzmatazz, something else thrown in, the climax, and then Lou, with
a drastic sense of finality, saw the curtain go up.

The scene was the campus of Bumble College, 1925. On-
stage the chorus in short skirts or white knickers began the
opening number, "Fourteen Freshmen." Even Lou, whose
immunity to theater of any kind was strong, thought it was
entertaining. Then there was some dialogue about the low
standing of the freshman class at Bumble, lacking a leader, a
rallying point.

"What we need to find is our Campus Queen!" cried a
young man holding a tennis racquet.

Then, in heavy tweeds, heavy shoes, glasses, and a flat hat, Charlotte made her entrance. So it was to be the Cinderella plot, caterpillar into butterfly; and here she was. She was an unknown face to the audience of course, but the New York people knew she was the lead, and there was a smattering of applause for her.

"Could anyone tell me where I might find the Dean?" she asked. They had not tampered with her accent.

Lou was rudderlessly at sea. In spite of her costume, he thought she looked enchanting. If something went wrong on that stage, he would die.

There was some conversation about Charlotte, or "Honey" as her character was named, being a student from "Abroad" including the predictable pun on "a broad," and then she had her first song, "Is a Sea Change a Me Change?" Lou felt he was giving her artificial respiration throughout it, and the cordial applause at the end hugely relieved him.

"It's all very silly, of course," mumbled Myron, "but sort of fun, don't you think? She's charming."

Lou nodded dazedly. "If she can't go on, I'm going to step in," he answered.

Myron looked at him. Behind this hyperbole there lay a fanatical Lou Colfax truth.

The Dean, in pince-nez and academic gown, was on stage now, doing a patter song about "Rules Are Made To Be Broken, You Know" which went over well.

Then Honey and the Dean came together to discuss what courses she would take.

"What do you want to major in?" he inquired.

"Goodness, I don't—"

"Goodness! What are you trying to do, young lady, destroy school spirit?"

"No, I mean, sir, whatever you think."

"Think, think? How long do you suppose I'd keep this job if I went in for that sort of thing. You—" gesturing to the blond second lead, "What do you major in?"

Blonde: Me? Goodness, I—

Dean (*in despair*): The college is doomed.

Blonde: No, sir, I mean, I major in Away-From-Home Economics.

Honey (*fascinated*): That sounds too too. What is it?

Blonde: That's how to manage eating, sleeping, dressing, jewelry, men, *everything*, when you're out and around, tea dancing and rumble-seat riding and on a party and *everywhere*, except at home. These days, a woman's place is away from home! *Anywhere* but home!

Honey: Good—oh no, I *am* sorry—my gosh, that sounds too daring for me. I only left my parents' home for the first time yesterday.

Blonde (*as the orchestra begins*): It's never too late to shed your stays.

During this song Honey was obscured behind other players who were working over her, and when they had finished she emerged stage center in a very short beaded orange dress and sang a reprise of "Is a Sea Change a Me Change?"

Lou sat transfixed through it. Now, in the glow of the footlights, she really did look beautiful. He was fascinated by her legs, shaplier than he had ever realized, and slimmer. Her ankles and wrists were so frail! And beneath her make-up Lou discerned the pallor of her complexion, that inescapable theatrical pallor all of the theater people he had met through her suffered from, dressing-room pale, rehearsal-hall colorless. But such vitality flowed from her! Frail, indestructible Charlotte, willing herself to be strong. Lou saw that she possessed the power to carry her role, carry the show, to do it, make it, arrive, succeed: reserves from somewhere inside her, currents she knew how to pull from the surrounding air, she could use and transform them and do it. She was not great; she was much better than adequate; she "had something," and her will had driven her to get this chance to demonstrate it on this stage here tonight. Lou settled back in his seat for the first time and exhaled long and slowly.

The rest of the play shot past his eyes at top Broadway speed. It was silly, knew it, laughed at itself, and was amusing. Charlotte's tensile ability to hold the stage never wavered. He saw that her career was not necessary, as some great actress' would have been. But she had something definite to offer on the stage. If she had chosen not to offer it the fate of the theater would have been unaffected, and she herself could have settled into another kind of life well enough.

She had chosen to make this act of will. Like any work of art, her performance was a provocation. Basically, it disconcerted Lou very much; for one thing, it made Charlotte sexier.

"You have to go back and congratulate her," confided Myron in his ear amid the hubbub. "She was good, wasn't she."

"I thought she was . . . okay."

They made their way up the aisle and out on the sidewalk, heading for the stage door. "I've had to do this so many times," murmured Myron. "It can be very painful, sometimes. *Vilma* did a play once. Yes. Well. There is always one comment you can make to the worst scenery-chewer in the business. 'You were *on that stage*' you can say, very forcefully, 'Yessir, you were really up there *on that stage!* '"

Lou looked sharply down at Myron's wry face, the face of a ruined boy, a self-disappointed face, finally a dangerous face, for those who have destroyed themselves have no reason not to destroy others, have in fact every reason to do so, misery loving company as it does. But Myron was too minor to be very destructive, too low-keyed, underenergized, passive. He gave provocative parties and let it go at that.

They pressed their way into Charlotte's jammed dressing room. Her dressing table ran the length of the left wall, and it was ablaze with artificial light, throwing illusory brilliance over the baskets of flowers, the New York people, most of all over Charlotte, in a blue silk dressing gown, seated by the table, chatting vivaciously with everyone.

Lou was now absolutely ambivalent about her. She was newly erotic and lovable; she was newly challenging and distant. "Hi, Charlotte!" he cried cheerfully.

"Oh you *were* there! Oh good. I *am* glad."

Playing the great lady: he could have killed her.

"Did I—was I—adequate?"

It was an appeal, she was vulnerable; he loved her.

"You were on that stage," he answered with ironic cheerfulness, denying his own deepest feelings; now he could have killed himself.

Charlotte looked puzzled for an instant, and then a man put his hand on the back of her neck and said, "When you got to those new lyrics in "Me Change" I could see the gears grinding in your head and then the smoke started to come out of your ears and I said to Sheila 'She's going to blow!' but you didn't! What a doll."

Charlotte smiled gamely back at him, her good-trooper smile.

Lou started to move away, but she called across to him, "You must come to the party. My suite at the Taft. No, you must come. Promise," and she indicated Myron's inclusion.

The sitting room of the suite had dull green walls, very subdued lighting, cigar and cigarette smoke, smoked salmon, bourbon, Scotch and gin, low music, and thirty subdued but genial—the aura of success around *The Bees Knees* was becoming clearer—guests. Host and hostess had not yet arrived.

"Very classy party," murmured Myron, still in his wry mood. "I remember when these things used to be like Fraternity Row on Saturday night. You see, the vitality is draining out of Broadway show business, even the opening night parties."

There was a stir at the door and then Charlotte came into the room on the arm of her husband. Her hair was cut short in the twenties bob; there was something charged about her, electric. Next to her her husband looked tall and broad-shouldered and competent, with nothing of show business about him. They seemed the image of a united, successful couple.

The Black House! It seemed a thousand years and a million miles away. How for granted he had taken her there. The Black House! Pathetic.

Myron found an old theatrical acquaintance and fell into

conversation. Lou retreated into a corner, as he always did at parties.

After a while Charlotte came across to him. "Louis, don't lurk here alone. Come and meet somebody or other. Who do you want to meet?"

"Well . . . your husband," he replied, because her husband was the last person in the world he wanted to meet and tonight he was locked in his self-destructive urges.

"Hello," said the producer neutrally as Charlotte introduced them, giving Lou a hard handshake. Then he turned and resumed the conversation he had been having.

"Who else?" said Charlotte, faintly embarrassed.

"Ah well, how about the baby?" he said casually, his mind in chaos.

"Asleep," she confided, pointing to a closed door. "That's why we only invited *quiet* people to this little festivity. That's all babies ever do," she added absently, seemingly to lose interest in the subject, "sleep. And eat."

"He must take a lot of your time. How do you do it, with rehearsals and all?"

"I've got Miss Hinkel, bless her, and she does it all."

"Must be frustrating, not to get to do it all yourself."

"It *is!* Still, she's better at it than I am."

"You planned to do it all yourself, once."

"Yes," she acknowledged softly, "but I sort of lost my, I don't know, *calling* for it, that . . ."

She had made her choice; he had made it for her, refusing to conceive their child in the Black House. Then she had been poised to live motherhood completely. After his refusal Charlotte had turned to the producer and to that definite if moderate talent for the theater she did possess. Her best energies went there, and that was why he found her so changed, electric, ironically sexier than when her ruling passion had been sex and reproduction. Faintly like a courtesan she was now to him. "Did you really like the show at all?" she asked, giving him a candid stare.

"I really did. You were on—" and then getting command of himself, "you were good, you really were."

"Thanks, love. I'm getting by, getting away with it at least, aren't I?"

"Much more than that."

"You're responsible for my career," she then said in a low voice.

"Yes," was all he could get himself to say to that.

"All for the best," she said, rather convincingly, but then she was an actress.

"Yes."

Then, in a totally new, public tone, she said more loudly, but not loudly enough for the producer to hear. "You must come round during the day and let Miss Hinkel show you Mark. He's quite divine. He had such fun playing about in the Black House the day I took him up there. Made himself thoroughly at home."

Those words sent a feeling like a cold knife stabbed into the top of his spine, paralyzing.

What had hit him? This is your son: that is what she was telling him, telling him publicly, coldly, before these strangers. And you can't have him, ever. Another stranger, one Miss Hinkel, will let you see him for five minutes maybe, and even perhaps let you touch him, once. Otherwise, buzz off, Buster.

That was what she was really saying in this cold public voice.

Lou shuddered and drew back toward his corner. "You haven't got a drink," said Charlotte, looking closely into his face. "What do you want?"

"Never mind, nothing or uh yes, but I'll get it," and he made off rapidly toward the bar in the other corner, where he poured himself a long straight gin.

The producer moved up beside Charlotte and put his arm over her shoulders. She leaned her head against his shoulder. Thus united, they talked to some people forming a half-circle in front of them.

Some time later, several gins later, Lou saw Charlotte coming across to him. "Come on," she said in an urgent whisper, "come with me."

She took his hand and drew him toward a closed door. She listened at it for a moment and then eased it open, drawing Lou after her into the darkened room. Diagonally across the room the bathroom door was ajar and some light shone into the room from there, enabling Lou to see a large crib with a small person asleep on it, small head, blondish hair, a tiny but sturdy person asleep. Near his hand in the crib there was a stuffed elephant, which Mark had been clutching before falling asleep and only released when he was unconscious. The elephant was still very close, to be recaptured the moment he woke up.

It was the sight of that elephant which undid Lou.

This little person had his intense loyalties and dependencies already, deep attachments to people and to things Lou would never know about. "Thank you," he whispered formally.

Charlotte nodded with a smile, and then straightened the sheet and blanket over the child. Lou saw that as a "bit of business" in the theatrical sense, an "improvisation" right out of the Actors Studio, Motherhood Image, Protective-Instinct Subdivision. Bullshit.

They returned to the party. "He looks very well," said Lou neutrally.

"Doesn't he?"

"He seems to look exactly like you."

"So they say."

From what Lou could see, the child was the image of Charlotte in a distinctly male recasting; even at fifteen months there was a certain shape to the nose and a set to the small shoulders denoting masculinity; but features, coloring, everything else was pure Charlotte. Any male on earth could be the father. But Lou knew in his guts who the father was.

And what was he going to do about it? Sue, fight, forget it? Argue, yawn, blackmail, plead?

No, he would do none of these things. The child was his, Charlotte was throwing his impotence to do anything about that in his face, publicly and privately.

Very well. There was only one thing to do: take the child.

. . .

The next morning first thing he went to the Yale Co-Op and bought *Baby and Child Care* by Dr. Benjamin Spock. For maximum concentration he took it to his cubicle in the stacks of the library and read it, making notes in the margin.

Bringing up your child won't be a complicated job if you take it easy, trust your instincts . . . every time you pick up your baby he's getting a feeling he belongs to you and you belong to him. ("Mark has never had that feeling about me.")

He isn't frail; you have a pretty tough baby ("That's a relief").

In the 3-to-6 year old period the child matures by means of an intense adoration of his parents ("Where will I be in his 3-to-6 year old period?").

A man can be a warm father and a real man at the same time ("Who could ever doubt it?").

We know that the father's closeness and friendliness to his children will have a vital effect on their spirits and characters for the rest of their lives ("!!!!").

To fold a diaper depends . . . When a new vegetable is added to the diet . . . Diphtheria, pertussis, tetanus inocula-tions . . . cowpox ("!") *. . . eczema . . . projectile vomiting in pyloric stenosis . . .*

By the time he finished his reading Lou was in a state of high nervousness at the vulnerability and complexity of babies. Nevertheless, he was going to have Mark.

Clement Jonaz looked into his cubicle. "What's that you're reading," inquired Clement, since Lou had instantly shoved the book out of sight, *"Fanny Hill?"*

"Yes."

"It is not. Don't lie to me. You can never lie, Lou. What is it?" he added with the small chuckle of the truly unshockable friend.

After gazing in a level way at this unshockable friend Lou slowly drew the book into view and let Clement see the title. Clement's reaction was not shock but amazement. "Baby care?" he inquired with quiet incredulity.

"Baby care." Then, to change the subject, Lou asked, "What can I do for you?"

"Take *care* of me!" Clement suddenly burst out irresponsibly.

"Shut up. This is serious."

"I'm not following your thought."

"Ah—Clement, what is it you wanted?"

Obscurely insulted, Clement hesitated, then plunged ahead. "I'm going to an art show, very special art show. Want to come?"

"Sure," said Lou, who had twelve urgent things he should have done instead. But his decision to take the baby had superseded all other duties, and until he figured out how to do that, only random behavior was possible. And what could be more random than this? "Where is it?"

"In the backyard of the Old Heidelberg."

A ramshackle saloon across the street from the back of Pierson College, the Old Heidelberg would normally have been thought the antithesis of all things artistic. But this art was different; this was the art of that small, arrogantly alienated group of Yale fringe people, Clement and his circle. "We're the *Salon des Refusés* and if you don't know what that refers to don't admit it." Lou then promptly recalled something he had read in a magazine about the *Salon des Refusés* five, no six years before: that was the name that an avantgarde group of Parisian painters gave many years before to an exhibition of their work which had been refused by the Academy.

So Lou was more or less prepared for what he was to see. They walked through Pierson Courtyard in the rain, crossed the street, and proceeded through the beerstench and past the battered tables of the Old Heidelberg, into the tacky backyard, where a very large dirty canvas tent had been erected. The rain tattooed strangely down on it, and in the mud milled Clement's circle—a half-dozen student artists, a couple of stray girls, several advanced thinkers from the faculty, and about twenty curious outsiders.

The works of art were fixed to the canvas walls of the tent or suspended on wires from bars holding the tent up, or on pedestals. The one which caught Lou's eye first was a block of wood about two feet high; it displayed one screw, and the label of the work read "Screw." There was a heavy carved black oaken frame suspended by wires, labeled: "Self-Portrait: Selden Leeming." The frame was empty. There was a small glass jar filled with a red substance. This work was labeled: "Life Study: Blood." By Selden Leeming again. "It's real, his suicide attempt," murmured Clement. There was a stuffed cat rampant, and a large black-and-white photograph of President Eisenhower grinning, labeled, "The Tic"; there was a big photograph of American soldiers dead on a Korean mountainside, titled "Tourists"; a surrealist oil painting of sexual intercourse; and quite a few more. "What do you think?" asked Clement guardedly.

"I don't know yet."

"Tell me when you know."

A very small blond-haired person crept up to them. "This is Selden Leeming, Lou Colfax." Lou put out his hand, which caused Selden to shrink back in alarm. Then he recovered, and murmured intensely, "These people here, these people here! They ought to be *censored*. Works and movies and books should never be censored, but audiences ought to be. They have no *right* to look at my work. Oh why did I ever agree to this, why?"

"Because you're a flaming exhibitionist and you know it," said Clement calmly.

Selden smiled trustingly: understood at last. "Do you like my 'Life Study'?" he inquired of Lou.

"Yeah. It's very engaging."

"Engaging! I mean that bottle of my *blood* over there."

"I know what it is. But you're right, engaging isn't the word. Let's see, it's . . . well, I don't know, I can't think."

Clement waited, powerless. Selden looked Lou up and down, from his black shoes up his black pants, up the black sweater, across the dark glasses to the long brown hair. "I sort of like you in an obscure way," Selden then said. "Who are you?"

"I'm an oceanographer."

"I wish I was," said Selden wistfully. "Do you want to buy one of my works?"

"I've never had any money."

"I guess that's why I like you. I only like failures."

"Oh I'm not a *failure*." Not yet anyway, Lou qualified to himself, and not if I take charge of my son, that will show I haven't it in me, haven't the temperament, haven't the chemistry, of a failure, that will prove it. Elated by this coming achievement, he said very cheerfully, "I also make mobiles."

"Like Calder's?" inquired Selden casually.

"Sort of. But mine are *stranger*. Calder I guess is a very happy man, child-like. Everything I'm not."

"You will be, you will be," murmured Selden.

"Will be what? Happy?"

"No, child-like. It just takes time, that's all."

"I suppose you're right," said Lou, cogitating.

"You been smoking with him?" asked Selden in an undertone to Clement.

Clement shook his head sternly.

"You mean he's not on anything and he still talks like this?" Clement nodded angrily.

Lou was uneasily intrigued: the marijuana group showing an edge of their submerged selves.

Inside the Old Heidelberg a group of sophomores began shouting a song, "Roll Me Over in the Clover" and then "Roll Out the Barrel" and several more in that repertoire, not to annoy the *Refusés* exactly but just to express themselves in their way as Selden with his bottle of blood did in his; the inescapable Germanic mood of American college boys on a spree began to engulf the old saloon and the tent behind it, the beer-cellar mentality moved in on them, dissipating the whiff of Baudelairean drug fumes Lou thought he had detected, putting to flight the Gallic pretensions of the *Refusés* and turning everybody toward Heidelberg, Germany, once again. "Zing, boom tarrera, sing out a song of good cheer," the sophomores yelled into each other's faces cheerily, and the Old Heidelberg was spiritually back on Fraternity Row.

"Balls," murmured Clement. "I think we'd better go."

Clement, Selden, Lou, and five of the *Refusés* repaired through the rain to Clement's rooms in the Graduate School. The room as usual was almost completely dark since all the light bulbs in it had been painted black. Lou could barely make out the low divan with cushions, the hookah, the Hindu art work, the Tunisian birdcage, the black rug, the very low Japanese table. On his record player Clement put a dirge of some kind, as different from beer-drinking music as possible, and then Clement said, "Who has the stuff?" Selden did and several cigarettes were rapidly rolled and distributed with almost sacramental care around the room.

Lou was very surprised that he had been so casually and matter-of-factly included in this kind of party, because while he had always known of the small marijuana-smoking coterie in Pierson College, he had also been aware of their labyrinthine security arrangements and self-protective devices. Clement had obviously guaranteed that Lou would not endanger their secrecy. Nor would he, of course, and now he would smoke marijuana because there was nothing else for him to do. He was very curious, and not a little nervous. On a nervous system of his complexity, what effect might the drug have?

It had no effect. Selden explained to him how to inhale and hold it and so on, and it simply didn't work. Deflated, Lou watched as others around the room began to pass into a cloud-like state, slowed and insulated and apparently restful, drifting, cushioned, bemused, philosophical, apart. He tried again. Nothing.

Clement moved to the bathroom and returned in a couple of minutes. "Try this," he murmured, handing Lou a lighted cigarette. Lou took several long puffs of that. Rather swiftly a suffusing enlightenment began to permeate his mind, freeing him, loosening endless holds which had restrained him, and he found himself. "What kind of marijuana is that?" he asked with slow happiness.

"That is not marijuana. That is keef dipped in opium."

"It is, is it," commented Lou sagely.

"Yes. Do you like it?"

"Yes, I do. I do. I do."

Across the room one of the beards was saying to another, "I don't want to break up the square world, why should I? What do I care? I just want to keep it off my back. I want to keep it and its beer kegs away from our art shows and things like that. Fighting society is a bore anyway."

Murmurs of agreement passed around the room.

"Why should I try to change anything? Why bother?"

"Don't you want to make your ideas felt in society?"

"Me? Are you jesting?"

"I'm going to realize myself," Lou announced to the world.

"Good," said Clement. "How?"

"I'm going to realize myself tomorrow," said Lou.

"How are you going to do that?"

"I'm going to realize myself tomorrow by taking what is mine."

There was a thoughtful silence in the dark room. The dirge-like music ground on.

"Brother," said one of the beards, "I'm so bored with myself all the time I don't know what to do. Except smoke, like this."

"There's always religion."

"Not in the West. There's Buddha, but he's far, far. Some day I will make my pilgrimage to Japan and to India, where there is religion."

"Good."

"I believe," Lou said quietly to Clement, "I have just solved perpetual motion. Nobody move. I may lose it if anybody moves."

Nobody moved. Finally Clement said, "Well?"

After a silence Lou said, "I have moved on, I have moved on."

"Good."

His brain had become a miracle of insight. It was time; he had solved time. Every problem he had ever had was rooted in his being *hurried*. This miraculous cigarette had slowed him to the pace his mind had always longed for and never achieved, slowed him to a pace at which he could notice . . .

notice everything. Blurred and hurried, his mind had skimmed the surface of the world, until now. Now he truly saw. It was a miracle. He could solve everything.

Time drifted very slowly on, at the exact pace Lou had always unconsciously longed for. As the day passed into evening the sequence of events became unfixed, and his awareness of them, while clear, was not sequential. There was a period spent in a booth at George and Harry's, a place Lou had always vaguely disliked because there seemed something cheerless and graceless about it. How could he have been so wrong? Tonight it radiated warmth and friendliness, a confiding aura of peaceful congeniality, and of studious festivity. Seated with Clement, Selden, and another of the *Refusés* in the booth, Lou discussed just how the endless peace negotiations over Korea could be terminated, how the two sides could be reconciled into fraternal sharing. It was so supremely simple.

There was a period spent on the fence inside the Old Campus, contemplating the universality of knowledge and the way November's frail moonlight fell on the roof of Connecticut Hall.

Back in Clement's room, either before or after these episodes, there was Selden's monologue, which was apparently a fixed recitative on such evenings.

"I know I'm not anybody and I know I never have been anybody," he murmured intensely, sitting in the middle of the floor of the dark room, legs crossed Indian fashion, "and I know there's absolutely nothing I or anybody else can do about it. I'm a cypher. Psychoanalysis? I've had, oh, seven years of it. I understand *everything* about my problems, I work out the meaning of every dream I have two minutes after I wake up, I understand the source of all my fears and anxieties and compulsions and everything else. But I never change. Nothing ever happens to me. There's an invisible screen between me and life so that I never touch anybody and nobody and nothing can ever touch me. I never *lived* a day in my life, and I never will. I was condemned to isolation the day I was born, or else in my mother's"—pronouncing this

word with special irony, "womb. Probably in the womb. I
constantly want to be loved and I'm always falling in love,
with women, men, dogs, footstools, but nobody ever falls in
love with me. Everybody always has and always will reject
me. I reject myself. I learned *that* the first six months of
psychoanalysis but it didn't help. Now I analyze everything. I
even analyze my analyzing. I'm a psychiatric basket case. It
didn't take. I even failed my neurosis."

Silence closed over his statement at last.

"What should be done?" Clement intoned finally. "We have
all considered Selden's problems many times. Louis, they're
new to you. What is your thought on this?"

Lou, head hanging contemplatively did not move or speak
for a while and then he finally said quietly, "I never heard
someone use the word 'I' so many times before," and that was
all he would say.

At another time in the evening Lou was standing alone in
the moonlight before the great white Classical façade of the
Freshman Commons, a memorial to the First World War dead,
speaking inwardly and exaltedly to some Eternal Presence,
well, to God:

"It must all come true. You must help me make it all come
true. You have given me . . . things in myself which I don't
deserve, they're so beautiful, so sublime. And now you must
help me realize them or else I will go crazy."

The next day he realized that the Freshman Commons
looked as much like a temple to the old gods, to Zeus and
Apollo and Athena, as any building in Connecticut, in America.

America. That word that night expanded and contracted
and was never still, never at rest, never fixed.

Sexuality never entered his mind. He had imagined drugs to
be orgiastic, the very semen of desire. Instead, for him, they
were like incense in a church, drifting his mind heavenward,
higher, higher.

Finally, at the gate of Pierson College, as he was going back
to his rooms at last, there was Clement saying, "There will be
no conflict between the East and the West. The coming world

conflict is between the North and the South, white versus colored."

Lou then went to his rooms. Gordon was sleeping. Lou picked up a copy of *Madame Bovary* in French, which he had been reading with considerable difficulty. He started to read it; miraculously the sentences fell immediately into place, transparently easy. He did not merely read French perfectly now, he reinvented French, he saw the roots and structure of the language and traced its conception and development and elaboration. Marvelous. Very much later he fell asleep.

The following morning Lou awoke to the most baleful hangover he had ever experienced or imagined. It was not his body—although that ached everywhere and felt totally exhausted—it was his mind. A depression and despair crushed his brain; a swirl of self-accusation knotted around it; blasted hopes stretched away from his thoughts in all directions, and at the core there was a devastating sense of nothingness and emptiness and vulnerability. He had never felt so awful in his life. This was the end.

But he would not let it be. Just as the morning he had bolted from his bed and driven to Stowe, Vermont, just as the other day when he had been about to fall, as usual, into despair and then a net of self-strength had borne him up, so now Lou struggled to reassemble himself.

Solve perpetual motion! The great "insight" which had broken over his mind had evaporated, gone with the fumes. Reinvented French! He opened *Madame Bovary* and stumbled through it as usual. He pictured himself sprawled in the dark of Clement's room raving about perpetual motion and felt filled with shame. And on the eve of taking over control of his son's life! For the first time Lou began to question the rightness of this course, whether he deserved it, was up to it. And this doubt was the most threatening of all. He just must not think; he must act, or else there might soon be absolutely nothing left of him.

Lou passed the next two days buying baby equipment and in the Payne Whitney Gymnasium, in the exercise room, in the swimming pool, in the steam room, until he felt sure that his brain and his bloodstream were completely cleansed. Dr. Spock accompanied him everywhere.

The third day, at 4:30 in the afternoon, risking all, he called Charlotte's suite at the Taft Hotel. A no-nonsense sounding woman answered.

"Miss Hinkel?" he ventured.

"Yes," she replied neutrally.

"This is Myron Stokes, the production manager over at the theater. I'm over here and—what? Excuse me a moment, Miss Hinkel. What did you say, Charlotte? Yes, I *am* seeing about Mark now. I've got Miss Hinkel on the phone here. Yes, all right, I'll hurry. Excuse me, Miss Hinkel. She wants Mark over here. There are some photographers from the magazines and they want some mother and child shots."

"Oh, lands, his best suit is at the cleaners. Never plan, you theater people," she softened that with a chuckle, "do you? Well, his nap is over but I'll have to make him all tidy and then we'll be coming over."

"Yes, you tidy him up. Charlotte, Miss Hinkel will be over with him in a little while. What? Look, why don't you talk to her yourself? Oh. Miss Hinkel, she's got her hairdresser here and can't move. She said would you go out to the store and get some kind of a new little sweater for him, something in a bright color, they're doing these pictures in color. And I'll pick up the baby and bring him over for some preliminary shots."

"Such a rush all of you are always in," Miss Hinkel murmured, resigned annoyance replacing the indulgent chuckle.

"I know. Well. Will he be ready in twenty minutes?"

"Twenty minutes. I see. What should I dress him in?"

"Ah why yes—she, uh Charlotte—or, darn it, they've gone down to the ah proscenium, she and the hairdresser. But she did say 'just everyday,' they want this to be a realistic picture story."

"Everyday, is it?" Sigh. "Very well. Good-by, Mr.—?"

For one glacial moment Lou could not remember the name he had given her. He took a deep breath, and then it came from nowhere into his brain, "Stokes. Myron Stokes."

Twenty minutes later, wearing his dark gray flannel suit and a white shirt, Lou knocked on the door of the suite.

Miss Hinkel had Mark ready in a little gray coat and a gray cap. She was holding his hand. He was so little, but sturdy and rather steady on his feet.

"Hello there," said Lou to him. "How are you?"

Mark studied him and then looked at Miss Hinkel. "Go along with Mr. Stokes to see your mother, and," to Lou, "don't let any of those people give him anything to eat, especially candy. Our stomach is not the strongest today."

"It isn't?" said Lou, stricken. Maybe he should postpone this to another day, to next year. Too late.

"No sweets," she straightened Mark's cap, and unlike Charlotte's straightening of the bedclothes, this action seemed routine but sincere, a genuine move. It shook Lou.

Rooted, he finally forced himself to take Mark's hand, willingly given, and they moved off down the hall. Miss Hinkel closed her door.

Mark was sitting on Lou's bed in Pierson College, playing with a toy steam shovel Lou had bought for him. Then Mark said, "Tick" several times. Show business had entered his vocabulary already. Or had Mark said "Tinkle" and meant he wanted to go to the bathroom? Lou led him there, put Mark on the baby seat, and waited. Mark waited too for a while and then began to squirm. They returned to the bedroom.

It was 6 P.M., dark outside, November dark, Gordon had not appeared, and Lou was improvising. Charlotte must know that the baby was gone by now, and, assuming she had recognized Lou from Miss Hinkel's description (he had not attempted a disguise, had not wanted to), she would go herself or send someone to the Black House, being sure that Lou had gone there. She would naturally never assume, nor would anyone, that he had simply returned to his rooms in Pierson with his son. So there they were, playing steam shovel and new words. Lou felt blissfully if unnaturally happy, he felt that his life was suddenly overwhelmingly purposeful and

significant, its wanness, the terrible college-boy purposeless-
ness which so often gripped him, had been conjured away.
"Watch," he said, pointing to his wrist watch.

"Wass," replied Mark.

Marveling at his precosity and a little intimidated by it, Lou
decided against offering to let him hear it tick, for fear Mark
would find that too childish. "Do you know how to read?" Lou
asked.

"Read," mimicked Mark. So Lou sat down on the bed, Mark
close against him, and together they began to read *The Little
Engine That Could.*

So Gordon Durant found them. "I thought for a minute you
had a young lady in here."

"This is Mark. I told you. . . . Charlotte's boy. . . . helping
her out . . . "

"Baby-sitting for the star, are you? Good-oh. Reflected
glory. What's the little tyke going to have for dinner?"

"Oh I've got everything here, hot plate and everything,
everything Dr. Spock—"

"You know, Lou, there *is* something kind of uncle-ish about
you. I never saw it before."

"Paternal," murmured Lou.

"Hmm? A baby in Pierson College bedroom—only you, Lou
Colfax."

Lou smiled brightly. "I'm taking him right back after giving
him his supper there . . . "

Thursday was Gordon's senior society meeting night and he
did not get back until well after midnight, when he went
straight to bed. At 3:45 A.M. he was awakened by a child's cry
echoing through the rooms. "That stupid son of—" he snarled
softly. "A baby! A baby! Even Colfax . . . "

Another child's outcry, followed by a subdued rumpus in
Lou's bedroom. Gordon threw on his dressing gown and
moved through the living room to the door of Lou's bedroom
and opened it. Lou had turned on the desk reading lamp and
was warming some milk on the hot plate.

"Colfax," Gordon said in an explosive whisper, "this is the
end. I'm going to call the police." This was of course pure

Durant overstatement. What would be the charge: aggra-
vated baby-sitting?

But Lou had paled to deathliness and Gordon looked with
new discernment at him. Then he said with some sympathy,
"Lou, what's going on?"

"Tell you in a minute," Lou whispered. "Bottle," and he
cocked his head at the large white crib which now occupied
the far end of the small bedroom.

Gordon contented himself with pacing up and down the
living room. Lou tested the milk for warmth with extreme care
and then gave Mark the bottle. The child began to gulp
eagerly. Was he supposed to gulp? Too late to consult Dr.
Spock. After draining the bottle Mark settled down and was
quickly asleep again. Had he burped? Had he burped?

Lou went nervously out into the living room, closing the
door after him. He and Gordon began to converse in hoarse
whispers.

Gordon said, "I knew show business people were crazy, but
leaving a baby with *you*, here! What kind of nut is she,
anyway?"

Lou, wearing a long, strange, white bathrobe, walked across
the room and then turned to face him. "She doesn't know the
baby's here."

Gordon looked at him very blankly.

"You see, I took him. He's mine. He's my kid and I have a
right to him and that's the way it is."

Gordon continued to look at him blankly.

"You see, I took him. He's mine. He's my kid and I have a
right to him and I'm not going to have all the meaning taken
out of my life by her or anybody else. I want to take on some
responsibility too. I wish you could have seen the group I was
with the other night. Smoking marijuana and raving, one of
them, the sickest of all, well, he was so sick because all he
could say was 'I.' There was no 'we' in his life and never will
be. Mark is my 'we.' It should have been Charlotte but, see, I
blew that, I was too much of a kid, too shaky to hang on to
Charlotte. And she wanted her 'we'—a baby, and I wouldn't
let her have it. Well, she did it anyway. And I've got to have

a—at least *share* in him, I've got to have that anyway."

Another silence and then Gordon said quietly, "Lou, you have and always are going to have a lot of personal problems. You've got my sympathy. But *I* don't want to get involved in your problems, I just don't, that's all. And you've just involved me now. You kidnapped that baby and you've just told me and I am now an Accessory After the Fact unless I report you to the police immediately."

"Oh no," said Lou quietly, in a Godforsaken voice.

"Oh yes."

"Will you let me just have ten minutes to try to explain things my way? They won't arrest you for ten minutes."

Gordon looked at him. Then he took a deep breath, and said "All right."

But ten minutes were all Lou needed. He had foreseen this possible emergency, and prepared his own special knock-out mixture. Now in the dark room he mingled it unnoticed with Gordon's favorite nightcap, Brandy and Benedictine, which he habitually tossed off in one Durant gulp. He sat listening to Lou's explanation for a short while, and then he began to blink and then his head fell, almost snapped back, and Gordon was lost to the world for at least five hours to come.

Charlotte, her husband, and *The Bees Knees* press agent were nearing the Black House. It was about 12:30 at night.

"I have a ghastly feeling he's not here," she murmured. "And I was so sure. But Louis would be sure of my sureness. I have a ghastly feeling I've fallen into his trap. We should have called the police."

"That kind of publicity," began the press agent, "it's the wrong kind of publicity."

"Publicity! *Publicity!* Are you crazy!"

"Now take it easy," said the producer. "We'll find him, and if we don't, we call the police. I'm not sure this publicity would be all that bad," he added under his breath.

Petrified, Charlotte turned to behold him.

.   .   .

Lou and Mark were passing through Riverdale at dawn.
Beautiful. The palest blue northern wash of an almost-winter
morning spread above whatever it was on the left, the Bronx
or whatever it was. They approached a bridge over a profound ravine. There was the Hudson River, majestic and still
in the deep shadow of its palisades below them on the right,
and further downstream there was the George Washington
Bridge, its structure still traced out with its nighttime lights,
arching in formidable lightness across the great river.

New York. Tingling from head to foot, Lou drove on toward
it. He had always, almost as a matter of principle, been
mortally afraid of New York. He thought of it as he was sure
it was: not dewy debutantes dancing at the Plaza, but of
middle-aged women running to drink and fat and turning into
cranks alone in cramped furnished apartments; not of major
league baseball and the Metropolitan Opera but of wan actresses and failed athletes waiting on table in greasy restaurants; not of spacious penthouse terraces but of grim slabs of
gray walls forming canyons which crushed everything natural
around them.

But today he felt utterly different about New York, as he
carried this child into it. Haven and hideout, blessedly anony-
mous, huge and dense as a jungle, it would shelter them
somewhere.

Mark slept in his little car-crib, securely fixed in the jump
seat. The Morgan wound through a park-like section of drive
above the river, empty as backwoods Connecticut at this
hour. They passed under the great bridge, and it forcibly
impressed on Lou the sheer inhuman scale of New York, and
of America as it spread away from its colonial seacoast beginnings; massive and manic, the country had built its office
buildings and bridges and highways and apartment complexes and housing developments many sizes too large. The
Morgan tore along the West Side Drive, miniscule amid the
scale and scope of Manhattan, and inside the little car slept
this very small person beside him, a person who had to survive
and even prosper in this crushing country. Lou then mutely
committed his life to bringing this about. It was a commit-

ment too deep to be deliberately chosen; he did not choose
this dedication, it chose him, there as the little car hurried
them into the huge city, and he could no more have refused it
than have rejected the color of his eyes.

He turned off the drive in the west Seventies and ventured
into the city's streets. The rattle and stir of a Manhattan
morning had already commenced, and amid the dated apartment houses, neglected hotels and thousand interchangeable
luncheonettes of the West Side the Morgan with Lou and
Mark picked its course.

But precisely where was he going? The precision was urgently called for because Mark was awake and fussing,
needed breakfast, needed a toilet, needed fresh clothes,
needed fresh air, needed to be read to, played with, was
bursting with babyhood needs. Where?

Lou pulled over beside a street-corner telephone booth and
dialed the number he had lifted from Gordon's address book
of Mrs. Norma Taloumi Durant. The baby needed a woman,
and since he had taken him unannounced (the word "kidnap"
was totally inadmissible to Lou) the woman had to be an
unconventional one, independent-minded.

When Lou had very briefly explained the situation Norma's
vibrant voice called back, "You will come here at once with
that child. At once. This morning air in the streets of New
York can be terrible! Hurry!"

Norma lived in a converted carriage house on a little cob-
blestone alley called Washington Mews, just off Fifth Avenue
close to Washington Square. She let them in, wearing a worn
black dressing gown, her blond hair in disarray, no make-up
whatever, not caring how she looked. Lou knew that she was
idly, abstractly attracted to him; he was deeply fascinated by
her and knew that she knew that; her receiving him exactly as
she looked when getting up in the morning therefore had a
revealing philosophic meaning: Norma scorned artifice in love
and in everything else; this is it, this is me and that is that,
that is what not even bothering to brush her hair before he
arrived meant.

Fists on hips, she stood in the doorway of her house and

beheld the Morgan, the car crib, the baby, and Lou lifting the child out. There was a formidable silence and then she said in her even, penetrating voice, "Louis Colfax, I think you have made a fool out of yourself!"

Lou looked up at her with an apologetic, I-admit-it little grin, and instantly noted that while she clearly meant her words the expression on her face was not really disapproving.

Inside, the house had an enormously high ceiling with a suspended curving staircase leading up to a couple of small bedrooms at the back of the house, an immense fireplace, huge Chinese screen, grand piano, immense couches, everything on the scale of the personality of Norma Durant.

At the back, in the kitchen, a housemaid was at work, and the two women turned full attention on Mark. Wide-eyed, too semi-asleep to be puzzled by all these changes, he was bathed, fed, dressed.

"Be careful with that sweater," Lou breathed as Norma prepared to slip it over Mark's head. "Remember, a baby's head is egg-shaped and you have to uh gather the sweater into a loop and slip it over the *back* of the head first—"

Norma cocked an eye at him. "I think you been reading a lot of books about babies. Did your books tell you the most important thing is that you really care about the baby, even if maybe you put the sweater on wrong?"

"Yes, I guess it did."

"So." She pulled the sweater straight down over the baby's head and into place.

Sitting with his steam shovel in the middle of the vast room Mark seemed reasonably content for the moment, although increasingly uneasy.

"He is a *vairy* good baby!" said Norma. "The best baby I ever seen. No crying."

Lou started at these words, stared at her.

A great drill erupted somewhere, signaling, like the cock's crow in the country, the day's beginning in New York. Mark's eyes rolled wonderingly at this strong, strange noise so close at hand, and Lou intensely watched that look. What is that little boy thinking? His mind is forming. How? Which ideas

are taking precedence, what emotions are gaining the upper
hand, what formulations will take place? If only I could lead
him! If only I could direct all that!

But in that wondering look on Mark's face Lou saw that an
independent mind was forming there, an autonomous life
force, and that that was as it should be, and that the best he
would ever do would be to aid.

"Louis, come here," ordered Norma, sitting down in an
unusual chair with a triangular base. "Sit down on the couch.
Leave Mark to play. He is okay now. A *woman* has taken care
of him so he is okay for the moment. Now. Tell me. What the
hell do you think you're doing?"

"I want to be with my own son, that's all."

"Are you sure this is your son?"

"Yes."

"How are you so sure?"

"I know it. I feel it."

"*Ech.* You feel it. You feel like killing people sometimes too.
Do you do it?"

"That's different."

She sat silent for a while, as though meditating. Then she
went on. "What do you feel about me? Am I an honest person,
would you say?"

"I think you're the most honest person I've ever met."

"No, you don't think that, you feel it."

Lou shrugged.

"You know when I say at New Haven that I take no
alimony from Gordon's father? It was a lie. I *take* alimony
from Gordon's father. I say that in the—hotness of the argument. It was a lie. I want to make my point with Gordon. It is
true that I do not take *as much* alimony as perhaps I could
get. I don't want the court fight, the private detectives, all
those disgusting things. Still. I took some alimony. And I lied."

Lou, elbows on knees, head clasped, stared at the floor.
"This baby is all I've got."

"And now you are being the *wrong kind* of fool! All you
have got! You have a brilliant mind, you have gifts. Say
something in German."

Lou looked at her and then said, "It is impossible ever to satisfy a woman," in German.

"When did you learn German?"

"A couple of summers ago. I had nothing to do at home in Connecticut so I bought the records and some books, and there's a piano teacher there, Klaus Broockmann, who is German and I talked with him, and I learned it."

"In a few months."

Lou nodded absently.

"And you got nothing but this baby," she said mockingly. "But tell me, why did you learn *German?*"

"Anyone who is interested in science is interested in things German."

"I suppose. There is much to admire about Germany, and Germans. I hate people who condemn any race, any nationality, completely. Only a Hitler can do that."

"But what I am saying to you is, you have some terror of emptiness inside you, and of meaninglessness in your life, and so, you commit a crime! We say the truth now. You kidnap this—"

"You can't kidnap your own child!"

"You kidnap this child from his lawful mother and lawful father. It was when you do not consent to have a baby with Charlotte that you lose your right to be a father. You cannot steal the right back now. It is too late."

These words tolled through Lou's desperate thoughts like the knell of his life. He would never recover from them. With a feeling of ice forming on his brain he said very evenly to himself: I am going to be a partial person all my life then. I will never be happy.

"Louis Colfax," she said, a smile drifting somewhere about her expression, "you have made a fool of yourself."

He was too harrowed to reply.

"You know something? I like you for that. I tell you something. People who are afraid to make fools of themselves never make anything of themselves."

It was a thought he had himself, once. He was pleased to find his mind so congruent with hers.

An hour or so later Norma looked across the room at Lou and said, "I would like to call the Taft Hotel in New Haven now. May I? You have met life head on, you have not evaded your problem. So, something much more good than you expect can come from this, *if you let me telephone New Haven now.*"

Lou sat staring at the boy. Quite simply, the boy could not flourish with Lou alone. There had to be a woman, Charlotte or a Charlotte-substitute. And Lou did not have one. He sat looking at Mark and thinking, not about himself and his needs and frustrations and humiliations and his lost chances, he thought about Mark.

He then ceased to be an 'I' and became a 'we.' "All right," he said quietly. And then a very poignant, suffusing emotion swept over him.

Norma got Charlotte on the phone.

"Hello," she said in an unexpectedly low, friendly voice. "I am Norma Durant, a friend of Louis Colfax—" a gasp at the other end, "yes, and he is here with . . . with your son, whom he loves very much."

"Is he—he is—"

"Everyone is fine." Norma heard Charlotte turn and tell the news to her husband, and heard the husband yell, "In New York? Get the address. I'll get somebody right over there."

Norma continued, "Louis wishes to bring the baby back now, after this short trip."

Both husband and wife must have been listening on the other end because the man answered, "Don't move and give me the address. I'll get somebody over there in ten minutes to get the baby."

And then Charlotte's voice intervened. "No. No. Ah, Mrs. Durant, you must know how grateful I am. Tell Louis . . . tell Louis to . . . bring Mark back now. I'll be waiting here."

"Thank you. I am so glad for that."

Tears at the corners of her eyes, she hung up and turned to Lou. "She ask you to please bring the baby back to New Haven now. Okay?"

Lou bent down to pick up Mark.

"She knows you well, doesn't she," said Norma.

He nodded. "So do you. In New Haven you said I was very unsure of myself, and here you said I was a fool."

Her smile blazed. "Exactly! That is why you are not to be a criminal or a failure or both. Louis Colfax, you are an uncertain fool, and so . . . you will be . . . okay."

Some time later, while the maid was taking Mark for a walk, Norma took Lou into her bed and they made love. To him this profound acceptance of him by this extraordinary woman seemed to be delivering him from evil. "You are not uncertain in bed!" she remarked brightly at the end, sitting up.

Early that afternoon, driving up Park Avenue just north of Grand Central Station, Lou for the first time saw New York as beautiful, unimaginably beautiful. The aspiring stone towers on either side reached toward a sky so endlessly and wisely blue that the contradiction between the stone and the sky was unresolvable.

It must have been some holiday: flags were flying brightly, urgently, as though on guard duty in front of the buildings. The four-square city reached into this topless, wondering sky and the most prosaic pedestrian along the avenue looked full of meaning and significance in the dying, theatrical, autumn sunlight.

In New Haven his delivering of Mark to Charlotte—her husband was not there—was brief and civil.

Five days later, in response to a note from her, Lou met Charlotte on a bench on the New Haven Green in a gusty afternoon's grayness.

They talked of this and that until finally Lou asked simply, "He is my kid, isn't he?"

Charlotte gazed at him, smiling quietly, and said, "Why do you want to think so?"

"Because if he is, no, *since* he is, you're criminal not to come and be with me, the three of us."

"Louis, to be with you, to be with you. I was willing to skin myself and wrap you in it if you'd said you were cold. I was. But you let that time pass, you were afraid, you wouldn't let me have your child. So I changed. I changed. But there was that time, I was ready. I would have dedicated myself absolutely to you. And you need, you demand that. You will have that or nothing, I think. Louis, you forced me to become somebody else, and I can't dedicate myself to you like that, anymore. But I could have, I could have."

Well then I'll kill myself, he said to himself.

Watching his face Charlotte now said, "You know in the theater I—we are going to have to travel a lot, be away and touring and all that, and I thought maybe you would like to keep Mark sometimes."

Lou started, thrilled.

"When he's a little older. Now he really is too young to be away from me. But later on, a man to take him to baseball matches or whatever it would be, I think it would be good for him. Both of us being in the theater, he might miss out on that otherwise. So that's what I thought, Louis: from time to time I would like to entrust Mark to you."

There was nothing left for them to say to each other. Walking back through the Old Campus toward Pierson through the obstreperous wind Lou thought: I may never be happy in the way I could have been if I'd agreed to have that child with Charlotte. Perhaps never. That was when all the gods decreed for me to say yes. And I, uncertain, said no. They may never ask me again. That refusal smashed that future into pieces. And now I am putting a future back together again, growing in another way, just as Charlotte had to grow in another way too. I may be only a partial person for the rest of my life because of that refusal.

But partial people do the great things in this world, don't they. So many of the scientists and artists and innovators did great work to make up for the inner knowledge that they were condemned all their lives to be incomplete people. Well, that may be it, that may be me.

And his thoughts drifted after a while to algae and plancton and then further, toward all the unplumbed secrets, the hopes for the world, swaying back and forth undiscovered in the depths of the seas.